THE NORTHS MEET

M·U·R·D·E·R

Books by Frances and Richard Lockridge

THE NORTHS MEET

M·U·R·D·E·R

FRANCES & RICHARD

LOCKRIDGE

HarperPerennial

A Division of HarperCollins*Publishers*

1329. 6106

Originally published in hardcover in 1940 by Frederick A. Stokes Company.

HarperCollins books may be purchased for educational, business, or sales promotional use. For information, please write: Special Markets Department, HarperCollins Publishers, Inc., 10 East 53rd Street, New York, NY 10022.

First HarperPerennial edition published 1994.

Designed by R. Caitlin Daniels

Library of Congress Cataloging-in-Publication Data
Lockridge, Frances Louise Davis.
    The Norths meet murder / by Frances and Richard Lockridge.—1st HarperPerennial ed.
        p.   cm.
    ISBN 0-06-092490-X (pbk.)
    1. Private investigators—New York (N.Y.)—Fiction.
    I. Lockridge, Richard, 1898– . II. Title.
PS3523.0243N67 1994
    813'.54—dc20   93-21275

94 95 96 97 98 ❖/CW 10 9 8 7 6 5 4 3 2 1

With the exception of Pete, the characters in this novel are fictional and have no counterparts in life. Pete is real; the authors live in his house.

• CONTENTS •

THE NORTHS MEET

M·U·R·D·E·R

• 1 •

TUESDAY, OCTOBER 25:
4:45 P.M. TO 5:15 P.M.

Mr. North came home rather early that Tuesday afternoon, and as soon as he came in Mrs. North realized he was in a mood. He was, for one thing, annoyed about the weather, because it was behaving so irregularly. He said that he was annoyed with the weather and that, as far as he was concerned, he wished it would make up its mind, because if it made up its mind to be summer all year round one could at least dress for it.

"As it is—" he said, going off into his own room angrily, and beginning to thump shoes.

"What?" said Mrs. North, from the living-room. She could hear that Mr. North was still talking, but not what he was talking about. In a moment, however, he came back in shirtsleeves and slippers.

"—in sixty-eight years," Mr. North said, coming back.

"What?" said Mrs. North. "What's in sixty-eight years?"

Mr. North looked at her and inquired, rather peevishly, if she hadn't been listening to a word he said. Mrs. North said that, if he was going to wander off whenever he started to say something—

"The weather," Mr. North said. "The warmest October in sixty-eight years. In the paper."

"Oh," said Mrs. North. She thought a minute.

"Why sixty-eight years?" she said. "It's always sixty-eight years, for some reason, and I've never understood why."

"Oh," said Mr. North, "that—well, the Weather Bureau's sixty-eight years old."

Mrs. North said, "Oh," and then said it was warm, wasn't it, and that she had a fine idea.

"So," said Mr. North, "have I. A very fine idea. Cocktails, or maybe Tom Collinses. And your making them."

"No," Mrs. North said, "I mean a really fine idea. I've had it since yesterday."

"Look," said Mr. North, "cocktails are enough fine idea for me. Just cocktails, or maybe Tom Collinses."

Mrs. North nodded and said that she thought that would be all right, too, but hers was a real idea. "And, anyway, you're getting so you want drinks every afternoon," she said. "I don't think that can be very good for you, do you?"

"Listen—" said Mr. North. Then he rose, coldly, and went to the kitchen. After a while he came back with two Tom Collinses. They sipped and said, "Ah!" and Mr. North, mollified, inquired whether it needed more sugar. Mrs. North said it was perfect the way it was, and watched while the drink slowly dissolved Mr. North's mood. He admitted it was dissolved by smiling at her and saying that the thing was, one got all set for cool weather, and then warm weather left its mark. "Leaves you drained," Mr. North said, leaving his glass in the same condition. Mrs. North nodded, and decided to go back to her fine idea.

"What would you think about a party?" Mrs. North said. Mr. North made small, discouraging sounds, so she continued rapidly. "Not an expensive party," she said. "Just a party upstairs. I thought of it yesterday and it's perfectly all right with Mrs. Buano, and we can dance. Wouldn't that be fun?"

"Upstairs?" said Mr. North, following at a little distance.

Mrs. North nodded.

"On the top floor," she said. "Where it's been vacant so long, poor Mrs. Buano, and we could fix it up and have the electricity turned on and take the radio up and—"

"Listen," said Mr. North, "I don't think I'm getting this. Why a party? Why upstairs?"

The party, Mrs. North said, because it had been a long time since they had had a party and she thought it was about time, and upstairs because there was so much room and she had just thought of it. "That's the fine idea," she said. "People can just leave their things down here." Mr. North pulled himself together and made more drinks, and afterward he went at the matter seriously, although he did not then, or later, clearly determine whether they were to have the party because Mrs. North had remembered the top floor apartment was vacant, or whether they were using the top floor apartment because they had to have a party. He tried to clear this point up for some time, too, because such points are among those Mr. North likes to have clear.

The top floor apartment was, in itself, clear enough, and Mr. North admitted to himself, and after a time to Mrs. North, that it would be a good place to have a party, other things being equal and if they were really going to have a party. And he agreed that Mrs. Buano, who owned the house, would probably be glad to let them use the apartment, which she advertised as a studio, since it was at the moment of very little use to her. It was a fine apartment, too, and neither of the Norths had ever understood why it was so difficult for Mrs. Buano to rent—why it was difficult to rent even before it was used for purposes which, for a very considerable time, made any thought of renting it out of the question.

The apartment occupied the whole of the additional story Mrs. Buano had had built on the house in a halcyon day when it seemed to most of the owners of old houses in the neighborhood of Washington Square that there would never be living space enough for those who wanted to rent it. Below the added story, the house was standard—the three-story and semi-basement brick house which was, for a great many years, the mean of New York domestic architecture. In such houses, almost all New Yorkers of sufficient duration and normally migratory habit have lived at one time or another.

Those houses were built, seldom less than fifty years ago, as dwellings for one family, but that did not last, as nothing in New York lasts. The families dwindled or moved or lost their money; the houses were remodeled into apartments and those were, around the square, occupied for some years by people convinced that everything south of Fourteenth Street was quaint. Those people dwindled, too, and after them came occupants not too unlike, except, of course, for timely change of mores, those who had lived in such houses first—save for change of habit, that is, and evident shrinkage, which permitted them to be content with a fraction of the space necessary to the fuller, and possibly in many respects, more arduous, life of their ancestors. Basements which had housed kitchens housed young couples engaged in advertising; parlor floors were occupied by the more solvent journalists or stock brokers, and the floors above were occupied by others of divers occupations and, in almost all instances, young or youngish or, at any rate, not old. In general, those living on the second floors did not know those living on the third floors; it was equally probable that they knew people who knew the people who lived on the third floors, so that always, leading a normally social life in that stratum, you were being introduced to people who knew people you also knew. As Mrs. North said, people overlapped.

The Buano house stood shoulder to shoulder with almost identical brick-front houses in Greenwich Place, from any part of which, since it is only a block long, one may hear the children playing in Washington Square, where children play at the tops of their voices. Mrs. Buano's predecessor had made it over; Mrs. Buano had given it an added head. And Mrs. Buano reserved the basement and first floor to herself.

The house was some thirty feet wide and perhaps seventy deep. The front had not been remodeled, so, facing it, one faced a broad flight of brown steps, leading up from the sidewalk to double front doors. At the right of the steps there was an iron railing, broken by a gate, and, going through the gate and down a few stairs to the left, one came to Mrs. Buano's basement front door, under the main stairs. Although Mrs. Buano had two doors opening off the common hall on the first floor, she and her guests commonly used the basement entrance as the more convenient, and in conformity with the unfailing human inclination to go downstairs rather than up them whenever possible.

Going up the brownstone stairs, you came to double doors, unlocked. Opening them you were in a square vestibule and facing an inner set of double doors, which were locked. If you lived there, you had a key to these inside doors and continued on your way. But if you were visiting someone who lived there, proceedings were slightly more difficult. Then you turned to the left wall of the vestibule and looked for your host's doorbell.

The left wall of the vestibule had set into it the four mailboxes of the tenants—Mrs. Buano, the Norths, the Nelsons of the third floor, and the fourth-floor box, at the moment unnamed. Each box was identified by a name card slipped into a slot, and the Nelsons' box was further identified by being full of the Nelsons' mail, which the Nelsons had not had forwarded when they went on vacation to California. Above the boxes was an open grating.

To the right of the mailboxes were four bells, each similarly identified with the name of one of the tenants. The Norths' identification card was cut from a calling card; the Nelsons' was typed; Mrs. Buano's was hand-printed in ink and the bell connecting with the fourth floor was, generally, unidentified. If you were calling, you pressed the suitable button and a bell rang angrily in the apartment of your host, usually making him jump convulsively. Then, in theory, he went to a wall telephone in his apartment and asked who you were, his voice emerging from a grating in the vestibule. You yelled back into the grating and told him. But these amenities were commonly dispensed with, because the system was usually obscurely broken down. Newcomers to the house yelled valiantly into their telephones for a couple of months, and their guests yelled valiantly back, but communication was seldom effectively established. Experienced tenants, like the Norths, who had been there six years, merely pressed a little button set into their wall telephone.

Pressure on this little button actuated a mechanism in the lock of the downstairs door, and set up a furious clicking there. Inexperienced callers stared at the inner vestibule doors doubtfully when this clicking began and then, catching on, threw their weight against them. If everything had gone properly, one of the doors then opened, letting them into the inner hall, with heavily carpeted stairs leading up. The hall, in spite of a skylight at the top of the house, was usually dark; now and then, when a bulb burned out, it was almost entirely dark. Like everything else in the Buano house, it was also very clean; in the winter it was usually too warm, but in the summer—because of the thick walls of the house and old-fashioned ideas of spaciousness—it was surprisingly cool. To reach the Norths, you went up one flight.

The Norths lived on the second floor—once the parlor floor—in two big rooms and two little rooms. The big rooms, one facing the street and the other the rear garden, had fireplaces and high ceilings and deeply recessed windows and were, respectively, bedroom and living-room. There was a hall and bath between them. Mr. North's study was hall-bedroom size, and at the front; and in the rear was its twin, the kitchen. Martha, the maid, almost filled the kitchen, but did not seem discomfited, nor, the Norths noted thankfully, handicapped.

The floor above the Norths was similarly laid out, although with lower ceilings, and was almost always rented. The plans for the top floor, however, had eliminated the study, and the living-room stretched the width of the house in front, with a sweep of windows admitting north light riotously. That was why Mrs. Buano called it the studio, and there had been painters in it. Recently, however, it had proved that everyone who wanted a studio wanted it for a piano and pupils, and on that Mrs. Buano, who had firm ideas, set a firm foot. Better, she said, vacancy than pianos, and pupils always on the stairs.

"Tracking," Mrs. Buano said.

Thus it was vacant, as per announcement on a swinging board on the front of the house, and available for the party.

"And," said Mrs. North, finishing her second Tom Collins, "I've got it all worked out. Come on."

"Come on?" said Mr. North. "Where?"

"We'll go look at it," Mrs. North said. "I know where we want the radio and you tell me what you think about yellow paper."

"Listen," said Mr. North, "why yellow paper, for heaven's sake?"

"Hallowe'en," said Mrs. North, "or, anyway, thereabouts. For decoration. Come on."

Mr. North sighed, but the Tom Collinses had mellowed him and he went on. They went up the two flights and came to the door of the top-floor apartment, which was closed.

"All locked up," said Mr. North, quickly. "We can look tomorrow." He turned, ready to start down again, but Mrs. North said, a little impatiently, that it wasn't locked, and proved her point by pushing it open. "I was up yesterday and it wasn't locked," she said. "Mrs. Buano leaves it unlocked so people can look at it without her going upstairs. Come on."

Mr. North, who wanted to go and mix another Collins, sighed and followed her in. It was, he saw at once, dusty and forsaken-looking. And, although a faint breeze came through a partly opened window at the rear, it was extremely hot. Mr. North looked around quickly and said all right.

"All right for the party," he said. "Fine for the party. Let's go."

Mrs. North put a restraining hand on his arm, and Mr. North stopped.

"Here," she said, looking around the smaller rear room, "we'll have the bar."

"Bar?" said Mr. North.

Mrs. North led him through the hallway to the big studio room.

"And dancing here," she said, "with the radio over there." She pointed. "And you'll have to get the electricity turned on, and see Mrs. Buano about the water."

"Water?" said Mr. North.

"It's turned off, too," Mrs. North said. "Everything's turned off, and we'll have to get somebody to clean, unless—"

"No," Mr. North said, "I certainly won't. We'll get somebody to clean."

There would, Mrs. North pointed out, be a lot of cleaning to do in the studio room, and in the rear room. The kitchen, since they could cook anything they wanted cooked in their own apartment, didn't mat-

ter so much. And there was, of course, the bathroom. That would have
to be cleaned, of course, because people—

"Yes," said Mr. North, quickly, "I see that."

Mrs. North's heels clicked on the bare floor as she went to examine
the bathroom. The bathroom door was closed, and she opened it quickly. The bathroom, without a window, was black vacancy, with only
faint light filtering in from the hall.

"A match," Mrs. North said; "we'll just look."

Mr. North, behind her, flicked on his lighter and held its wavering
flame above her shoulder. Both peered into the bathroom. And then
Mrs. North's breath came in, with a kind of shudder, and Mr. North
shook out the light and, seizing her shoulders, drew her back against
him, holding her firmly.

"All right," said Mr. North, quickly, and keeping the shake out of
his own voice. "All right, Pamela." The voice came through to Mrs.
North, and she managed not to scream, and in a moment he had pulled
her back from the door, and was saying, over and over: "All right, kid.
All right."

She was quiet after a moment, and nodded, although she still did not
dare to try to speak. Mr. North held his hands for a moment firmly on
her shoulders, and then flicked on his lighter again and went back,
because he had to, to look at what they had seen. It was not a pleasant
thing to look at.

Whoever had hit the man who was lying in the tub had hit him
much harder than was necessary, even admitting a murderer's necessi-
ties. The head lay against the sloping end of the tub with a peculiar,
horrible flatness, and that, quite clearly, was because blows had
crushed in the back of the head. The face, too, was battered and discol-
ored, but there did not seem to be any other mark on the body. Mr.
North could see that, because the body was entirely naked—naked and
white in the uncertain light of the little flame. After Mr. North had
looked at it a moment it seemed to him to begin to float, and then Mr.
North turned and went out of the bathroom, closing the door behind

him. Mrs. North was standing where he had left her and she looked at him once. Then she was clinging to him, shaking, and saying something he could not understand about the party. He thought she did not understand what she was saying, either, because she seemed to feel that there was something horrible in their having planned to give a party.

• 2 •

TUESDAY
5:15 P.M. TO 7 P.M.

Mrs. North was still trembling a little when they reached their own apartment, but she was sure that she was perfectly all right. "Only it was awful," she said, "just when we were talking about a party." She had, she said, always wondered how people felt when they discovered a murder, and then she looked a little puzzled, and said that even now she didn't know, really.

"Things happen too quickly to have feelings about them, don't they?" she said. "I mean, by that time things are over, and you begin to have feelings about the kind of feelings you had. And it isn't as if we knew him, of course."

She was, Mr. North saw, coming out of it quickly—much more quickly, as a matter of fact, than he was, and he thought that it must have something to do with speed of perception. He, for example, was only now really shaky and glad to sit down. He sat down and reached for the telephone. "Police?" Mrs. North said, and Mr. North nodded.

"You know," he said, "I never called the police. I never really thought I would." Mrs. North nodded.

But, an indefatigable reader of directions, Mr. North remembered

10

how to call the police, and dialed the operator. She was cool and impersonal and a long way off, where nothing had happened.

"I want the police," Mr. North said. Then he remembered the phrase. "I want a policeman," he said.

"What?" said the operator, as if it had come to her very suddenly. Perhaps, Mr. North thought, she has never called the police, either. Mr. North told her again and gave his name and address. "It seems to be murder," he added, because he wanted to tell somebody about so strange and awful a thing.

"Thank you," said the operator, and cut off, leaving Mr. North with a sense of incompletion. He was still glad to be sitting down, but he was feeling better. Mrs. North seemed virtually all right again, excited instead of shocked.

"You know," she said, "they'll think we did it. They always do."

It seemed, momentarily, odd to Mr. North that things, including his wife, were going on as usual; that they were talking as usual, and no more clearly or dramatically than usual. Then he decided it was not odd at all.

"People who find bodies," he said. "Yes, they do usually." He paused, thinking it over. "And, as a matter of fact, they're usually right," he added. Something was bothering him.

"You didn't see it—him, I mean—when you were up there yesterday?" he said. "I mean, of course you didn't, but—"

Mrs. North looked at him, and a slight, affectionate quirk appeared at one corner of her mouth. Her voice was very serious, however.

"No," she said. "I'd have mentioned it." She waited until Mr. North looked up.

Mr. North had a moment to feel that things were all right again. "I—" Mrs. North began.

But then there was a wailing in the street, and an angry screech of brakes, and the sound of feet hurrying grittily on the steps outside. A moment later the Norths' bell rang, in the way only a policeman, or perhaps a boy with a telegram, rings bells.

"Cops," said Mr. North, and clicked them in. There were only two of them, at first, and they were in uniform.

"North?" the one who was ahead said, as if he suspected Mr. North of being hard of hearing. "Gerald North, 95 Greenwich Place? What's going on here?"

"We—" Mr. North began. But a great hungry wailing of sirens in the street outside poured in through the open windows of the apartment and drowned his voice. More brakes wailed, and in the background of the sound there was the distant rise and fall of other sirens.

"My," said Mrs. North, who was at the front windows. "My—cops! Come and look."

"I've got cops," Mr. North shouted back, before he thought. The leading cop said: "Hey, you!" But by that time there were two more cops coming up the stairs.

"Six cars, every which way," Mrs. North called, excitedly. "They don't pay any attention to one-way streets. Seven cars, and there's going to be a crowd. Oh—!"

Mr. North faced four policemen, and more were coming. It was all rather absurd—absurd and disproportionate, and for a moment Mr. North thought of the awful quiet upstairs in the bathroom and the faint light on the white body, and how it had begun to float. And now everything was so overwhelmingly alive, and full of sound.

"Upstairs," Mr. North said. "Top floor, in the bathroom. We found him."

The first two cops pounded on up the stairs. The next two went after them, but two more stayed with Mr. North.

"Well, buddy," one of them said, "what's going on, here?"

Mr. North looked at him, and said: "Oh, for God's sake."

"Listen, buddy—" the cop said.

"Where do you think you're going? To a fire?" Mr. North said, loudly. He was angry, all at once.

"There's another one, now," Mrs. North called, in what was clearly a pleased tone. "A big one, just like anybody's. And another little one."

"I guess it's the squad car, Buck," Mr. North's adversary said to the other policeman. "Get on inside, buddy." He said this last to Mr. North, in a tone of dislike, and Mr. North backed farther into the apartment. The two policemen came in with him, and stood looking at him. Then a much quieter voice spoke from the doorway, and the two policemen turned to face another man.

"What's going on here?" the new man said, but in a different tone. He said it as if he really wanted to know what was going on there. The policemen saluted.

"We just got here ourselves, Lieutenant," the spokesman said. "Some of the boys have gone on up."

"Some of them?" the lieutenant inquired. "Well, go up and bring some of them down. Before they take it apart." He spoke quietly, and did not seem excited or angry. "And you are the man who telephoned?" he said, to Mr. North. "Mr. Gerald North?" Mr. North nodded. "And you found a body, right?" Mr. North nodded again. There seemed, now, to be more connection between the white body upstairs and all this confusion—a connection, as yet remote, but which might grow tangible.

The new policeman looked at Mr. North as if he saw him, and spoke as if he were speaking to another man. It also helped that he was in ordinary clothing—an ordinary blue suit, with a white handkerchief in the breast pocket, and a soft gray hat, worn tilted forward on his head. He did not seem angry about anything at all, but only interested, and he was, Mr. North guessed, in his late thirties. There was nothing special about him, except an air of interest.

"Right," he said. "I'm Lieutenant Weigand, Homicide Bureau. William Weigand. I'd like to talk to you, after a bit. If you'll just wait until I look around upstairs? Right?"

"Of course," Mr. North said, and Mrs. North, who had left the window and come to the door, nodded. Weigand stood aside, rather obviously, and the two policemen went out. The policeman who didn't like Mr. North looked at him once more, forbiddingly, but he went. Mr. North closed the door and went with Mrs. North to the front window. The street was full of police cars, all right. They had come in, obviously, from both ends of the block and jammed to stops at any convenient angle. Up at the corner, Mr. North could see a policeman turning cars and trucks aside. Windows across the street were filled with people leaning out and, as they looked down, Mrs. Buano came up from her basement and spoke to one of the policemen. Then she looked up at the

Norths, wonderingly, and on up at the windows of the top floor. Across the street people were standing, looking up at the same windows, and more people were coming. Then there was the whine of another siren and an ambulance found a gap to stop in. A young man in white, wearing a cap with "Surgeon" on it in absurdly large letters and carrying a black bag, jumped out and trotted to the steps. He disappeared inside.

After that not much happened, for a while, except the sound of police voices in the common hall and on the stairs. Most of the policemen seemed to be saying "O.K." to one another. Then another car came, and men with cameras got out of it, and then there was an especially big car, and three rather big men got out of it. They did not run to the steps, but went with heavy dignity and, in spite of the thick carpeting on the stairs outside, Mr. North could hear them plodding up to the top of the house. But after a very little time he heard them plodding down again and they got in their car and drove away.

"I guess they didn't like it," Mr. North said. "Maybe it isn't big enough for them."

Then two taxicabs came up, almost at once, and young men jumped out of them. The young men had cards stuck in their hats. "Reporters," Mr. North said. The reporters stopped suddenly after they had run up the outside stairs, and the Norths, with the windows open, could hear them arguing with policemen in the vestibule. "What the hell," they heard one of the reporters say. "What's going on here?" It seemed to be the question of the day. Then there was a knock at the door of their apartment. Mr. North went and let in Lieutenant Weigand, and another man in ordinary clothes. The other man looked precisely as a police detective ought to look—he had a square face and a square torso, and Mr. North decided he was an inspector; perhaps even a deputy chief inspector.

"Now," said Weigand, "I'd like to have you tell me about it. This is Mullins—Detective Mullins. Take your hat off, Mullins." Mullins took his hat off and said, "O.K., Loot."

"We may as well sit down," Mr. North said. "Although we don't know much. He's dead, of course?"

"Very dead," Weigand said. "Quite a little while he's been dead. And you found him. Right?"

"We both found him," Mrs. North said. "It was dreadful." For a moment her face changed, as she remembered how dreadful it was.

"Yes," said Weigand. "Right. So you both found him. And how was that?"

"Well," said Mrs. North, before Mr. North could say anything, "it was because of the party, really. I was just showing Jerry about the party and we wanted to see if the bathroom was clean."

"The party?" Weigand said. "Yes, I see. What party?" He looked a little puzzled and confused.

"The party we are going to have up there," Mrs. North said; "only now we won't, of course. Would you?"

"No," said Weigand, "I guess not. Why have a party up there, though? Why not here? I don't think I get it, entirely, Mrs. North. It is Mrs. North?"

"This is Lieutenant Weigand, Pam," Mr. North said. "He's from the Homicide Bureau. This is my wife, Lieutenant."

"Right," said the lieutenant, and Mrs. North said, "How do you do?" and, "Why don't we sit down?" Everybody sat down but Detective Mullins.

"Sit down, Mullins," the lieutenant said, and Mullins said, "O.K., Loot," and sat down. It was evident that he was not a deputy chief inspector.

"Now," said Weigand, "let's see if I've got this right. You, Mrs. North, planned to give a party in the vacant apartment upstairs, and so this afternoon you and your husband went up to look at it, just—just why, Mrs. North?"

"To see how it looked," Mrs. North said. "Why?"

Weigand looked puzzled and a little alarmed, and evidently before he noticed it said, "What?" Mr. North observed the spread of Mrs. North's influence, and felt that things would probably be all right.

"I wanted to show Jerry where we were going to put things," Mrs. North said. "I decided yesterday, but he wanted to see, too. Didn't you, Jerry?"

"No," said Mr. North, "but it was all right. At first, anyway."

"Well," said Mrs. North, "I didn't know about that, of course. It wasn't there yesterday, and you don't expect them to be. Certainly not in bathtubs."

"Listen!" said Weigand. "Let's get this straight. Right?"

Both the Norths stopped and looked at him, for a moment honestly puzzled. Then they both laughed.

"I'm sorry," Mr. North said. "We get to talking. Pam was up there yesterday, and there wasn't any body then. That's all."

But Lieutenant Weigand was suddenly very interested, and there was nothing puzzled or doubtful in his expression as he looked at Mrs. North. He took a cigarette from a pack as he looked, and lighted it before he said anything.

"What's this about yesterday?" he said, then. "You were up there yesterday, too? Both of you?"

"No," said Mrs. North; "I was up there."

"And there wasn't any body?"

"Not when I was up there," Mrs. North said. "At least, I don't think—" She paused, and thought. Slowly her face changed, and there was something like fear in her expression, or perhaps, Mr. North thought, more a shrinking from something unpleasant than fear. "I don't know," Mrs. North said. "I didn't look in the bathroom, I don't think. Just in the other rooms. And the bathroom door was closed, so perhaps—" There was no doubt about the look, now. "I'm glad I didn't," she said. "Not alone."

"Look," said Mr. North, "when was it—when was he killed?"

"He was killed yesterday," Weigand said. "Sometime between noon and six in the evening, for a guess." He paused. "Somebody hit him hard on the head," the detective went on, slowly and clearly. "With some flat, heavy object. And crushed the skull."

Weigand looked at the Norths, neither of whom said anything. Mrs. North looked a little pale.

"He had a thin skull, probably," the detective said, "and it simply caved—caved inside, but hardly broke the skin. That's why there wasn't much blood. Then whoever did it beat the face."

Mr. North nodded. He remembered.

"Well," said Weigand, "there it is. Yesterday afternoon, sometime, and probably a blow to stun and then several more blows. And no struggle, so he wasn't expecting it. And now, Mrs. North, about yesterday—I think you'd better tell me all about yesterday. Just to get things straight. Right?"

"Everything?" said Mrs. North. "About threading the needle and Pete?"

Both Weigand and Mr. North looked at her, speculatively; Mr. North thought how accurately the detective's expression pictured his own feelings.

"Well," said Weigand, "of course I can't tell until I hear it. I only want what is pertinent, but perhaps you'd better start everything, anyway, and I'll stop you if it doesn't seem important. Right?"

"Do you always say 'Right'?" Mrs. North inquired, with interest. Weigand got a little red, and then he smiled. "All right," he said. "Habit. Now, as to yesterday—"

Mrs. North said she had got up late, rather, and had had breakfast— "with an egg, because it was Monday," Mrs. North said—and then had had to do some mending, which took a large part of the morning.

"That was because of the needle," she said. "I had an awful time threading it. It's the eye, you know. Smaller, or something. So it always splits, or just peeks through and I can't catch it."

She paused and looked at the detective inquiringly.

"All right, kid, be yourself," Mr. North said, and Weigand looked at him with enhanced friendliness. So Mrs. North had had lunch, rather late, and begun to think about having a party. Then she had thought about the vacant apartment on the top floor and had asked Mrs. Buano—there was a moment's pause, while Mrs. Buano was identified for Weigand—if she might use it. Then she had gone out for cigarettes and a newspaper and then, about three o'clock, she thought, had gone up to look at the apartment. She had looked at it and come down again and—

"Now," said Weigand, "let's go into that. Right?"

Mrs. North looked interested.

"Tell me about the apartment," Weigand said. "Everything you remember."

Mrs. North said it was, then, much as it was today, and that Mr. Weigand had, after all, just come down from it. There was a big room in front, she said, and then a narrow hall, with the bathroom opening off it. The thought of the bathroom sobered her and she became suddenly concise. "But you've seen that," she said. "It was hot and dusty, yesterday, and I thought of opening a window, but I decided it wasn't worth it and—" Then she stopped suddenly. "There was a window open today," she said. "Open when we went in."

"Yes," said Weigand. "Neither of you opened it. Right?"

They shook their heads.

"And—?" Weigand prompted.

But there was, it seemed, nothing more. Mrs. North had looked at the two big rooms, mentally placing a table to serve as a bar, and the radio; mentally decorating the room with paper from Dennison's. Then she had come down. That was all.

"Yes—?" said Weigand.

Then nothing else had happened, except that Pete had got lost.

"Pete?" Weigand said.

Both the Norths said, together: "Pete!"

And, after a dignified pause, Pete came out, waving his black tail. He was, Weigand agreed, a very handsome cat, with his black back and white—er—

"Chest and belly," Mrs. North said. "Yes." She looked at him. "Wash yourself, cat," she said. Pete looked at her and stretched. Mrs. North said he seemed to have got dusty somewhere, while he was lost. The lieutenant was more interested than Mr. North had expected in Pete, and wanted to know about his being lost.

He was lost, but only for a little while, after she had come down from upstairs the afternoon before, Mrs. North said—she thought she had come down about a quarter after three. She had seen Pete when she came down, but after about half an hour she called him and he had not come. Then she had looked all over and found he wasn't in the apartment, and realized he had gone out the window onto the roof.

"The roof?" Weigand said. Mr. North, realizing that it would save time, and probably confusion, took him to the rear windows in the living room and showed him the roof. The roof resulted, Mr. North explained, from another of Mrs. Buano's improvements.

She had extended the house at the rear to make room for a kitchen and an extra bedroom. The flat roof of this made a porch outside the Norths' windows. On it, the iron fire-stairs ended; from it an iron fire-ladder ran down the extension wall to the ground. Pete often went onto the roof, for the sun, and the Norths had frequently thought of making it into a terrace for summer, but never had.

"He goes out," Mrs. North said, "and then sometimes he goes on up the fire-escape and sits on the landing or even jumps to windows. The Nelsons often let him in."

"The Nelsons, yes," Weigand said. "The floor above, aren't they? And they've been in California for a month. Right?"

"Right," said Mr. and Mrs. North in rather embarrassing unison.

Pete had, Mrs. North thought, been gone fifteen minutes, perhaps, and then he had come in, sure enough from the roof. And that was all yesterday—Weigand looked as if he doubted it. He said he didn't want to lead her, but he wondered if there wasn't something else. "Pertinent?" said Mrs. North. "I don't think so." Martha cleaned the apartment and went marketing and then had gone home, Mrs. North said.

"And, of course, we went to Mr. Edwards' party in the evening," Mrs. North said. About seven, she thought, and they had a buffet supper. "You know, sliced turkey and ham and salads and lobster and things," she explained. "I didn't feel so well this morning, either, probably because of something I ate. The ham, maybe, or—" She paused a moment. "The lobster tasted a little flat, too," she said, reflectively.

Lieutenant Weigand said that he didn't suppose Mr. Edwards' party had anything to do with it, and both the Norths agreed.

"Nothing else?" Weigand wanted to know. "Nothing out of the ordinary? Nobody called?"

Mrs. North said no. Then she thought of something, but it wasn't out of the ordinary.

"There was Western Union," she said. "But it was the wrong house."

"Yes?" Weigand said.

It was, Mrs. North pointed out, nothing of interest. The doorbell had rung and she had clicked and then when nobody came up, opened the door of their apartment and called down the stairs. It had been Western Union, looking for a Mr. Shavely, or some such name, and she had told him there was no Mr. Shavely. Western Union had said "sorry" and gone away, and that was all.

"You're sure he went away?" Weigand asked. Mrs. North was. She had heard the door of the vestibule, which closed noisily, slam as she was closing her own.

"Did you see him?" Weigand persisted.

She hadn't, nor could she say anything about his voice, and was obviously puzzled at the detective's interest. And then, a moment before Mr. North thought of it, she said, "Oh!

"You mean—?" she said.

"They had to get in someway," Weigand pointed out. "Or one of them had to get in, and let the other in. And they would have needed keys to get from the vestibule to the hall. Right?"

The Norths nodded.

"So the simplest dodge would be to ring somebody's bell and then pretend to be looking for someone else, and then pretend to go out by slamming the door from inside. I think we can assume somebody did that."

"The murderer?" North said.

Weigand nodded.

"Or the victim," he said. "Either could have got in first, of course. So you see why the voice is important, Mrs. North."

Mrs. North said she did, but that she couldn't help. It was just a voice, and sounded as if the man had a cold. That was all. Weigand nodded. "Probably held his nose a little, or talked through a handkerchief," he said. "You didn't hear anybody go up?"

Mrs. North hadn't, and Weigand said he didn't suppose she would have. The stairs, he pointed out, were solid and the carpet was heavy. Nobody wanting to be quiet need be heard, he thought. Somebody, knowing about those things, and the darkness of the hall and the habits of the tenants, had almost certainly got in that way.

"The murderer, undoubtedly," Mr. North said, but Weigand shook his head and said there was nothing to tell. They would have to know more of what had happened, and something of whom it had happened to, before they could decide. But Mrs. North shook her head at that, and both the men looked at her. Mrs. North said that of course it was the murderer.

"Why?" Mr. North said.

"Because of the trouble," Mrs. North said. "He had to go to the trouble of planning how to get in and then of getting in. So of course it was the murderer."

The men looked at each other and shook their heads in a puzzled way. Mrs. North, seeing this, said, with a little scorn, that it was perfectly obvious.

"Nobody," Mrs. North said, "is going to that much trouble to *get* murdered. But if you're going to murder somebody, you expect to go to a lot of trouble. I would."

"Well," said Mr. North and then he looked at Lieutenant Weigand. Lieutenant Weigand was looking at Mrs. North in a startled way and, once again, Mr. North recognized an expression which, he knew, he himself often involuntarily assumed. He had an impulse to help the detective, and then he realized that there was nothing he could do. Lieutenant Weigand would have to learn his own way about, like other men. And when he did, Mr. North thought, he would learn that Mrs. North was very likely right. Mr. North himself was now entirely convinced that it had been the murderer who had pretended to be Western Union looking for Mr. Shavely, although he could see that Lieutenant Weigand might, quite reasonably, remain unpersuaded. The lieutenant would, Mr. North thought again, simply have to learn.

"Of course—" Weigand said, after a minute. Then he broke off and said suddenly, "Mullins!" The Norths were startled because they had forgotten Mullins was there, sitting in a corner; Mullins apparently was startled, too, for he said, first "Huh?" in an awakened tone and only then, "O.K., Loot."

"Go up and see how they're coming upstairs," he said. "And then go and ask the landlady, Mrs.—"

"Buano," North said.

"Buano, if she let any strangers into the house yesterday. And then come back."

Mullins said, "O.K., Loot," and went away. Weigand sat a moment, thinking, and paying little attention to the Norths. When he did speak, it was more to himself than to them.

"Jumping at conclusions, of course," he said. "The Western Union boy may have been a Western Union boy looking for a man named Shavely. The murderer might have come in any time earlier, and hidden when she was up and—"

"No," said Mr. North, "I don't think so. The window, you know. It was closed when she was there, open later." Weigand said, "Umm," thoughtfully.

"Then there couldn't have been a body there when I was," Mrs. North said. "I'm glad because I would have been frightened."

Both Weigand and North thought that one over, but neither said anything.

"It gives you the time if it was the Western Union boy," Mr. North pointed out. Weigand nodded. Then Mullins poked his head in and said they were about through up there. "D.O.A.," Mullins said, "and no M.E. yet. I'll buzz Mrs. Buano, huh?" Weigand nodded and Mullins started off. Then Weigand called him and asked if the Doc had made a guess on the time of death. "Just a guess is all I want," Weigand said. The Doc had, it appeared: "Not much more than twenty-four hours, not much less than eighteen." Weigand looked mildly reproving, and said he hoped the Medical Examiner would do better. "Not that he will," Weigand added, a shade morosely.

"What's D.O.A.?" Mrs. North asked.

"The man upstairs," Weigand said. "Dead on arrival, the ambulance surgeon said. And M.E. is Medical Examiner. Right?"

Mrs. North said, "Thank you," and then both the Norths waited while Weigand thought. Then Mullins, who seemed now to be moving very rapidly, came back and stuck his head in again.

"She says no," Mullins said. "She didn't let nobody in."

Weigand nodded and after a while nodded again, more decisively.

"It starts us, anyway," he said. "We'll call it the Western Union boy, anyway until we know better. It gives us a time, about—About when, Mrs. North, as near as you can come?"

Mrs. North thought a minute, and said that after she had come down she had had to wash her hands, because she touched something dusty up there, and then she had sat down to read and then the bell had rung. It had been about ten minutes, or perhaps fifteen, after she had come down. She thought around three-thirty, one way or the other. Weigand nodded.

"Probably before rather than after," the detective said. "People tend to overestimate time, usually. Say 3:25, or even 3:20."

"That's one limit, then," Mr. North said. Mr. North was acutely interested and was, he discovered, forgetting how horribly real the body had been. Weigand nodded.

"But any time from then on," North pointed out. "From, say 3:30 to midnight?"

Weigand hesitated for a moment, and then did not answer directly. Instead, he said that there was something upstairs he wanted them to look at, and stood up. The Norths got up too, and followed him upstairs. At the door they stopped, startled at the number of things which seemed to be going on, illuminated by harsh floodlights. Men were, apparently, looking for fingerprints everywhere, and two men were taking pictures. There were flashes from the bathroom and Mrs. North came closer to her husband and put a hand on his arm. He closed his free hand over it, reassuringly, and after a moment she smiled at him. Several of the men looked at the Norths briefly, nodded to Weigand and continued their work.

"Here's what I want you to look at," Weigand said, and led them to the open window. He pointed to the broad, dusty sill. The dust had been disturbed, irregularly, and the Norths looked at it, puzzled. Weigand apparently expected them to say something. He looked at Mr. North inquiringly. Mr. North had just begun to shake his head, when Mrs. North spoke.

"Pete," she said. "See, there's a paw. And there—" she paused for a moment. "There's where he sat," she said. "He came up here when he was lost and the window was open—why, Pete saw it!"

Weigand said that of course they didn't know it was Pete.

"But it was a cat," Mr. North said, "and it's hard for a cat to get here, unless it climbs the fire-ladder, and it wouldn't."

It occurred to him that he sounded rather like Mrs. North, but it was perfectly clear to him. It was clear to Weigand, too, evidently, since he nodded. He said that it probably was Pete, all right, and that the murderer had arrived in time to open the window while the cat was lost. That was—? Mrs. North guessed it as between 3:30 and 4 o'clock.

"But he wouldn't go straight up," she said. "He never goes anywhere until he's smelled the porch roof, and it would take him a minute or two to make up his mind to come in after he came down, unless—" She stopped, and Weigand nodded again.

"Unless he was scared," Mrs. North went on. "Then he'd bolt home and what would scare him there but—" She stopped suddenly. "He saw the murderer!" she said. "And it scared him, poor kitty."

Weigand kept on nodding, and said it could be that way; could very easily be that way. "I was wondering about the marks," he said, "and then you told me about the cat being lost. But would it scare him, do you think? Or would he just be interested?"

The Norths consulted briefly, and silently, and Mr. North said he thought Pete would be scared if there was sudden movement, or a struggle or if anything fell.

"And then he'd run home at once?" Weigand asked. Mr. North thought so and Mrs. North was sure of it. Weigand nodded slowly, and said that that might do it.

"That would make it around four o'clock," he said. "A little before, or after. Just before he came back. It isn't final, obviously, but it's something to go on. Tentatively. Right?"

He did not give them time to answer, because just then there was a stir near the door, and somebody yelled: "O.K., bring it up." Weigand looked over toward the door, nodded at a man entering with a physician's black bag in his hand, and said to the Norths that probably they'd better go down to their apartment and stick around. Mr. North lifted inquiring eyebrows at him and he nodded.

"The basket," Weigand said. "They're about ready to take it away. That was the Medical Examiner. You don't want her—" Weigand nodded at Mrs. North, and Mr. North realized that the detective was quite right, not only as regarded Mrs. North, but as far as he was concerned, too. "No more bodies right now," he thought, and guided Mrs. North out and down. Weigand remained behind, talking with the Medical Examiner.

"Well!" said Mrs. North, when they were downstairs again and had the lights on. Mr. North felt, he said, precisely the same way, and they looked at each other with surprised expressions. Then Mrs. North said that things certainly were funny, when you didn't expect them. After a moment she added that the detective was nice, and not what she would have expected. She said she had thought derby hats.

"I thought derby hats and cigars," she said. "But he's just like anybody. You wouldn't think he was."

"That's what he keeps Mullins for," Mr. North suggested. "Mullins couldn't be anything else, and he guarantees Weigand."

Mrs. North agreed that that was probably what they had Mullins for.

• 3 •

TUESDAY
7 P.M. TO MIDNIGHT

Lieutenant Weigand looked thoughtfully, even a little wonderingly, after the Norths' when they started downstairs; he smiled a moment reminiscently and then recalled himself sharply to the business in hand. There was, clearly, an abundance of business. He talked to the Assistant Medical Examiner for a moment, learning that he agreed with the ambulance surgeon as to the approximate time of death, that a post mortem might—or, on the other hand, might not—give more accurate information and that the body would be posted at once.

"Then if he's eaten recently you'll know about when he died," the physician observed. "That is," he added, "if you know when he ate."

Weigand thanked him and thought he might as well eat himself. He collected Mullins, left word that everything should be rushed as much as possible and all data sent to his office at Headquarters, and led Mullins out. Walking with Mullins, who was so inescapably a detective, always made Weigand feel, obscurely, as if he were under arrest. Mullins was often helpful, however; just now he knew a swell place around the corner to eat. He led the way to it, and into a long, noisy barroom, with tables in the rear. There was a noticeable lessening of the

26

noise when Mullins entered and everybody looked at Weigand curiously, and with sympathy. Weigand stifled a rising suspicion that any
kitchen in the establishment would be there merely as a legal device,
satisfying the statute which, in New York, requires a readiness to serve
food on the part of all who want to serve liquor.

Weigand, reflecting that he was on duty, drank two quick martinis,
after which things were noticeably better. Mullins had an old-fashioned,
and another old-fashioned. Weigand looked at the menu and had another
martini, which gave him strength to order. He looked at the New Eng-
land Pot Roast which resulted and speculated on the desirability of
another martini, but decided against it. There was, after all, Deputy
Chief Inspector Artemus O'Malley. Artemus was no teetotaler; on the
other hand, he would view any tendency to stagger with disapproval.
Weigand ate quickly, nervously, and waited for Mullins, who ate slowly
and thoroughly. Mullins finished his pie and showed an inclination to
talk.

"It's a funny one, all right," Mullins said. "Why do we get the funny
ones, huh? Why not just ordinary blastings? The kind you just give a
couple of guys a going over for?"

Weigand shook his head, not knowing the answers. It was a funny
one, all right—a bare man in a bare apartment. You couldn't start more
completely from scratch, if you came to that. Weigand moved his head
again, nodding this time to show that he agreed with Mullins.

"With a blasting, you know where you are, and can just round guys
up," Mullins added, plodding after his thought. He smiled at the
thought when he overtook it. Mullins liked to round guys up. His smile
was succeeded by a somber expression, and Weigand could chart the
arrival of realization that there was nobody to be rounded up. Then
Mullins brightened again.

"How about these North guys?" he said. "They'd talk, all right." He
looked hopefully at Weigand. "They're screwy, anyhow," Mullins
urged.

Weigand shook his head, and Mullins' hopes visibly subsided. He
sighed deeply, and looked at the menu again, seeking comfort. But
Weigand shook his head once more.

"We've got to see the chief," he said. "Dear old Arty. And how he'll love it."

They rose, Mullins reluctantly.

"And don't tell Arty that one about the Norths," Weigand warned. "The idea's screwier than they are. Right?"

Mullins said, "O.K." without enthusiasm. The more he thought about the Norths, his face reported to the lieutenant, the more he thought it would be a fine idea to go over them a bit. They would be easy to round up, too. But maybe the Loot knew best.

They picked up their car and Mullins winked on its red emergency lights. Then, to the accompaniment of a stimulatingly alarming noise from the siren, they went down to Centre Street. Mullins went, on order, to the Homicide Bureau office and inquired with decision whether a lot of things were being done. They were, because the police department knows ways of starting from scratch; because a naked body, male, 165 pounds, five feet ten inches, brown hair and eyes, age about forty, has ways of speaking even after the tongue is stilled. Department experts, without direction from Mullins, were trying to make it speak.

The Medical Examiner's office was taking it apart with knives, and reserving portions for analysis, and sewing it up again. Fingerprint men had long since photographed and enlarged the prints of the dead fingers, and found that there were none in the department files to match them. Copies of the enlargements had been started by air mail to Washington and the Federal Bureau of Investigation, and there more experts compared them with yet more files, and found nothing. To the Federal Bureau, too, went precise physical descriptions, backed by measurements, and those, reduced to punch marks in a key card, sent thousands of other cards whirling through a machine, and expelled a few of them—including cards which gave names and last addresses and other significant details of three men long since dead, two serving life sentences and another at that moment awaiting trial for bank robbery. This was not as helpful as it might have been.

And the body's teeth were examined. They turned out, to everyone's annoyance, to be remarkably healthy teeth, showing only a few small fillings and no really intricate dental construction. It was a set-back; nevertheless, dental charts were prepared on what data there was, and sent circulating among dentists, on the off chance. The Bureau of Missing Persons came into it, checking the description of the body against those of men who had wandered, unreported, from their homes, and one or two promising leads were turned up. Detectives hurried with photographs to consult worried men and women who might prove to be relatives of what had been found in the bathtub of 95 Greenwich Place, and men and women looked at the photographs fearfully and sighed over them with relief. For that came to nothing, too.

While this went on, and Mullins waited, Lieutenant Weigand went to see Deputy Chief Inspector Artemus O'Malley, in charge of the Homicide Squad, and of Lieutenant Weigand—in final charge, too, of the body which had turned up in the bathtub. Inspector O'Malley had once been rather like Mullins, only several times as bright. Like Mullins, he preferred blastings, and regarded amateur murder with distrust. Murders like the present, which were not only amateur but bizarre, irritated Inspector O'Malley. Thus, although not an unamiable man, as Deputy Chief Inspectors go, he growled at Weigand when the lieutenant entered, and wanted to know, profanely, where he had been. Weigand said he had stopped for a bite of dinner; he tried to make it sound as if he had scooped a sandwich off a counter and chewed as he ran after clues. The inspector looked at him coldly, and Weigand was gratified that he had avoided the fourth cocktail, but felt slightly uneasy about the third.

"Well," said Inspector O'Malley, "what's going on there? It sounds screwy to me."

Weigand told him what he knew—about the Norths finding the body, about the battered skull and the nudity, about the Western Union boy who probably was not a Western Union boy, and about the cat. He told about the cat with misgivings, because, among other prejudices, Inspector O'Malley did not like cats. He did not even like to have cats mentioned. He frowned disgustedly.

"A cat!" he said. "For God's sake!"

Lieutenant Weigand was sorry, and said so. Nevertheless, there it was. A cat had got into it and, when you looked at it carefully, to good purpose. It fixed the time, if you could believe it.

"A cat!" said Inspector O'Malley, with distilled disgust.

The inspector glared at Weigand, blaming him for the cat. Weigand waited suitably and went on.

"Well," said the inspector, when Weigand had told him all he could think of that was pertinent, and omitted only the conversational waywardness of Mrs. North, which he doubted the inspector would appreciate—"well, it's your baby, Weigand. It's certainly a screwy one."

Weigand nodded. There was no doubt of that.

"Let's have a report," the inspector directed. "Let me know when you get an identification. Did you see the press?"

O'Malley preferred the press to cats, but by a narrow margin, and his tone revealed it. Weigand had seen the press, as a matter of fact; for a moment amid other moments. He had told the press there was a body and murder, and described the man. He said that that was all he knew, thinking it was enough for the press to know—from him, at any rate. The press could go to O'Malley, for more. The press would, it assured him, and he warned the inspector. The inspector thanked him for nothing; the press was on the doorstep, howling. Weigand thought of something, and suggested it, as a lieutenant suggests things to an inspector. He thought it would be better if the exact time of the killing were kept from the press. The inspector agreed.

"Even if we knew it," he said. "A cat!"

Weigand left it to the inspector to tell the reporters that he, Deputy Chief Inspector Artemus O'Malley, had the matter well in hand and expected an arrest soon. The inspector, Weigand knew, would "have the case in hand" and be "working on it unsparingly" until, in the end, he solved it. And if it were not solved, the inspector would take Weigand in hand. The lieutenant did not resent this; it was a course proper to inspectors.

Weigand went back to his office and looked at the reports, which were coming in. Prints not in the files; the body not that of Mr. Irwin Bokandosky, missing since September 26 from his home in the Bronx; not that of Alexander K. Churchill, absent only since the tenth day of

October from his home in Queens—and also from his cage in the City National Bank. This last did not surprise the Police Department in the least; it had ideas already about Mr. Churchill. Mullins reported that it was a damned screwy case, and was deepeningly pessimistic.

Weigand studied the report sent along by the Assistant Medical Examiner, Dr. Sampson. It was technical, but clear enough, and Weigand translated it to himself. The man had been dead about twenty-four hours, but it might be as short a time as twenty or as long a time as twenty-eight. He had eaten several hours before he died. Death resulted from severe brain lacerations, and several blows had been struck. The blow which had partly disfigured the face, breaking the nose, had been delivered after the man was dead. Perhaps, Weigand thought, out of sheer rage. The weapon had had, apparently, a circular, flat face. ("Maybe a croquet-mallet," Sampson had written along one edge of the report.) Weigand conveyed the gist of this to Mullins, who took it badly.

"Men with no clothes, croquet-mallets, cats and screwy people," he said, indignantly. "And the guy ain't even got a record," he added, piling on what was evidently the last straw. Weigand agreed this made things difficult, as did the battering of the face. The last was, intentionally or not, a shrewd move on the part of the murderer, since it made it highly improbable that the newspapers would publish photographs taken of the corpse, and thus blocked one quick channel of identification. Weigand sighed and reached for his hat.

"Let's go look at it," he said. "Maybe we'll see something."

Mullins heaved himself up, sadly, and Weigand led the way to their car. Mullins switched on the red lights, which made him more cheerful, and almost smiled as the siren cried their coming. A morgue attendant got the body out of its refrigerated drawer, where Dr. Sampson had left it. Weigand examined the hands, and pointed out the deep cigarette stains on the right hand.

"You get that from holding on when you drag," Mullins assured him. "If you let go, you don't get them, see?"

Weigand said he saw, saying it abstractly as he examined the face. The wound told him nothing, but he looked thoughtfully at the bristle on the undamaged cheeks. The beard had grown since death, but it seemed to have grown irregularly—here and there the detective saw hairs much longer than those around them. And the short sideburns, instead of ending sharply, were irregular. The man had shaved hurriedly and badly when he shaved the last time and—then Weigand realized why, and rubbed his own cheek reflectively. He, too, had recently bought an electric shaver, and was having trouble learning to use it. Unaccountably, it missed hairs now and then, and it was hard to get a clean line at the sides. It left stray beard hairs standing belligerently among their clipped neighbors.

It might, Weigand realized, put them on to something. With his own razor there had come a guarantee blank, valid only when it had been filled in with the name and address of the purchaser and sent to the district office of the manufacturer. If, now, this man filled out such a blank and mailed it, his name and address would be on file with the company—along with, he added sadly to himself, hundreds, perhaps thousands, of others. If he had bought the same kind of razor Weigand had bought himself; if he had sent in the guarantee blank as, thinking of it, Weigand remembered he himself had not. "Do it tomorrow," he thought, and pulled himself back to the matter at hand. Was it, he wondered, worth the trouble? He decided it was, and looked sympathetically at Mullins. Mullins caught the look, which he knew of old, and an expression of foreboding overspread his face.

"Now, Loot," he began, "listen—"

Weigand told him, crisply, what he had to do—he and Perkins and Washburn. Mullins' expression lightened a little at the news he was not to be the only victim. They would get hold of the manager of the Clipper Shave Company and he—with Perkins and Washburn—would go over the records of guarantee slips returned. They would copy out all showing identified purchases within two weeks—"better make it three," Weigand corrected himself—and tomorrow they would get enough men on it to make the rounds.

"Tonight?" said Mullins, drearily. "I gotta work all night?"

Weigand's sympathy was mild and his instructions unaltered. "Tomorrow you can get some sleep," he promised. Mullins went unhappily to the telephone to break the news to Perkins and Washburn, and to try to persuade one of them to uncover an officer of the company. Mullins said "Yeah" and "That's what I told him" into the telephone, glanced around to see if Weigand had relented, learned he had not, and, eventually, went about his chore. And now, Weigand realized, he would do it diligently and exactly, missing nothing. Weigand looked at the body and had another idea, but decided it could go until morning. He could, he decided, do with some sleep himself, and went home to get it.

• 4 •

WEDNESDAY
8 A.M. TO NOON

He went to sleep in his small apartment uptown thinking that it might be rather fun to be married to somebody like—well, like Mrs. North. He awoke in the morning and groaned to find it day again, and constabulary duty to be done. He made himself coffee and toast and decided the world was screwy; he smoked his first cigarette and was mildly dizzy for a moment; he answered the telephone. Mullins, sleepily, reported a list of four hundred and thirty-two names, all over town, and said he was turning it in and going to get some sleep. Weigand called Headquarters, reported, and found that the squad could allow him three men to check the four hundred and thirty-two names, and felt that preliminary work, at least, could be done by telephone.

"Arty doesn't think so much of the idea, anyhow," the office lieutenant informed him.

Weigand hadn't thought Arty would. Nor did he suppose Arty would think so much of the other idea, which was for a canvass of cigar-stores with pictures. The canvass might, Weigand thought, begin in the neighborhood of the murder, although there was no particular reason to think the murdered man lived there. Afterward it might

34

broaden out. The Bureau decided, reluctantly, it could give five men to that and Weigand realized the murder was making a stir. He got his newspapers from in front of the apartment door, when he had finished with the telephone. The murder was making a stir, all right; it had, Weigand gathered, everything. There were pictures of the house, and of the bathroom—without body—and of the Norths. Mrs. North looked surprised and interested, Weigand noticed. There were no pictures of the body, except a few shots in one of the tabloids, taken at some distance and after the body had been covered. Nobody, the newspapers reported, knew the identity of the victim, nor the time of the murder. The Norths, he was pleased to notice, had evidently been cautious about what they said to the press.

Weigand went downtown to Headquarters and waited for reports. It was dull business, and he took a hand in telephoning to the purchasers of electric razors. Most of them were alive and well, or had been when they left home that morning. Two wives who answered gave small shrieks, and, apparently, fainted. About every fourth call gave no response and had to be put aside for further investigation, along with a smaller pile of reports which left matters in the air. It was slow work and probably, Weigand thought, futile. He was explaining to an alarmed Italian woman that her husband was, so far as he knew, in perfectly good health and importing the olive oil he had gone forth that morning to import, when a call came. He hung up on expostulations, and said "Yes?" into the other telephone.

"Detective Stein, Lieutenant," the voice said. "Got him, I think."

Weigand was flooded with pleased astonishment, and demanded particulars. Stein was, he said, in a United Cigar Store on Sixth Avenue, about three blocks from Greenwich Place. It was only the third store he had tried, and the clerk was pretty sure.

"Fellow named Brent, he thinks it is," Stein said. "A lawyer."

Weigand told him to stick around; that he would be up. A squad car took him up. The clerk was certain, by now, and pleased with himself.

"He's been coming for three years, Mr. Brent has," he said. "That's him, all right." He pointed at a photograph, retouched to lessen the facial injuries as much as possible, taken in profile to hide them still more.

"That's the angle he always stood at," the clerk said. "Put one elbow on the counter and talked a minute, he did. Came in almost every day and just stood there while I got the cigarettes; always the same brand, always two packs. He didn't ever have to order when I was on."

His name was Brent, which was as far as the clerk could go. He could go so far because Brent had come in once or twice with friends who had called him by name. Once one of them had said, to Brent, something about "you lawyers" and after that, when they were talking, the clerk had asked Brent if he were a lawyer and Brent had said he was.

"I like to find out about customers," the clerk explained. "Makes the job more interesting, somehow."

Weigand agreed that it would do that, and started things rolling by telephone. It was easy to find the Brents who were lawyers. There were only three of them. It was easy to discover, by telephone, that two of the legal Brents were in their offices, deep, it proved, in conference, and that the third had not yet come in. It was not, indeed, difficult to detect an undercurrent of uneasiness and uncertainty in the voice of the secretary whose employer had not arrived—the secretary of Mr. Stanley Brent, of 34 Fifth Avenue, with offices in East Forty-second Street, who lived within such comfortable walking distance of the United Cigar Store on Sixth Avenue near Tenth.

Weigand came out of the booth, thought a moment and went back in, calling Headquarters and the squad room where the check of electric shaver purchases wearily continued. He told the detective who answered that they could lay off a while, and to find out if the name of Stanley Brent, 34 Fifth Avenue, was on the list. It was, and Weigand was pleased with himself. It was on the list of those whose telephones had not answered, but that had been almost two hours earlier. Weigand went around, with Stein.

• 5 •

WEDNESDAY
NOON TO 2 P.M.

There was nothing homely and nothing old about the apartment house at 34 Fifth Avenue; it belonged to a different era than the comfortable, spacious one which had given rise to the Buano house and its multiple replicas. The apartment house at No. 34 rose sharply in dispassionate façade and kept on rising for a long way. It was sleek and indifferent—the very model of what lower Fifth Avenue had become. A doorman gave the door a starting push for Weigand and Stein, making the action a haughty ritual. A uniformed attendant permitted them to ask that he announce them to Mrs. Brent, but his dignity slipped a little when Weigand gave his name and rank—Detective Lieutenant Weigand, from Headquarters. Curiosity and surmise passed hurriedly across the attendant's features and left troubled ripples behind them.

Mrs. Brent would see them; Mrs. Brent, after a slim, dark maid in a pale green uniform had momentarily intervened, saw them. Mrs. Brent was tall for a woman. Summer tan was still on her face and arms; smooth tan, well acquired. She moved with compact grace as, greeting them at the door of a long living-room, she led them a little way in and then turned, her eyebrows lifting politely. She said:

37

"Lieutenant Weigand? Yes?"

She said it, Weigand was gratified and a little surprised to observe, to him. Stein's recognition was condensed to an inclination of the head. Her eyes, Weigand noticed, were gray and steady and seemed to be ready for something. Weigand thought how to begin; began by suggesting that she sit down. It told her something, apparently.

"Stan?" she said. "Mr. Brent—?"

"It may be," Weigand said. "We're not certain, yet. But a man who may be Mr. Brent has—has had an accident."

She moved a foot or two and sat down.

"Dead?" she said. The voice had lost resonance. It was as if it were going on by itself. "He's dead?"

"It may not be Mr. Brent," Weigand said. "We don't know—there were circumstances. Was he home—" Weigand hesitated. "Was he home last night, say? Or yesterday?"

Mrs. Brent shook her head, and said she didn't know.

"I just got back," she said. "I was in the country. I've been in the country since Saturday, until just now—closing the house. But I thought Stan would be here this morning, and his office—"

Her voice still seemed to be going on of itself.

"I was going to call you," she said. "Somebody, I mean—the police. He hasn't been at his office since Monday morning." Her hands clenched and unclenched on the arm of the chair. "Tell me—" she said.

Weigand told her part of it. But it might not be her husband. It was merely a possibility. Her husband was about forty? His hair and eyes were brown? He—? Mrs. Brent nodded with each question, and her eyes grew wider and seemed to grow shallow. It was horrible to tell people things like this, Weigand thought, and now she knew; there was no doubt, really. Her voice was still deadened when she spoke—deadened and certain.

"The man—" she said. "The man who was killed? In the papers?"

"We don't know," Weigand said. "That's it—we don't know. You'll have to tell us. I'm sorry, Mrs. Brent, I'm—" But there was no word to fit. "I'm afraid I'll have to ask you to come with us," he said. He was formal, as a policeman. He would, at the moment, have liked to be something else; he would have liked to sell cigarettes to cheerful, chatting men who leaned elbows on showcases. These were the worst moments in a murder case. You grew used to the ones who were killed, used to bodies and coldness and horrible things. But you never got used to the ones who were still living; never learned what to say to them.

Mrs. Brent stood up. Weigand nodded imperceptibly to Stein, and the other detective moved so he could reach a hand to Mrs. Brent's shoulder, if it were needed. But it was not needed. Claire Brent walked quite evenly to the hall and adjusted the hat the maid handed her, slipped into the coat. Her voice was quite level when she spoke to the maid, saying she would be gone for an hour or two. All the way downtown in the taxicab the doorman got for them, with the dignified cordiality reserved for tenants and now extended to the companions of tenants, Claire Brent sat quietly, with her hands still in her lap. At the morgue she waited with unswerving quiet while the refrigerating drawer was opened and the body moved to a marble-topped table under a light. Even when the face was uncovered, she only nodded, slowly and with a horrible stiffness. Then her two hands on the sides of the table tightened for an instant and relaxed and Weigand caught her before her loosened body reached the floor.

"And that," he said to himself, "is that."

He sent Stein home with Mrs. Brent and Stein called a doctor and directed the frightened maid. Mrs. Brent was conscious again by that time and her eyes were open, looking at nothing. They still had a strangely shallow look, and it was impossible to believe that she was seeing anything through them; anything that was there and then. . . .

Weigand went on to Headquarters, reported, set things rolling again. Two hours later the newspapers were excited with the news that Stanley Brent, Yale graduate and attorney, member of the firm of Strahan, Mahoney and Brent, was the man found murdered so curiously in a bathtub in the village; found "nude" the previous day, in case the readers had forgotten, by Gerald North, connected with the publishing firm of Kensington & Brown, and Mrs. North; husband of Claire Brent, before her marriage Claire Askew and well known a few years before as a tournament tennis player who once had reached the quarter-finals at Forest Hills before she was eliminated by Helen Jacobs; father of no children, member of several clubs. He was generally thought of, the papers said, as one of the more promising of the younger members of the city's bar. He had had a short but brilliant career several years before as an Assistant District Attorney. A former State Supreme Court Justice spoke very highly indeed of Mr. Brent, as a prosecutor and as a man.

Detectives settled down on the law offices of Strahan, Mahoney and Brent. They learned from Brent's secretary, who fluttered with excitement and now and then wept, that Brent had left the office at lunchtime Monday, saying he would not be back and not saying where he was going. She had canceled several appointments for him, at his direction. She had wondered when he did not come to the office Tuesday and had told Mr. Mahoney. (Mr. Strahan had, it seemed, been dead for several years.) Mr. Mahoney had suggested that she telephone Mr. Brent's home, which she had done, getting no answer. Mr. Mahoney had then said that, probably, Mr. Brent had gone to the country to help Mrs. Brent with the closing of the house, and been prevented from telephoning, or thought it unnecessary. She had telephoned the apartment again that morning, and still got no answer, and had been about to ask Mr. Mahoney for further instructions when Mrs. Brent telephoned and was told her husband had not been at the office since Monday.

Detectives settled down in Brent's office; experts with training as accountants began going through books. Mr. Mahoney spluttered and was calmed. Nothing confidential would trickle through the police hands and minds. But the police wanted to find out things—names of clients, details of appointments, names of correspondents who might, as correspondents sometimes did for one reason and another, write personal letters to a lawyer at his office. When they left they took a good many things with them—check-books, appointment blanks, not a few letters which were, clearly, extremely personal. Back at Headquarters they made out reports, attaching exhibits, and sent them along to Deputy Chief Inspector Artemus O'Malley, who looked at them with a detached air and sent them to Detective Lieutenant Weigand.

Inspector O'Malley then saw the press and reported that he and the men working under him were, they felt, making rapid progress. Without saying so, he left the implication that an arrest was extremely imminent. This implication encountered the tough, experienced minds of reporters who knew Inspector O'Malley, and many other policemen. The implications bounced, at which nobody was surprised, not even Inspector O'Malley.

Weigand was at his desk when the reports came in, and decided to defer them, for the moment. People first, Lieutenant Weigand believed. Then documents. Then, with both people and documents in mind, people again. He looked at his watch, confirming his suspicion that it was lunch-time. He lifted a telephone and instructed the police operator to get Detective Mullins on the wire. Detective Mullins came on the wire. He said:

"Hey, listen, Loot, you said—"

Weigand said he was sorry, but that things were happening. Mullins could eat breakfast while he ate lunch and meet him—well, meet him at 95 Greenwich Place. They would go on from there. Mullins groaned.

"O.K., Loot," he said, aggrievement in his voice.

Weigand went on to lunch. After lunch he walked a dozen blocks, thinking. There was not, he found, much to think about, as yet. But, at any rate, he had the victim; had something to work on. He would talk to a few people now, before they thought too much, get what he could find from the desk Brent almost certainly had in his apartment. Then he could spend the evening putting things together, if they would go together. The trouble with this business was, he thought to himself, that you never got enough sleep. You never knew enough facts, either.

Lieutenant Weigand went down into a subway entrance, hung to a porcelain strap and stared for a few minutes at a map of the Independent Subway System, and emerged at West Fourth Street. From there it was only a few blocks to the Buano house. When he got there, Mullins was standing in front of it, leaning on the railing and looking suspiciously at a negro houseboy who had come out of a house across the street to polish the doorknob and look suspiciously at Mullins.

Weigand gathered Mullins up and together they summoned Mrs. Buano. She had never heard of Stanley Brent. He had certainly not occupied the house while she owned it. She had been consulted by Mrs. North on Monday about a party in the vacant apartment—"studio"—on the top floor, had seen nothing odd in the request and had readily agreed. Yes, Mrs. North had said she was going up to look at the apartment. Mrs. Buano had told her that the door was unlocked; it had not been locked since the previous tenant moved out. Why, when you came to that, should it be locked? There were the four walls, nothing else and, in any case, the front door of the house was always locked. Nobody could get in.

"Well," Weigand said, "somebody did. Right?"

Mrs. Buano, a middle-aged, incisive woman, with coiffed gray hair, agreed that somebody had, more the pity was. It didn't, she pointed out, help the house—thank heaven the Norths weren't apt to be frightened away, however. She did not, it became clear, blame them for finding the body. It was, as a matter of fact, just as well they had, since it had to be found sometime.

"That might have been a long time, as a matter of fact," Weigand pointed out. "With the bathroom door closed, and the apartment door closed—heavy doors, heavy walls, top of the house. And the bathroom has a ventilator, of course? Right?"

Mrs. Buano agreed. Ventilators were required by the building code. Weigand nodded.

"And with a window open, too," he said. "The murderer may have counted on its being a good while before anybody noticed. You wouldn't have gone up in the normal course of things, would you?"

Mrs. Buano agreed that she wouldn't. Not with the October renting season past, although one could never tell. But it might, certainly, have been several weeks, in the ordinary course of things; even a month or two. With the ventilator and everything, and the doors closed.

"He may have counted on that," Weigand said. "He may have thought, if it was long enough, we couldn't identify. Right? We would have, though."

Turning from that, he confirmed that Mrs. Buano had admitted no one to the apartment Monday afternoon; as a matter of fact, she was away for a couple of hours in the middle of it. She had heard nothing of the Western Union boy, but that, she added, meant nothing. She might have been away; she might have been in the rear of her own ground floor, where she would have heard nothing in the hall in front. There were, she was certain, no keys to the front door loose in the world. She had a set, and her maid; each tenant had two each. She had the two keys which would have been issued to tenants of the top floor. The Nelsons, on the third floor, might, to be sure, have given their keys to somebody, but she thought it unlikely. They were very particular people. Either of the Norths, and particularly Mrs. North, might easily lose a key, but if either did he would report the loss and she would change the lock. Only a few months before, indeed, Mrs. North had lost a key, and Mrs. Buano had had the lock changed. But since then no keys had been missing; the key lost by Mrs. North the spring before would be useless in the lock now on the door.

That seemed, Weigand agreed, to be that. He thanked Mrs. Buano, hoping he would not have to bother her soon again. She bowed; Weigand bowed. On the sidewalk again, Mullins said that, to him, it was still screwy. He was morose about it.

Weigand thought that, while they were there, they might as well talk to the Norths—to Mrs. North, anyway, assuming Mr. North would be at his office.

Mrs. North was home, and clicked them in. She leaned over the banister and beckoned eagerly. She was excited.

"I was just trying to get you," she said. "I know who did it!"

"What?" said Weigand.

"The murder," Mrs. North said. "I know who did it! He left his name!"

"Well," said Weigand, and then, because no word he could think of seemed adequate, "well . . . " Then there seemed to be only one next remark.

"Who was it?" Weigand said. "That is, I mean—who was it?"

Mrs. North said that, if he would come in, she would tell him all about it. He went in. Mullins went in behind him.

"Screwy," Mullins murmured, darkly, just loudly enough for Weigand to hear. "I told you it was screwy."

"Well," said Weigand, when they were sitting in the living-room.

"You'll tell me about it, right? Who left his name? Where?"

Mrs. North said she wanted to begin at the beginning. The beginning, she said, was the Mortons, who were coming to dinner that evening. "And flowers," Mrs. North said. "There's a man over in the doorway who sells them for almost nothing. And—"

"Listen," said Weigand. "He left his name? Right?"

Mrs. North said she was coming to that.

"It's a big clue," she said, "but it goes in order or it doesn't mean anything. It was when I was going out to buy the flowers because the Mortons are coming to dinner tonight. Right?"

"Right," said Weigand.

Mrs. North had gone downstairs, on her way to get flowers, she said. It was about—"What time is it now?" Mrs. North said. It was a quarter of two, near enough. Then it would have been about an hour ago. Between 12:30 and 1. She looked in the mailbox to see if there was any mail for them, and there wasn't. "But there was a letter in the wrong box," she said.

"The wrong box?" Weigand asked.

"The fourth-floor box," Mrs. North said, "and I thought I'd wait and see if it was for us." So she had waited, knowing the postman was due about 1:30. "Timothy," she said. "That's the postman's name. Timothy Barnes." He was the regular carrier and the Norths both knew him. "Because he brings so many books," Mrs. North explained, "and they won't go in, so he has to ring."

Weigand felt that he was galloping, but he was getting used to it. Once you got the hang, you could keep up quite easily, playing leapfrog with words. He nodded.

"So Mr. Barnes said he would look to see if it was for us," Mrs. North explained. "He thought it might have been the substitute carrier on the 11 o'clock delivery." She was being very clear and careful, now, Weigand could see. Mullins made an occasional low, bewildered sound, and tried to take notes. Every now and then he would look at his notes and make a discouraged sound.

Mrs. North said the carrier had looked at it and it was, so he let her take it out.

"And was that the clue?" Weigand said. Mrs. North looked at him, as if he should have known better. She said certainly not, it was an announcement from Saks of a private sale. The clue was under it.

"Under it?" Weigand said.

"In the bottom of the box," Mrs. North said. "After I got the letter out of the wrong box there was still something in the bottom."

"Of the fourth-floor box?" Weigand said. "Where the murder was?"

Mullins made an even lower and more discouraged sound; now, the sound said, the Loot was getting that way. Weigand himself felt oddly elated and triumphant.

It was the fourth-floor box, Mrs. North agreed. And after she had taken the letter out there was still a little slip. She had known at once it was a clue. She had persuaded Mr. Barnes to leave the box open while she went up and got a pair of manicure tweezers and she had fished it out with them.

"Not touching it," Mrs. North said. "Fingerprints, you know."

Weigand said he knew.

"And it had his name on it," Mrs. North said.

"Whose?" said Weigand. "I mean—can I see it?"

That, of course, was what she was explaining for, Mrs. North said. It was a clue, so naturally it was for him. Nobody had touched it except with the tweezers. "Right?"

"Exactly right," Weigand agreed. Mrs. North said she would go and get it, and she went and got it, bringing it out in the tweezers. They laid it down on the coffee-table and looked at it. It was a slip of rather stiff paper, an inch and a half long, and about half an inch wide. There was a name lettered in ink on one side of it. The name was: "Edwards." The size and shape suggested something to Weigand and he almost had it before Mrs. North spoke.

"You see what it is, don't you?" she said. "It came out of the little slot by the bell."

That was it, Weigand realized. Each bell in the vestibule downstairs had a slot by it, into which a slip bearing the name of the tenant could be inserted. This slip would fit the slot; it had been cut for the slot. It had, he realized, almost certainly been in the slot. But it might—

"Did anybody named Edwards ever live here?" he asked.

That, Mrs. North told him, was the point. Nobody had; not, at any rate, since they had been there, and that was a long time. It couldn't have been there all that time.

"Don't you see?" she said. "It's the murderer's name! He put it there so the other man could ring."

It could, Weigand realized, be that way. He checked it over, aloud, while Mrs. North nodded.

"The murderer," Weigand said, "came about—what did we say?— 3:20 or 3:25. He had this slip ready, and put it opposite the bell of the fourth-floor apartment. Right?" Mrs. North nodded. "Then he rang your bell and pretended to be Western Union when you let him in. So— Then he went upstairs and into the apartment. Right?" Mrs. North nodded again.

"Then," said Weigand, "he must have already made an appointment with the man he was going to kill; made it for, say 3:30 or a little later, and given the man this address and false name." Mrs. North looked dubious. Why, she said, false? And if false, why did the other man come? Weigand thought false, because nobody would use his own name. It didn't stand to reason.

"He, the murderer, talked to his man by telephone, probably," Weigand explained. "Perhaps around noon Monday. He said he was Edwards, which means that the victim knew somebody named Edwards who might call him up and arrange an appointment. Right, so far?"

Mrs. North still was a little dubious, but she nodded, and Weigand went on.

"The murderer—" he began.

"Call him X," Mrs. North said. "People always do."

"Right," Weigand said. "Call the murderer X. So X telephoned the victim, Brent."

"Brent?" said Mrs. North.

Weigand said he had assumed she had seen the papers, but she shook her head. "Only the mornings," she said; "he was still just nobody in the mornings."

He was, Weigand explained, Brent in the afternoons and told her, in a few words, something about Brent. But they would let that rest for the moment, and where were they? They were, Mrs. North said, with the murderer being called X, and X calling up the victim, Brent. Weigand said, "Right.

"X called Brent," he said, "and described himself as Edwards. Brent knew somebody named Edwards, and had some reason for wanting to see him but he didn't know where Edwards lived—" Weigand studied a moment over that. "Or," he said, "X, posing as Edwards, said he had moved and gave this address. It's close enough to October 1 to make that plausible—you expect everyone to move then. X told Brent to come around at 3:30 and Brent did. Sure enough, when Brent got in the vestibule, there was Edwards' name by a bell, and he rang the bell and X let him in. And X killed him."

"But would it ring?" Mrs. North said. "The fourth floor bell, I mean, with the electricity off up there?"

The bells, Weigand told her, would be on the general house circuit, unconnected with the apartment circuits.

Mrs. North nodded, still a little hesitatingly.

"Why couldn't it really have been Edwards?" she said. "Somebody really named Edwards?"

That, Weigand pointed out, was perfectly clear. If the murderer were really named Edwards, he'd take mighty good care not to leave his name around. Edwards, he said, was one name they could rule out—it might be Smith or Jones or Finklestein, but it wouldn't be Edwards. Mrs. North said she saw what he meant.

"But why leave any name?" she said. "Why leave anything, any slip? Why put the slip in the mailbox, as the murderer must have done, instead of just throwing it away?"

It was Weigand's turn to nod, puzzled. He had, he agreed, got that to worry about. At the moment he couldn't think of the reason. He picked up the slip and looked at it, still using the tweezers, and shook his head over it. Then he slipped it into an envelope.

"It's a clue, all right. It was quick of you to notice it, Mrs. North. It may tell us things. Now, a couple of other points. Did you know a man named Stanley Brent?"

Mrs. North shook her head, decisively. But there was something about the decisiveness—

"Ever hear anything about him?" he asked, more sharply.

"Somebody—" Mrs. North began, and stopped. "No," she said, "that was somebody else. No, I never heard of Mr. Brent."

There was, Weigand thought, a change in her manner. He slipped that change in manner into a mental envelope, to be considered later.

"And Edwards," he said. "Do you know anybody named Edwards?"

"Three," said Mrs. North. "It's a common name. Only, one of them's the laundryman."

Still, Weigand said, he might as well take down the names of the three Edwardses Mrs. North knew, including the laundryman. The laundryman was, it turned out, William Edwards. Then there was a Dr. Richard Edwards, who was Mrs. North's dentist. And Mr. Clinton Edwards, who was a broker or something.

"We knew him best," Mrs. North said. "We've been there to dinner."

Weigand nodded, absently.

"Monday night, as it happens," Mrs. North said. "That's a coincidence, isn't it?"

Weigand nodded, although it seemed a rather mild coincidence. He was wishing the name had been one less common than Edwards; it would be helpful, he thought, if men's names differed as infallibly as their fingerprints. There would be columns of Edwardses in the telephone book; columns not in the telephone book. Mrs. North knew three—out of thousands. Still— He would, he supposed, have to check up on them. Meanwhile—Meanwhile, there was, next, Mrs. Brent to question, if she could see him. It wasn't pleasant, but it had to be got through. And there would be Brent's desk at home to be looked over, if he had a desk at home. He would have, Weigand thought. Life was full of duties.

Leaving, Weigand met Mr. North, who was coming, on the stairs. Mr. North looked faintly surprised for a moment, then nodded and inquired how things went.

"I wish I knew," Weigand said, going on downstairs.

· 6 ·

WEDNESDAY
2 P.M. TO 5:15 P.M.

Emerging from the house, Lieutenant Weigand looked to Mrs. North, who was watching through a front window, precisely as if he were in the custody of Mullins. Looking down on and after Weigand, as the two walked up the street, Mrs. North realized that it was going to be difficult to think of him as a detective. "For everybody," she said to herself, thinking it probably helped him. He looked, seen from this angle, very slight, although he was tall enough, and rather surprisingly young. His hat was canted forward anxiously, somehow, and he walked lightly, like a much younger man. Mrs. North tried to think who he looked like, "because everybody, almost, looks like somebody," she told herself, and for a moment could not place any resemblance. Then she decided he was like, more than anyone else, an associate professor at Columbia they had met a few weeks before and who had turned out to be, for a professor at any rate, amazingly gay and frolicsome.

"He'd be frolicsome, too, if he weren't a policeman," Mrs. North thought, of Weigand. "People with blue eyes and chins like his are, usually. Stubby chins."

"What?" called Mr. North from the other room, making Mrs. North realize that she must have been speaking aloud.

"Stubby chins," Mrs. North called back. "Friendly, sort of."

There was a considerable pause, and then Mr. North said, "Oh," vaguely.

"Don't you think so?" Mrs. North called, still looking out the window.

"No," said Mr. North. "Anyway, I wouldn't call his that. It's got a point."

Mrs. North continued to look out the window, watching a man across the street, who was burrowing into the waste in a trash-can, and every now and then finding something and dropping it into a burlap bag he carried.

"Listen," said Mrs. North. "We're being watched. He's put a tail on us."

"What things you must read!" Mr. North said, coming in to look. He looked.

"It's just a rag-picker," he said. Mrs. North looked disappointed, and said she thought sure it was a tail.

"After all," she said. "We found it. I think it would be very irregular if we weren't tailed. As if we weren't important."

"Nonsense," said Mr. North, but he looked at the rag-picker more closely. The rag-picker still looked like a rag-picker. "Nonsense," said Mr. North, more firmly. "You've been reading things. It was Weigand you meant about the chin?"

Mrs. North nodded, and said he didn't look much like a detective to her. He was too—Mrs. North stopped.

"Well," Mrs. North said, "he talks just like anybody and he took off his hat and he smokes cigarettes, so he's not like a man from Headquarters. But did he talk about jade?"

"Jade?" said Mr. North. "I don't get it."

"No," said Mrs. North, "he didn't. So he's not like an amateur. He's just like anybody else—brown hair and blue eyes and a little tall, but not very, and just thin like anybody else. And he dresses like anybody else."

Mrs. North's tone was, Mr. North thought, vaguely accusing, as if she didn't like the detective he had provided for her.

"Well," Mr. North said, "he's a lieutenant. So he must be all right."

Mrs. North nodded, and said there might be something in that.

"He's nice," Mrs. North said. "As a person, he's nice. But he seems very irregular to me. Not like Mullins."

No, Mr. North agreed, he wasn't at all like Mullins. Mullins represented type casting.

Weigand and Mullins turned the corner and went on toward Fifth Avenue and Mrs. Brent. They came to a drugstore and Weigand turned in and found a telephone booth. He telephoned Headquarters and had a man assigned to keep an eye on the Buano house and its occupants, which could be done from a café in the semi-basement across the street. Half an hour later, Second Grade Detective Cohen found the café and was pleased to discover that he could sit at the bar while keeping the Buano house under his eye. It was only a slight flaw, he decided, that he would have to stick to beer; after all, there were peanuts to go with it, and peanuts were fine. Looking back on it afterward, Detective Cohen decided that it was one of the pleasantest cases he had ever worked on.

Weigand and Mullins left the drugstore and went on to No. 34 Fifth Avenue. A crowd stood outside it and stared aloft, and a couple of uniformed men told it to move along and open up, and pushed it aside when it threatened to block the sidewalk. Inside the lobby two more uniformed men peered through an increasing haze of cigarette smoke at half a dozen reporters; and the doorman, who had retreated from the outside crowd, expressed dignified disapproval, as well as some furtive enjoyment, of the whole matter. The reporters got up when Weigand entered, and sat down again when he shook his head at them. He went up.

The face of the Brent maid reflected suitable gravity and her voice was hushed. She would see if Mrs. Brent could see Lieutenant Weigand; Mrs. Brent was feeling very indisposed, but the maid would see. "She's grieving," the maid imparted, in a suddenly lowered tone.

Then she left and, after a moment, returned. The detectives followed her across the foyer and into the living-room, done in soft grays and reds. Mrs. Brent rose from a chair near the window and said, "Lieutenant Weigand." Her voice was low-pitched and steady, but there was still shallowness in her eyes. She was very pale, under tan. She moved forward and Weigand noticed that she moved with that balance which becomes instinctive to a dancer, or an athlete.

She was a little above the usual height of women, and muscularly slender. Standing quietly, and waiting for Weigand to speak, she lifted a cigarette to her lips, and as her arm rose Weigand could see the supple stir of muscles under the pale brown skin of her forearm. Weigand could feel Mullins beside him thinking "She's a good-looker, all right."

She was, Weigand agreed, mentally. Her features were regular and disciplined; her jaw compact and liable, he suspected, to become prominent as she grew older. Youth softened it now, but it was the jaw of a lady who knew her mind. Her hair was blond and—Weigand's experienced eyes hesitated imperceptibly—yes, naturally so. Her gaze at him was steady, unrevealing and unperturbed.

He apologized. She would understand that there were certain questions they must ask; certain things they must find out. He would like to give her more time; knew the shock she had experienced. But in such cases it was hazardous to waste time; every hour made their task more difficult, as she would realize.

She said, "Yes, Lieutenant, of course," in her low, steady voice, and motioned toward chairs. She sat again herself, in a fluid, balanced movement which Weigand envied. That sense of balance you had to be born with; could never fully acquire if you were not. He had seldom seen it more completely embodied than in Mrs. Brent; never, he decided, in a woman. Watching her move, he wondered why she had not really attained top flight as a tennis player, and decided that it must have been because she had not wanted to, or had lacked something of the peculiar spirit necessary. Or perhaps, and that was always possible, she lacked that supernormal coordination of vision necessary for greatness as an athlete. Certainly what she had not lacked, he realized as she waited composedly for him to continue, was poise.

There were routine questions, about herself and her husband—questions for the record. She was thirty-two; they had been married a little over seven years. Before her marriage she had been Claire Askew; had been born upstate at Binghamton and been educated in private schools. Her husband had been five years older, a native New Yorker, educated at Yale. He had been a member of the law firm for about five years. Before that he had been, for a short time, an assistant in the District Attorney's office. Latterly, she thought, his practice had been almost entirely a civil one. The firm represented several corporations.

She had last seen her husband on Saturday, when she went to the country to close up their house there. Her level voice checked a moment, and went on. She looked straight at Weigand, waiting for each new question, with her hands quiet in her lap.

"The country house?"

"It is a little way out of Carmel," she said. "It is a week-end place, really, although we often spend a month there in the summer—longer if Stan can get—" She stopped suddenly. "It is hard to realize," she said. "That was what we used to do."

"I'm sorry about this," Weigand said. "You understand it isn't what I'd choose to do?"

She nodded. She quite understood; she was sorry if she was making it more difficult. She was keeping him at arm's-length, Weigand realized. Perhaps she was, in a way, keeping herself, also, at arm's-length.

"It's about two hours from town by car," she said. "Sometimes a little less. I was there from about Saturday noon until this morning. I drove in."

"Yes," said Weigand. "Thank you."

He waited a moment while Mullins finished a page of notes and flipped to a new page.

"Now," he said, "there are a few more things. Do you know, or did your husband, anybody named Edwards? A man or, perhaps, a woman?"

Mrs. Brent's eyebrows rose almost imperceptibly in inquiry, but the question appeared to be no more than faintly puzzling. Her eyes deepened as she thought. There was, she said, a laundryman named

Edwards, or perhaps Edmonds. And there was an old school friend of
hers who had married a man named Edwards. They lived in Chicago.
She couldn't answer for her husband, of course—he might know many
others. She had met a Dr. Edwards a month or so ago at a party and he
had played the piano delightfully for an hour or more, but she had
never met him again. Yes, her husband had been at the party.

"Do you know a Mr. Clinton Edwards?" Weigand asked.

Mrs. Brent nodded, and said, "Just.

"Stan had some business relations with him, I believe," she said. "A
year or so ago, and we both got to know him slightly—never well. We
went to his parties once or twice, and he came here, I think, once. But
all of this was some time ago; I haven't seen, or thought of, him for
months."

And her husband? Had he seen Clinton Edwards recently? Mrs.
Brent couldn't, of course, say definitely. But not so far as she knew.
Weigand said, "Right," and that he would pass on. Did she know
whether her husband had enemies? Had he ever mentioned them?

"I don't think people nowadays have 'enemies,' in that sense," she
said. "Do you? I suppose some people didn't like him. There were people we used to see, and don't see now"—she corrected herself, and her
voice went dead on the correction—"hadn't seen recently," she said.
"Some of them didn't like him, any more; or didn't like me. Some of
them we didn't like. But I don't think people like us really have enemies."

Weigand more or less agreed with the theory, but the facts seemed
against it. He nodded.

"No quarrels?" he said. Mrs. Brent thought.

"He and Ben Fuller swore at each other, once," she said. "They
were both a little tight, and nobody knew what was wrong. I don't
think it was very much, really. I don't know of anything else."

"Right," Weigand said. "It doesn't sound like anything." But he jotted down the name of Benjamin Fuller, just on the chance. He collected, also, the names of relatives. He inquired about insurance, and again
Mrs. Brent's eyebrows raised themselves slightly. It was routine, he
pointed out. "We like to get the picture," he said. She thought her hus-

band had carried rather a good deal of insurance, but she was not sure. Weigand could doubtless find out. He agreed. And if Mr. Brent had had a desk in the apartment, might he look through it? And among the papers in the safe, if there was a safe? Mrs. Brent, whose eyes were growing shallow again, and who seemed to be looking beyond him, agreed with a nod. The maid would show him the desk and the wall safe. But she did not know the combination of the safe.

The desk showed two things. In one pigeonhole a note of two lines, reading:

"Both my wife and I have had enough of this. I'd advise you to quit your little pranks."

It was signed "B. F."

The desk also yielded, very conveniently, a list of numbers which might be the combination of the wall safe—might be, and, as it turned out, was. The safe disclosed a few bonds, and stock certificates, none of great value; insurance policies on a car and on household effects, and a life insurance policy. The last was for $50,000, with a double indemnity clause which might, Weigand thought, be applicable in event of death by murder. He jotted down particulars, and put the policy back.

"A hundred thousand," he said to himself. From where he sat it was a lot of money. The policy named Claire Brent as beneficiary. Weigand said, "Um," and listened while Mullins told him what he had learned from the maid, Mary, and the doorman.

Mary had gone with Mrs. Brent to the country, to help close the house. The cook had been given Saturday, Sunday and Monday off, Mr. Brent saying he would prefer to eat out rather than in the apartment alone. Mary and Mrs. Brent had been busy both Saturday afternoon and Sunday; by Monday noon they were done. But it was a lovely day, so Mrs. Brent had decided not to go in until the next morning. She, Mary, had "jes sat around in the sun," but Mrs. Brent had driven off on Monday.

"She took the things she paints with and jes drove off," Mary explained. "She came back before it got dark."

Pressed, she had thought Mrs. Brent might have left between one and two o'clock, and got back at six-thirty. She had said she was going to the Danbury Fair.

"Huh?" Mullins had said at this point.

"The Danbury Fair," the maid had repeated. "At Danbury. She goes right often."

It took Weigand back to Mrs. Brent. He was sorry, but there was one other point—pure routine. Monday afternoon? Did she remember? She had driven off—?

"Oh," said Mrs. Brent. "You want to know—?" Her voice had a new note of strain, but it was still unshaken. "Yes, I drove over to the fair at Danbury. I paint sometimes, you know, and I usually try each fall to do something at the fair. There is a way the light comes in through the main exhibit tent and falls on things—cans and prize vegetables and cakes. I've always wanted to get it on canvas. I spent most of the afternoon there Monday."

"Did you get it?" Weigand wanted to know.

"No," she said. "I was further off than ever. That evening I scraped the canvas."

She had seen no one she knew at the fair.

Weigand thanked her. It was, he reflected, perfectly reasonable; perfectly likely. It was also completely unprovable, so far as he could see. She might have driven into New York in plenty of time, and back afterward in plenty of time. She seemed shocked by her husband's death, but she might be shocked even if— People who killed were shocked, sometimes, at themselves when they thought about it afterward. And terror, too, might shock. Mrs. Brent did not seem terrified, but— And there was the hundred thousand in insurance.

"Well—" he said to himself, walking slowly back to the living-room, where Mullins stared out of a window and down at the crowd below. There was one—Claire Brent. Motive, money. Opportunity, possible. Alibi, none. There was Mrs. North, who was hiding something about her acquaintance with Brent, or her knowledge concerning him. There was a Benjamin Fuller, not further identified, who had quarreled with Brent. There was some one named Edwards, whom Brent obviously had known. And there was Clinton Edwards, broker

and party giver, who might be the man. There was, of course, Mr.
North, but he was a suspect only if men who found bodies were necessarily suspects. The odd thing about that was that men who found bodies were, quite often, the men who had quenched the life in the bodies
they found. He could name half a dozen such, from experience and his-
tory.

"Well?" he said to Mullins.

Mullins had interviewed the doorman and elevator man on duty
Monday. The doorman remembered it had been a fine, warm day. The
elevator man remembered that Mr. Brent had come home about one
o'clock that afternoon and gone out again several hours later. He
remembered it because it was unusual for Mr. Brent to come home in
the daytime. Weigand said, "Um?" and Mullins shook his head. Mr.
Brent was by himself; nobody came to see him while he was in the
apartment. If he had telephoned, he had used his private telephone and
not gone through the house switchboard; he had the choice. He had
gone in, stayed a while—until three, maybe—and come out and gone
off to be killed. While inside he had, the elevator man thought, changed
his clothes. He was wearing a brown suit when he went out, unless the
elevator man was wrong. "I could be wrong, all right," the elevator
man assured Weigand, when the detective checked as they went out.

"If you ask me, we ain't getting anywhere," Mullins announced
gloomily as they walked toward the corner. "Give me a case where you
can round people up, O.K. But these fancy cases—" Mullins' voice
withdrew into a cave and rumbled.

"Here," it said, coming out again, "here we got how many men on it,
Loot?"

Counting the precinct men, the men trying to trace the clothes of the
murdered man, the auditors and others at the law offices, the sergeant
and two detectives questioning the staff there, perhaps twenty, Weigand
thought. When it came to alibis, if it came to alibis, twice as many.

"And precinct and squad men doubling up, probably," Mullins
remarked. "Falling over each other. And where do we get? We know
who got killed!" Mullins was disgusted. "Twenty-four hours, pretty
near, and we know who got killed," he said. "Guys who don't have

prints!" Mullins was still, Weigand realized, annoyed at the victim for
not being on file. They had, Weigand pointed out, done rather well, as
a matter of fact. They had been lucky. Identification might just as well
have taken weeks. Mullins was not pacified.

"These fancy cases," he said. "People you can't round up. People
who talk screwy, so you can't understand them. People who paint vegetables!" Mrs. Brent's activity on the afternoon of the murder, providing it had in truth been her activity, had done nothing to assuage Detective Mullins, Weigand realized. "Now who tells us funny stories?"

"Edwards," Weigand told him. "Clinton Edwards. Did you get his
address?"

Mullins had got the address, and it was little more than around the
corner—another remodeled house, this time, or, rather, a series of
remodeled houses thrown together. Edwards had a duplex apartment
on the third and fourth floors of one of them, and was served by an
automatic elevator. He was also provided with service stairs, in case he
wanted them. Looking at him, after they had gone up, been admitted
by a serious-faced Japanese and shown into a long living-room,
Weigand decided that Edwards would have little personal use for
stairs.

Edwards stood up and looked very affable when Weigand and
Mullins were shown in. He had just risen from a deep chair near a window, and he had a copy of an afternoon newspaper in his hand. Half
across the room, Weigand could see the headlines about the Brent murder. Edwards was a large man, tall and wide and thick, and somehow
rather billowy. He had a high forehead from which the hair was retreat-
ing and an irregularly shaped nose, and his voice was a soft, cushioned
bass.

"Yes, gentlemen?" he said, in the soft, cushioned bass voice.
"Inspector Weigand?"

"Lieutenant," Weigand corrected. Edwards spoke, somehow, like a
man who, knowing city magistrates by the dozen, is still affable to traffic policemen. The city magistrates would also be treated affably,
Weigand thought, so that they would never guess that Edwards guessed
there was a difference in social level—or would think they were not

supposed to guess that Edwards perceived any such distinction. "Very complicated," Weigand told himself.

Edwards' room, on the other hand, was uncomplicated. It was thirty feet long by perhaps twenty wide, and the ceiling was his height again above Edwards' head. But the chairs were low and the fireplace was broad; there were a great many chairs, Weigand noticed, but the room did not seem as if it held a great many chairs. There were tables near the chairs, with ash-trays and room for drinks and, all in all, the room looked as if it were ready for a party. There were flowers on the mantel and more flowers sprawling from a low vase on a table by the windows. All, Weigand thought, very nice.

"Won't you sit down, gentlemen?" Edwards said. "And tell me what I can do for you?"

He spoke the words of each sentence with full, measured precision. Weigand and Mullins sat, sinking deeply into chairs.

"Perhaps a drink?" Edwards said. He was, clearly, being very affable. Mullins looked expectant.

"No. Sorry," Weigand said. "We're both on duty, you see. Regulations—"

Mullins looked at Weigand in grieved astonishment, but Edwards nodded with a nod that was almost a bow, and said he quite understood.

"Then—?" said Clinton Edwards, with an inflection that rose smoothly and with the utmost cultivation.

"We're investigating the Brent Murder," Weigand said. It sounded very crude.

"And you have learned that I knew Stanley Brent, no doubt?" Edwards said.

That, Weigand thought, was getting it before you asked. He found himself wishing he were not so deeply sunk in so comfortable a chair. It invested the proceedings with undesirable lassitude.

"Yes," Weigand said. "That, among other things. You knew him—?"

"Yes," Edwards said. "Certainly I knew him. Professionally and socially, although never intimately." He paused. "No," he said, "never intimately."

"Huh?" said Mullins, suddenly. Weigand glared at him, and he subsided to note-taking.

Edwards would, it appeared, be delighted to give any helpful information, although he hardly saw how details of his acquaintance with Brent would prove helpful. He had known Brent and, to be sure, Mrs. Brent, for several years, first when Brent made with him "certain small investments."

"I am a man of business, as you probably know," Edwards said. "Merely a man of business."

Later, through this business relationship, he had got to know the Brents socially, and they had come several times to "my little parties."

"I often give little parties," Edwards said. "Many people come to my little parties. I should, indeed, be delighted, Lieutenant, if you—"

"Quite," said Weigand. "Very good of you. And the Brents came often? You got to know them rather well?"

Edwards' heavy shoulders lifted just perceptibly, gesturing disclaimer. Who, Edwards inquired, could say? "Our nearest friends," Edwards said, and left it open.

"Certainly," he said, "I did not know Brent well enough to imagine why he might be murdered. It was hardly a friendship. He was an acquaintance. We spoke when we met, he came to my little parties, I once went to his. It was all casual. You and I, Lieutenant, know so many on that basis, don't you find?"

"Right," said Weigand. "Did you know anybody who disliked him; did you know of any enemies he might have?"

Again the question seemed rather crude and direct. Edwards, however, hardly smiled at its crudity.

"The inevitable question, is it not?" he said. "Any enemies. I should not say that I knew any enemies, although no doubt some people liked Mr. Brent better than others did. I don't suppose, for example—but I must not gossip, of course."

Weigand waited, and let Edwards see he waited.

"But no," Edwards said, sweetly and reasonably rumbling from his deep chair. "It would not do to gossip. You will agree, Lieutenant? And I know nothing, really. But nothing."

Weigand still waited. Mullins waited with his pencil poised.

"Ah," said Edwards, "you will have my thoughts out of me, I see. But it is only gossip, and certainly no motive for murder." He paused, and Weigand continued to wait. "You know of Mr. Benjamin Fuller, perhaps?" he inquired. Weigand nodded. "I see you do. Then there is nothing I could tell you, and it is, of course, of no importance. You agree?"

"No," Weigand said. "I don't agree, or, at any rate, I should like to know. Did Fuller dislike Brent? Did he, in any way, have it in for him?"

One of Edwards' large, soft hands brushed aside the vulgarity of the phrasing. Not, he said, "in for him." Certainly not. There was, to be sure, friction—but definitely, one might say, friction.

"But that," Edwards said, and the large, soft voice was edged with melancholy, "is so very often found, don't you agree? So much friction, in such cases."

"Listen," said Weigand. "Assume I know nothing of anything between Brent and Fuller. Right? Just tell me."

There was, Edwards said, so little to tell, and that so—how should one phrase it?—conventional.

"Brent and Mrs. Fuller," he said. "They—you understand? But I am sure that Fuller, at bottom, took a most civilized view. He was, shall we say, irritated? But he is, naturally, quite modern in such matters. We are all so modern, don't you find? I sometimes think—"

Weigand found he was not listening to what Mr. Edwards sometimes thought, as Edwards purred comfortably through the relationship of morality to modernity. The relationship seemed to be, in any event, vague. Weigand was thinking that Fuller had popped up again, accompanied this time by a wife. Jealousy and, er—well, call it outraged love. That took in both Fullers, one way or another. They seemed to pop up, certainly.

"You know this?" he asked. "I mean, it is generally understood that Brent and Mrs. Fuller are—or were—lovers? Is that the general understanding among their friends?"

Edwards' shoulders deprecated such forthright, encompassing statements.

"Among their friends?" he repeated. How could one postulate a general understanding, outside one's ken? "Lovers?" It was, the lieutenant would understand, a matter of speculation on Edwards' part. "They had not gone away together, certainly. There was, shall I say, nothing direct." But, personally, Edwards had implied there was little room for doubt. One knew, in such cases, Mr. Edwards suggested. There was—how should one say?—an atmosphere. But one could not, of course, be certain—in the very nature of such things. Edwards' affability was bland and worldly.

There was a pause for mental digestion. Then Weigand resumed.

"What really brought us to you, Mr. Edwards," he said, "was another matter—a rather curious matter." He paused, and Edwards looked expectant.

"The murderer seems to have used your name," Weigand said. He had the satisfaction of seeing Edwards start perceptibly.

"That will jar him," Weigand thought with interest. He explained about the slip bearing Edwards' name. He regretted, disingenuously, that the slip was now being examined by experts, else he would have liked Mr. Edwards to see it. But it was, certainly, the name "Edwards." Hand printed, in ink; blue ink.

Edwards seemed at a loss for a moment, and shook his head. It was a grave, unpleasant business, the shaking head implied. Then it spoke.

"One can hardly imagine," Mr. Edwards said. "For any one to throw suspicion on me, deliberately, as it seems, is—" Words failed him; words were found again. "I am such a harmless person, so friendly with everyone. I think I may say that I feel friendlily toward everyone. It is very—" he paused for a word and found one that was a little, it seemed to Weigand, inadequate, "—disheartening." Edwards thought about it. Then he brightened slightly.

"But it is, of course, such a very common name," he said. "It does not seem to me that the connection is—?"

"Right," said Weigand. "We thought of that, of course. It may very well be merely a coincidence. You were friendly with Brent and—"

Edwards raised a hand to stop him. In all honesty, Edwards said, he could not let it stand at that. Lately, he was sorry to say, there had been a certain coolness. Representing a client, Brent had been, should he say, in opposition? Edwards was, should he say, regretful?

"He was representing a man named Louis Berex," Edwards said. "A man toward whom I feel, shall I say, like an older brother—yes, like an older brother. An inventor and a very excitable young man; the son and nephew of two men I knew well and valued very highly. Louis himself is, shall I say, innocent of business knowledge and I felt that he had, although it seems a harsh way of putting it, fallen into Brent's hands."

How, Weigand wanted to know, was that? Edwards hesitated; made deprecating sounds. How it bore—?

Weigand admitted that, probably, it did not bear at all, except in so far as everything they could discover—matters of psychology as well as of speech and action—might bear to complete their picture. Edwards, looking a little troubled, nodded.

"I am," he said, "Louis Berex's man of business; I am many people's man of business. In Berex's case I manage a trust fund set up for him by his uncle some years ago. Now and then I act as his agent, because he is really quite incapable of acting wisely for himself in such matters." Edwards paused. "I would not have you misunderstand," he said. "Louis is, in his own way, brilliant and quite practical. One of his minor inventions, indeed, brings him a very decent sum annually, as I happen to know. But in matters solely of finance he is, as his uncle realized, totally without experience. So I administer and advise, in his behalf."

"Yes?" said Weigand.

Edwards hesitated and looked rather unhappy.

"Lately," he said, "there has been, or perhaps I may now say was, a misunderstanding on Berex's part. He felt that I—this is rather difficult, as you will understand, because I wish to be fair—that I had not been managing the trust as efficiently, shall I say, as it might be managed." Edwards paused, and smiled, forgivingly. "It is difficult for practical men like you and me to appreciate how utterly without experience such men as Louis Berex may be in practical matters," he said. "Securities, changes of value, rearrangement of investments—all things of that sort—are completely a closed book to Berex. He thinks, I believe, that securities somehow lay money, like hens." He smiled, understandingly. "He felt that his securities were not laying well, as indeed, during the past year or so, they were not. He wanted an immediate explanation, but he could not understand the explanation when I gave it. Then he hired Brent."

Weigand nodded.

"It was, I suppose, quite a natural thing for him to do," Edwards said. "I was, perhaps, a little hurt, but I could understand. But I felt, at the same time, that a man of Brent's experience was—but one should not speak ill of the dead."

"You felt that Brent was stringing him along, for the fee?" Weigand inquired, bluntly. Edwards thought it over, and in the end, nodded reluctantly.

"Something like that," he said. "I felt—ethics—" He looked at Weigand hopefully, and Weigand nodded.

"Right," Weigand said, and made mental notes. It was another matter to be looked into. He might, Weigand explained to Edwards, as well see Berex too, since, for the moment, one could not tell what might be learned from anyone who had known Brent. He got Berex's address, and saw that Mullins noted it. He turned to another point, assuring Edwards that it was purely routine, and for the record. Would Mr. Edwards outline his activities on Monday?

Mr. Edwards looked, momentarily, pained, then nodded. If, of course, he could remember—but yes, he could remember, as it happened. He had been out of town Sunday and part of Monday morning, reaching home a little before noon. He had changed and gone to his office, but only for a short time. Then he had returned to the apartment. That evening he was having a small buffet supper for some friends; some twenty friends. There was much to be done in preparation, particularly since he had been away the day before and could attend to nothing, and there was little exigent to do at the office. "My hours are always rather short at the office, I am afraid," he said, with the smile of an apologetically indolent man. "Here, for example, I am at home at what is, for so many business men, the middle of the afternoon." He had spent Monday afternoon making some preparations himself, and directing Kumi in others. "Kumi is my servant," he explained. "My only servant. I live alone and very simply—but very simply." He smiled, deprecatingly.

"I even tried my hand at cooking," he said. "As, indeed, I often do. You may perhaps regard that as, how shall I say—an odd activity for a man? And flower arranging, too, no doubt? I always arrange the flowers myself."

"No," said Weigand, "I wouldn't think anything about that, particularly." Edwards beamed on him.

"And you were alone all afternoon, or only with Kumi?" Weigand asked. "Kumi was here when you came, of course?"

Edwards nodded to the first question, and nodded again to the second.

"Not much of an alibi, I am afraid," he said. "But it could hardly have taken all afternoon—I mean, isn't from twelve to, say six rather a long span of time? For an hour or so, perhaps, I might be more precise. If you could—?"

Weigand thought it over and decided he might, within limits, be more specific. He said they could, roughly, call it between three and four-thirty. Did that help?

Edwards shook his head, with a disarming expression, and said he was afraid it didn't.

"It is quite ridiculous," he said. "About then I must have been preparing the lobster and Kumi was probably cleaning upstairs. I started him on that, I remember, not long after I returned from the office. That was about the time the lobsters came, and I was, I am afraid, rather annoyed."

Mr. Edwards was annoyed, it turned out, because the lobsters should have been delivered during the morning, when Kumi could have shelled them while he was putting things to rights on the lower floor. As it was, Mr. Edwards, feeling that time was growing short and that there was much to do, had been forced to shell the lobsters himself, a process at which he was, he admitted, by no means expert. It was, he had found, very hard on the hands to shell lobsters. Perhaps he was shelling lobsters at the very time that—He paused, delicately.

66   FRANCES & RICHARD LOCKRIDGE

"And I fear the lobsters cannot substantiate my alibi," he said. "They were, shall I say, unresponsive at the time and now, I fear, are long since digested entirely." He looked thoughtful. "I hope," he added. "And Kumi, while certainly in the apartment, was upstairs during most of the period you fix, so I fear—"

Weigand nodded and was consoling. No doubt it was of no importance. Still, Mr. Edwards might think it over and, if any details occurred to him, keep them in mind against the further question or two which might be necessary. "To complete the record," Weigand assured Mr. Edwards, pleasantly. For now, he could think of nothing else; Mr. Edwards had been most helpful. Mr. Edwards expressed himself as pleased to have been helpful, and offered to be even more so. He would, for one thing, be glad to make the records of the Berex trust available to investigators, since the matter had come up, and if Weigand had, remaining, any doubts. Weigand deprecated the necessity, but said he would, to complete the record, send auditors around.

Weigand leaned forward to rise from the chair and a nickeled watch popped, somehow, out of a vest pocket. It popped out and slithered across the carpet almost to Mr. Edwards' feet. Mr. Edwards retrieved it, as one instinctively retrieves articles which roll to one's feet, and handed it back to Weigand, who accepted it with apologies for his clumsiness and replaced it in his pocket, holding it lightly by the stem. He shook hands with Mr. Edwards, which was like shaking hands with a small, smooth cushion, and led Mullins out.

It was, he thought, probably foolish to go to so much trouble to get Edwards' fingerprints on the watch, carefully polished for the purpose, but so long as he had he might as well have them brought up. Mullins approved that, but was rather cross with the lieutenant for not pursuing the alibi further.

"We oughta talked to that servant," he said. "If there's anything screwy going on there, they can cook something up together."

"Do you really think there is?" Weigand asked. Mullins started to answer, with some emphasis. "About the case, I mean," Weigand added. Mullins, rather grudging about it, shook his head.

"Not that guy," he said. "Flowers! Cooking! Huh!"

They walked back toward the subway and were, Weigand realized, hardly a block from the Buano house. While they were there, he thought, they might as well check up a point or two with the Norths. He looked at his watch—not at the nickeled watch, but at one on his wrist—and found, rather to his surprise, that it was after five. Presumably Mr. North, also, would be at home. He might as well, Weigand decided, find out where Mr. North was on Monday afternoon, for the sake of the thoroughness Inspector O'Malley so much prized.

· 7 ·

WEDNESDAY
5:15 P.M. TO 5:45 P.M.

The Norths were home, and at cocktails, which they urged on Weigand and Mullins. Weigand said that, of course, they were on duty—Mullins looked very unhappy—and that they would be very glad of cocktails. Mullins beamed, and his beam grew when Mr. North, after a quick look, suggested he might prefer rye. Mullins did prefer rye.

"I was telling him about the murderer's leaving his name," Mrs. North said. "Was he?"

"What?" said Weigand. "This is where I came in," he said to himself, bewildered.

"Was he the murderer, of course," Mrs. North said. "The man who left his name—Edwards. The laundryman."

Weigand said that he hadn't, as yet, seen the laundryman, although no doubt it would be attended to. He had, he said, seen Clinton Edwards.

"And is he?" Mrs. North said.

"Listen—" said Mr. North. "You shouldn't ask him things like that. Murders are confidential."

"Right," said Weigand. "However, I don't think he is, as a matter of

68

fact." He remembered something. "You had dinner at his house Monday evening? Right?"

"Right," said Mr. North.

"Did you have lobster?" Weigand asked. Both the Norths looked at him in astonishment. He nodded, confirmingly.

Mr. North said he had a vague idea they had lobster and Mrs. North said certainly, from her receipt. "Recipe," she said. "Only I was brought up saying receipt."

Weigand explained about Edwards and the lobsters. He supposed, he said, that one could spend considerable time preparing lobsters? Both the men looked at Mrs. North, who said that one certainly could, particularly by her receipt.

"Hours," said Mrs. North. "Simply hours."

"Literally?" said Mr. North, interested.

Mrs. North nodded, adding that, of course, it depended on how many and where you started. If you started with live lobsters, it was one thing, but she never did because of the claws and putting them in boiling water. She couldn't, she said, bear to think of lobsters in boiling water, so she had it done at the market. But even with the lobsters boiled, there was the problem of taking them out of the shell, and then boiling the shells.

"The shells?" said Weigand. Mr. North, at whom the detective was looking, nodded.

"She boils them," he said. "For the flavor. But I usually take them off. It takes time, all right."

It didn't seem, to Weigand, that they were going much of any place.

"Well," he said, "anyway—"

Mrs. North said she could get him the receipt, if he liked, but Weigand shook his head, just in time to save Mullins from choking on his drink. Recipes for lobster would, Mullins' face reported, be entirely the last straw. "Screwy!" Mullins' face said, with exclamation-points.

"I could send it to you," Mrs. North said, pursuing the subject. Weigand nodded, abstractedly. He said there were one or two other things.

"The slip," said Mrs. North. "What about the slip? Show it to him."

Weigand hesitated a moment.

"After all," Mrs. North said, "who found it?"

Weigand shook the slip from the envelope to the coffee-table and they bent over it.

"Handwriting?" Mr. North inquired.

Weigand shook his head. Printed as it was, and so small a sample, it would be very nearly hopeless, he imagined. The experts could try, of course. They looked at the name, and it told them nothing new.

"How about the other side?" Mr. North said. "Blank, I suppose?"

Weigand realized that he hadn't looked, because he supposed so, too. He flipped it over with the torn end of a paper match. It was, as everyone had expected, blank. They stared at it, and all three saw at the same time that it was not quite blank. At one end of the slip, on the edge, were two small marks. Mr. and Mrs. North pointed at it together, and said, "What's that?"

The marks were tiny and only a fraction of an inch apart; they slanted diagonally away from each other. The Norths leaned back and looked at one another, while the detective studied the marks. Mrs. North said she bet she knew what it was.

"Part of a letter," said Mrs. North. "Somebody cut a letter down the center." She looked very pleased. "I think it's a fine clue," she said. Mr. North looked at the marks again.

"What letter would be like that?" he said.

Mrs. North's lips moved faintly as she ran through the alphabet.

"K," she said, triumphantly. "If you cut a K just to the right of the fork and left it on, it would look like that."

Weigand and Mr. North looked at her; even Mullins allowed his attention to be distracted, momentarily, in the direction of the slip.

"It could be," Mr. North said. "It could be, at that, Weigand."

Weigand look at it again. It could, at that.

"Or an X," he said.

The Norths looked at it again.

"Any other letter?" Mr. North said. Separately, but more or less in unison, they ran over the alphabet. They all looked at one another, and shook their heads. It couldn't, they decided.

"It could be K going away or X going either way," Mrs. North said. "But nothing else."

"That's right, too," Mr. North said. "Only, of course, it needn't be a letter at all. It can be just a couple of marks, meaning something else."

Weigand agreed; Mrs. North didn't.

"It has to be a letter," she said. "Part of a letter, anyway. It looks like it. We ought to look at it through a glass."

Weigand nodded. It would, he agreed, be a good idea.

"Got a glass?" said Weigand.

"No," said Mrs. North. That seemed to be that, for the moment. Using his match, Weigand wheedled the slip back into the envelope.

"I'll have it examined," he said. "They may turn up something." They sipped their drinks a moment, and Weigand said there were a couple of other points.

"Do you people know the Fullers?" he said. "Benjamin Fuller and his wife."

"Jane," said Mrs. North. "Ben and Jane."

"Right," Weigand said. "Then you do. Do you know whether they knew Brent?"

Mrs. North started to shake her head, but Mr. North said, "Yes."

"Oh, Jerry," Mrs. North said. "Now you've brought them in!"

Mr. North looked surprised and said, "But they did.

"My God," said Mr. North, "hundreds of people did, probably. But they didn't all kill him. There's no harm in that."

"Well," said Mrs. North, "I still don't think we ought to. I didn't earlier, when he asked. Did I?"

Weigand tried to remember; did remember that she had assured him she had never heard of Brent; put two and two together and came out with, he supposed, about three and a half. The lacking half represented a faint probability that Mrs. North might have had some other reason. He said, in answer to Mrs. North's question, that she hadn't.

"But you had heard of Brent?" he said.

Mrs. North said, all right, they had because of knowing the Fullers.

"We've known the Fullers for two or three years," she said, "and seen a good deal of them. But it was before that that they knew the

Brents. I think they knew them rather well at one time."

"How well?" Weigand wanted to know. Mrs. North hesitated and said she thought "quite well." Weigand nodded.

"Did you ever hear that Brent and Mrs. Fuller were—well, playing around? I mean, you probably know people who knew them then, and things get around. Right?"

The Norths looked at each other; Mr. North nodded agreement to Mrs. North's glance, and Mrs. North said that, as a matter of fact, they had heard something of the kind. Gossip, it was.

"But of course, it could have been true, for all that," Weigand said. "A good many people thought it was true, didn't they? Edwards did, for one—does, as a matter of fact."

"It's just their minds," Mrs. North said. "They want to think that, because they like to think things are happening. I know it wasn't true, ever, and isn't now."

"Know?" Weigand said, doubtfully.

Mrs. North nodded in a decided way.

"You always know," she said. "It's always perfectly clear, and Jane Fuller wasn't playing. I know Jane, so I know she wasn't."

It wasn't, Weigand thought, as easy as that, but there was no point in an argument. It would, he thought, be pleasant if it were as easy as that; detecting would be much simpler, for one thing.

"But they didn't see each other just before Brent was killed?" he said.

Mrs. North shook her head vigorously, but Mr. North nodded his, reluctantly.

"As a matter of fact," he said. "I think they did—I heard they did, until quite recently. I heard somebody talking about it, somewhere." Mrs. North said, "Oh, Jerry!" Mr. North said that, of course, that might merely be more gossip.

"Look," he said, "why don't you ask the Fullers? I mean—all we know is gossip, and I don't like to be passing it on. And, anyway, we get all this second or third hand. There were rumors, and they lasted until quite recently—that's all we know, really. And the Fullers are friends of ours. Right?"

"Right," Weigand said.

"But there wasn't any truth in anything about Jane Fuller and Brent," Mrs. North said. "That's perfectly clear."

"Right," said Weigand. "What kind of people are the Fullers, aside from the fact that she wouldn't play around."

The Norths had trouble getting together on that. They agreed that Fuller was tall. Mr. North stopped there in describing him, and Mrs. North said he was homely in an attractive sort of way. "The red-haired sort of way," she added, in explanation. "He's very full of energy," she said, further. Mrs. Fuller, they both agreed, was much smaller, and dark. "Very attractive," Mr. North said. Mrs. North looked a little doubtful at that, and shook her head hesitantly. "I wouldn't say she's good-looking, exactly," she said. "She's got lovely hair and eyes, though. I think she's a very sweet person, really."

"I always felt, somehow, that he would have a nasty temper, under the proper circumstances," Mr. North said. "He looks it, somehow."

"Why, Jerry!" Mrs. North said.

Weigand said, "Um." Mullins produced a curiously artificial cough and looked at Weigand knowingly when Weigand looked at him.

"Bad temper, eh?" said Mullins, significantly, and retired into his drink.

"But listen," Mrs. North said. "He isn't—"

"Right," Weigand said. "I'll see him, anyway. Make up my own mind. Right?"

Mrs. North seemed a little mollified, but not entirely satisfied. "Prejudice," she said, to nobody in particular. "Prejudicing detectives."

Mr. North poured more cocktails and gestured Mullins toward the rye tantalus. Mullins said he didn't mind if he did, and proved it. Weigand said there was, while they were on it, one other point.

"I gather neither of you knew Brent, personally?" he said. "I asked Mrs. North and she didn't. How about you, North? Did you know Brent?"

Mr. North, rather to everybody's surprise, nodded. Mrs. North said, in a shocked tone, "Why, Jerry!"

"I only thought of it a moment ago," Mr. North said. "There was something about the name ever since I saw it in the paper. I knew him slightly, as a matter of fact. He was counsel for the plaintiff in a suit against us."

"Suit?" said Weigand. "Against you?"

It was, Mr. North said, against the publishing company—plagiarism suit.

"We brought out a book, and some woman argued it was stolen from something she had written," Mr. North explained. "She'd sent us the manuscript earlier, as it turned out, and we'd sent it back. They tried to argue that we had given the idea to Peterson, our author. Nonsense, of course, and it was thrown out of court. And—"

"Oh," said Mrs. North. "Was that the time you got so mad—" She stopped, as if she had stepped on something, and flushed. Mr. North grinned at her.

"All right, kid," he said. "I was coming to that—no brick dropped."

"I was on the stand," he explained to Weigand, "and Brent cross-examined me. He tried to make it appear I had passed the idea on to Peterson, because I had completed arrangements with him. All nonsense, of course, but rather annoying. As Pam says, I was annoyed. But it was nothing, really."

"Look, Jerry," Mrs. North said. "I'm sorry. I talk too much."

She was, it occurred to Weigand, talking too much now, but that was all right with him—or ought to be all right with him. It was all right with him as long as he remembered he was a policeman.

"It was nothing," said Mr. North. He seemed flurried and upset, and he was conscious that he must appear so, which annoyed him still more. "Molehills," Mr. North said, rather explosively. "For God's sake—"

"Right," said Weigand. "Obviously. All very silly." He realized, however, that his next question was going to come in rather embarrassing juxtaposition.

"This is purely routine," he said. "But the inspector will want me to have asked. Where were you Monday afternoon, Mr. North? At your office, I suppose."

"Why, yes—" Mr. North said, and then he stopped, while a tiny tingle of alarm went through him. He hadn't been, now he came to think of it. He had been—

"Damn it all," Mr. North said, exasperated. "As a matter of fact, I was at a reception for one of our authors. At the Ritz. There was a mob of people from about five o'clock on."

"Well," said Weigand, "if you left your office a little before five—"

That, Mr. North said, was the whole trouble. He had been reading a badly typed manuscript most of the morning and missed lunch and then, in the middle of the afternoon, turned up with a headache. So he had left the office about three.

"And?" said Weigand.

"Took a walk," said Mr. North, rather desperately. "Just took a walk, in Central Park. But, for God's sake, I didn't even remember I knew the fellow then! If you'd said 'Brent' to me it wouldn't have meant a thing. Not a thing." He looked at Weigand anxiously, but Weigand was finishing his cocktail. He looked at Mrs. North, who looked back at him, Mr. North disturbedly realized, bravely. She looked at him as if she believed in his innocence.

"Listen!" said Mr. North. "Listen."

"There," said Mrs. North, "I'm sure he believes you. It's just a coincidence, really. You're going to be perfectly all right."

"Damn it all," said Mr. North. "Of course I'm going to be all right. It isn't even a coincidence—it isn't anything at all. Of all the—"

Then he saw Mrs. North's face again and suddenly grinned at her.

"O.K., kid," he said. "Have your games."

But the point was, he thought, whether Weigand was playing the same game. He couldn't tell from Weigand's face. "But Weigand drank my cocktails," Mr. North told himself. "Only," he told himself, "that was before he knew I knew Brent." He tried to remember whether Weigand had kept on drinking after he had known, and couldn't be certain. The detective had, to be sure, had his glass up to his lips, but perhaps it was already empty. Mr. North felt, on the whole, pretty worried. "If I only knew," he thought, "whether there was anything in the glass—that would tell me." Then he thought of offering Weigand another cocktail, but Weigand was beginning to stand up.

Mullins took a final gulp and stood up too.

"Well," said Weigand, "thanks. We'll have to be getting along." He paused. "You've both been helpful," he said. Mrs. North smiled at that and Mr. North started to. Then he realized that Weigand might mean several things by that.

"Damn it all," he said. "I *was* walking in the park."

Weigand looked at him, and there seemed to be the beginning of a smile on his lips.

"Of course," Weigand said. "Who said you weren't?"

Nobody, Mr. North realized, had even hinted that he wasn't, except, of course, himself.

"Well," Weigand said, "we'll be seeing you."

Weigand and Mullins went along, and the Norths looked at each other. They both looked a little taken aback.

"I was playing, of course," Mrs. North said. "You knew that."

Mr. North said that he did, obviously.

"The point is, did he know it?" Mr. North said. Mrs. North thought it over.

"The point *really* is," she said, "is *he?*"

"Is he what?" Mr. North said.

"Playing," Mrs. North said. "Or does he think you did?"

They stood a moment and looked at each other, wondering. Then Mr. North said maybe they had better have some more drinks.

• 8 •

WEDNESDAY
5:45 P.M. TO 7:15 P.M.

When they were on the sidewalk again, Mullins appeared happier. (He also appeared, Weigand noticed, mellower.) Mullins fell into step and made knowing sounds.

"That guy Fuller," he said. "There's the guy, all right. There's a guy that fits—motive, bad temper, everything. There's a guy to round up and go over. O.K., Loot?"

Lieutenant Weigand wasn't, he said, as sure as all that. But he saw what Mullins meant, and they would certainly have to go over Fuller, in one way or another. Mullins looked interested and expectant and said, "Now, Loot?" Weigand elevated his hopes and dashed them.

"Now," he said, "but not you. You've got a couple of other things to do. Round up this laundryman named Edwards and talk to him, just to cover that. See if he knew Brent and ask him if he killed Brent. Tell him we'd sort of like to know. Then see that this slip gets over to the laboratory boys in Brooklyn. Tell them we want whatever they can find and see that they notice that little mark on the back. Did you see the little mark?"

"Sure, Loot," Mullins said. "What dja think?"

77

"I thought you were wading into the Norths' rye," Weigand answered, quite truthfully.

"Listen, Lieutenant," Mullins said. "Who says I was wading into rye? Ain't I on duty?"

"Right," Weigand said, and told him to get along. Mullins went along, showing that he was very much hurt, when they came to the corner of Fifth Avenue. Weigand watched him go, grinning, walked over to Sixth Avenue and went into Goody's Bar. He looked Fuller up in the telephone book and found a Benjamin Fuller conveniently in Grove Street. He found a gap in the bar fringe and ordered a dry martini. He sipped it, noting that North did them better and deciding that, whatever the experts said, he liked them with a twist of lemon rind. He thought it would be comfortable to stay leaning against the bar the rest of the evening, perhaps in the end persuading the bartender to twist lemon peel over martinis. He looked at his watch, found it was almost six, and toyed with the idea of letting Fuller go over until tomorrow. Already, he told himself, he was beginning to feel like a house to house canvasser.

"Well," he said to himself, "I may as well have some company."

He withdrew wearily from the bar and went to the telephone, calling Headquarters. It was dimly and, he realized, a little morbidly, satisfying to send detectives out to keep eyes on the Brent apartment house and Edwards' front door, and to trail along if either Mrs. Brent or Edwards went out. It would almost certainly come to nothing, in either case, but it would be nice to know what a couple of suspects were doing—assuming that Mrs. Brent and Edwards constituted a couple of suspects.

Weigand came out of the booth and looked at his watch again. It still lacked some minutes of six and the bar was temptingly near.

Six o'clock was, Weigand told himself, a nice even hour, and if he didn't leave until six Fuller would have plenty of time to get home from his office, assuming he went to an office. What Weigand needed before the next interview, he told himself, was a martini, with lemon peel, to last him until six o'clock. He explained to the bartender that he wanted a very dry martini with a twist of lemon peel and the bartender, after looking him over, said O.K., buddy, he was the doctor. It was all right this time, but still not up to the couple he had had over at the Norths', Weigand thought, sipping it. He reached over for the salted peanuts.

Force of habit is a compulsion, particularly when you are fifty-seven and tired; when your feet are tired and your shoulders ache, a compulsion which sends you home at the end of the day is an easy one to accept. The rather stooped man in the gray-blue uniform, with its official buttons, almost went his usual way down the stairs leading to the uptown platform of the subway at Fourth Street. Then he remembered what he had decided that noon, sitting at the tiled lunch-counter and reading a newspaper while he drank pale, sweet coffee from a white mug. He remembered it and sighed and wished he had never thought of it. But he had, and there you were.

You were an official of the government—yes, you could call it that. When you knew something that ought to be known by authority the duty on you to tell authority what you knew was a little more exigent than on an ordinary man, a layman. When you had seen something that might be important and remembered what you had seen you had to go and tell about it, because there was no likelihood that anybody would come and ask you about it. You nodded over the newspaper and made up your mind, and finished the last cup of pale coffee, sweetest toward the bottom, and went back to duty until your time was your own and you could go to authority and tell what you had seen a little before four o'clock on Monday afternoon at 95 Greenwich Place. It might be nothing; probably it was nothing, except for the strange, direct look you had got. But perhaps the suitcase was important, too; you never knew.

The man of fifty-seven had thought about it off and on all afternoon, as he grew tireder, and once or twice he almost persuaded himself he could let it go until the next day. If he had been only a layman and not, in a way, a government official—yes, you could say a government official, really—he probably would have put it off until the next day. Then he would have gone down the stairs leading to the uptown platform and got a Grand Concourse express and got off and gone home to the second floor of the frame duplex house far up in the Bronx and had dinner and told the wife about it. He and the wife would have talked it over and agreed that he should go in the morning and tell authority about it, and then, perhaps they would have talked about the days which were to come in a few years, after he was retired and the pension started, when they would leave the Bronx and go to a small town upstate and have a garden. He had never had a garden, but he had often thought about having a garden. Flowers, he thought.

Every now and then he could remember, with sudden clearness, how things were when he had been a boy in a smaller town and had helped his father in the backyard and how daffodils started to come through the ground in the early spring while there was still snow in sheltered places.

Even although he had decided definitely what he was going to do, he almost failed to do it, because habit guided him imperceptibly to the stairs leading to the uptown platform. He remembered when he had gone down only a step or two, however, and went back to the sidewalk and crossed the street to the downtown stairs on the other side. The downtown platform was crowded with people going home to Brooklyn, and going down to the Hudson and Manhattan terminal for New Jersey, but it was not as crowded as the uptown platform across the tracks. That was jammed, as always—well, there was that, anyway. By the time he was ready to go home the crowd would have thinned and he might even get a seat. That would be a novelty.

There were plenty of people on the downtown platform, but not so many that he could not get into the front rank, waiting in a long line along the edge for the downtown express to come in. If the door opened, by chance, where he was standing he would only have to step through and, inside, he might get a seat—a seat even for one station was something, when you had been on your feet all day. It shouldn't, he thought, take long to tell what he knew, and make a statement, and then he could go along home, knowing that duty was done. He shifted his weight from one tired foot to the other and, with the others, looked up the track to see if the train was coming.

It was; its red lights were already at the end of the platform, the rails were clacking in front of it, and its individual roar was dominant over the roar of other trains. He started that recoil which is the safety gesture of all subway riders who have got near the edge of the platform and see the train coming; that subconscious gesture toward safety which is the New Yorker's almost invariable response to the juggernaut under the streets. He shrank back—

But something stopped him as he shrank; somebody was pressing against him, ending his retreat. Ending his retreat; then pressing him forward—forward into that perilous, inches-wide margin between his feet and the edge. Somebody was in an almighty hurry, he thought; somebody had better watch out. Some kid who didn't know any better, but it was dangerous, all the same. Even now—but now the pressure was increasing, now, suddenly, it was resistless. He tried to turn in protest, to cry a warning.

"Hey!" he cried. "What—"

But then the pressure suddenly stiffened, grew hard and purposeful. His arms flailed wildly and there was a strange, horrible scream through the station. The scream hit the low, concrete ceiling and reverberated down; it glanced from pillars and echoed in his ears; it rose terrifyingly, madly, above the roar of the train and it was tearing in the ears of the man who was falling, and detached from him. His hands clutched momentarily, desperately at nothing and he had time to think, "This isn't me—this is somebody else—this isn't happening—" before he did not think; before he died with his own scream in his ears.

The motorman of the train did everything a man could do, and then shut his eyes. The wheels of the train screamed against the brake-shoes and against the track. Standing passengers were swung helplessly on their straps and several fell. But there was not time for a man to do anything of real importance. The train was, to be sure, going hardly five miles an hour when the first wheels cut through the gray-blue uniform. The screaming, mercifully, had died an instant before; falling, the man had hit his head on a rail, and had so been spared that last appalling second of hopeless consciousness.

There were screams on the platform, and men and women ran and shouted; the crowd knotted where the train had stopped, and people struggled out of it, white and with their faces working. The dispatcher in his booth at one end of the platform set signals against following trains, reported to the district operations office, telephoned the police. The motorman of the train set his whistle wailing; its sound reached the street through ventilating gratings, and after a moment, brought a traffic policeman from Eighth Street running down the stairs. He had hardly reached the platform when the first radio car spewed out two more uniformed men; within ten minutes everything was under control and within fifteen ambulance surgeons, who did not need even a glance to tell them there was nothing for them to do on the track, were reviving several women who had fainted and quieting the several more who were hysterical. A crowd collected on the street above and stared at the radio cars and ambulances.

The police cleared the platform and turned people back at the entrances. Behind the stopped train, traffic was rerouted from express to local tracks and proceeded, after some delay, almost at normal speed. Orders to accomplish this went out by routine; the New York subways provide a devastating agency of destruction for many who decide against further living.

No reporters accompanied the police. Volunteers called the afternoon newspapers and reported that service was interrupted; the newspapers investigated by telephone and ran short accounts. The New York City News Association sent out, after a time, a brief report, stressing, as was natural, that the disturbance of traffic had occurred during the evening rush hour.

Weigand came out of Goody's Bar when it was hardly any time at all after six o'clock and noticed that something had happened at the subway station down the avenue. Uniformed men were standing around waving people on; radio cars half blocked the street and two ambulances were wedged among them. He looked a minute and shrugged.

"Some poor devil," Weigand said to himself, glad it was a precinct job. He crossed Sixth Avenue and found Grove Street after a moment's search. He went along it looking at numbers. He was getting near, he realized, when a couple of cats began fighting in the middle of the street and he stopped to watch. They went at it with savage yowls, tangled and rolled in a whirl of yellow and gray. Weigand, who liked cats, was wishing he had a pail of water to douse the fighters before they did serious damage to each other, when a car turned the corner ahead, moving at a moderate speed, and came up the street.

A man with an angry face was driving. Weigand could tell by his expression when the man in the car saw the cats; the expression, strangely and unpleasantly, was a gloating one. The car suddenly leaped at the cats, and the cats disappeared under it.

"Why, you—!!" Weigand yelled, whirled and noted the number. Then he whirled back to look for the cats. There was, miraculously, only one cat and it, with every hair bristling and a furious tail, was staring after the car. The other cat was a flash of movement in an areaway across the street. Both, amazingly, had been missed by the wheels.

Then, from the door of a three-story red brick house near where Weigand was standing, a tall, angry man burst, yelling.

"You—!" he yelled. "If I could—!" He was, Weigand saw, yelling after the man in the car. He was, Weigand thought, as angry a man as he had seen in a long time, or wanted to see. The angry man ran a few steps toward Weigand, and after the car, and then stopped. His rage was cooling, Weigand decided. Now he could see the detective.

"That—" the angry man said, describing the motorist grimly and, Weigand felt, rather exactly.

"Yes," Weigand said. "I agree with you. But they came out all right—the cats, I mean."

"No fault of his," the angry man said. "That—"

"Well," said Weigand, "you find all kinds about." He glanced quickly at the number of the nearest house, checked the probable address of the red brick house, and took a chance.

"Would you be Mr. Fuller, by any chance?" he said. "Benjamin Fuller?"

"Well," the angry man said, anger still under his voice, "as a matter of fact I am. Yes." He looked at Weigand more carefully. "I don't know you, do I?" he inquired.

"Weigand," the detective said. "Lieutenant William Weigand, of the Homicide Bureau. I was coming along to see you."

Fuller did not seem greatly surprised, or, for that matter, greatly pleased.

"I thought you would," he said. "Or somebody. About that ———— Brent, I suppose." He described Brent unfavorably.

"Well," said Weigand. "About Brent, yes. No friend of yours, I gather."

"No," Fuller said, "no friend of mine. Come along in."

They went along to the red brick house which was, Weigand discovered, apparently occupied entirely by the Fullers. "In the money," Weigand thought. "Pretty well in the money, anyway." Aloud he said:

"Was one of those your cat?"

"No," Fuller said. "I keep a dog. I don't like cats, much."

Weigand said, "Oh," and decided that Fuller must have a bit of temper.

"But any animal," Fuller said. "The louse."

Weigand nodded, and they went into a living-room which seemed to run the full length of the house, and was furnished in substantial modern blocks. The chairs looked as if they had been made by sculptors, chiseling out hollows and shaping forms from cubical masses. There was a table all of glass, and the rear wall of the long room was of glass brick. The lamps were hooded in metal and glass, and Weigand, who had always assumed he disliked modern furniture, found his dislike subsiding. He took the chair Fuller gestured toward and was pleased with it.

Fuller lighted a cigarette and said, "Drink?" inquiringly. Weigand, after a moment of temptation, said he didn't think so.

"Not with suspects, eh?" Fuller said, sharply. He stood in front of the frosted glass fireplace, with a space for a real fire, and looked down at Weigand.

"Not on duty," Weigand said. "Rules. Sit down, won't you?"

Fuller grinned. He had rather a crooked, attractive grin. He seemed about to say something, decided against it and sat down.

"Well," he said. "Where do we go from here? Did I kill Brent? No, the answer is. I didn't kill Brent. Did I have a motive to kill Brent? Yes. Did I have opportunity? I don't know. I don't know when he was killed."

"Well," said Weigand. "We can go on with this the rest of the night, I suppose. Or I can ask you some questions and you can give me some answers. Or we can go down to Headquarters and we can ask some questions there. Or whatever you want. Right?"

"Right," Fuller echoed. He stared at the detective a minute. "All right," he said. "I'm keyed up, probably. Wipe it out, and we'll start over. Did I kill Brent? No."

"But you're just as well pleased somebody did?" Weigand said. Fuller thought it over a moment.

"Well," he said, "literally, no. Of course not. He was a nuisance to me and I didn't like him, any more than I like the man who tried to run down the cats. That doesn't mean killing, or being glad of killing. People don't kill, really, nowadays."

"Yes," Weigand said. "Yes, they do, sometimes. For some reasons. Somebody killed Brent, for example. There seems to be a pretty general impression going around that you didn't like him. Why?"

"That," Fuller said, "seems to be my business."

Weigand nodded and said if Fuller chose to take it that way, certainly.

"If you choose to take it that way," he said, "I'll get along. I'll go along back to Headquarters and send up a couple of the boys. They'll bring you down there. And then you don't have to talk without a lawyer. And then we'll lock you up as a material witness. No third degree, or anything. Just lock you up a while, until your lawyer springs you. Then we'll lock you up on suspicion. Then, maybe, we'll sort of keep you from getting the sleep you'd like to have, and half a dozen of the boys will take turns questioning you. It's just as you like. Why didn't you like Brent?"

"Listen," said Fuller, "how about talking to you as another man? Suppose you're not a cop, for a while?"

Weigand shook his head, and said he was always a cop.

"Which doesn't," he said, "mean I tell everything I hear, or want to make mistakes in my man. I'm after the man who bumped off Brent. I'm not after anybody else." He paused. "Or anything else," he said. He was weary of saying it. "My God," he said, "what your wife does is her business, and yours. Only who killed Brent's my business."

The blood flooded hotly under Fuller's skin. He had red hair, all right. He half started up, and then settled back a little.

"You've been hearing things," he said. "They're lies."

"Right," Weigand said. "I've been hearing things. I've been hearing that Brent and your wife were great friends. I've been hearing—"

"That they were perfectly swell friends," Fuller said. "That I could go into divorce court on how good friends they were."

"O.K.," said Weigand, mildly. "Right. That's what I've been hearing. So what? I don't have to believe it. You could calm down, if you wanted to. You could tell me about it, and why you didn't like Brent, if it wasn't because he was running around with your wife. We wouldn't have to fight about it, unless you wanted to."

Fuller lighted another cigarette and took a drag from it. Then he took another, and another. He watched the smoke and Weigand waited. Finally Fuller said, "All right.

"You may as well know the truth of it," he said. "You've heard everything else, apparently, from our friends." The word "friends" was harshly accented. "You've heard that the Brents and the Fullers used to be great friends?"

Weigand nodded.

"Well," Fuller said, "I'll tell you about it." He dragged at his cigarette and hesitated.

It took a good many cigarettes and many pauses for words before he finished his story.

The couples had met, as couples, about four years earlier, he said. Fuller had known Claire Brent, first; had known her before she was Claire Brent, while she was still Claire Askew. "She was a tennis player, you know," Fuller said. So, Weigand learned, was Fuller. He and Claire Askew had met in the marquee at Forest Hills. Fuller paused to clear up a point. "I was no good," he said. "Never was any good; any real good. The best I ever did was to get through the first round, against another bunny who was even worse. She was better, in her class, but no world beater. Quarter finals she got to, once. And lost to Jacobs in love sets."

"Right," Weigand said.

"We played together a few times in mixed doubles," Fuller said. "Not tournament play; just for fun. She didn't have much but an overhead game. She could smash if they set them up for her." He grinned. "Which they didn't, if they knew anything," he added. "It made her mad, that."

"Yes," said Weigand. "And—?"

They had, Fuller explained, got friendly and for a while seen a good deal of each other. Then she met Brent and in a little while married him; Fuller himself married a few months later. There had been nothing more than a casual friendship between himself and Claire Askew, Fuller indicated; it had continued with Claire Brent, and, as such things happened, with her husband, Stanley. "The four of us got to going around together a good deal for a while," Fuller said. "To theaters, and night clubs sometimes, and bridge. It made an agreeable foursome."

Things had jogged on that way, Fuller said, for a couple of years, and then Brent began to pay special attention to Jane Fuller. "He began to edge in," Fuller said. "Nobody else wanted it that way; Claire and I didn't feel that way. Nobody felt that way but Brent. At first, anyhow."

"And then?" Weigand said.

"Then—all right," Fuller said. "Suppose she did get flattered? And suppose she liked Brent? What about it?"

"Right," Weigand said. "What about it?"

It became, after a time, inescapable that Brent was making a play for Jane Fuller. Nobody could ignore it, or pretend it wasn't happening. So Fuller had had a showdown with Brent and broken up the foursome. Claire, who was angry and hurt, had agreed that was the only thing. Brent had laughed about it. "I damn near knocked his block off," Fuller said. "But—well, it was a mess anyway you took it. It was a mess already."

"And how did Mrs. Fuller take it?" Weigand asked.

Fuller thought a moment before he answered. To understand, he said, you would have to know Jane, and it was hard to explain her.

"Damn it all," Fuller said, "what do you want me to say? She's my girl, man!" Weigand nodded—and waited. Well, then, put it this way: Jane thought it was a storm in a teacup. "She thought I was making a lot out of nothing," Fuller said. "She said people nowadays didn't need to take such things seriously; she thought she could bring him around without breaking up the group. She said you had to be kind to people, because people were restless and lonely, and that I could trust her."

The point was, Fuller insisted, that he did "trust" her, when it came to that. And that he wouldn't, in any case, try to apply compulsion. It was up to her, but what he did was equally up to him, and he wasn't seeing any more of Brent. It was merely a way he felt, he had told her—it was nothing to argue. As far as he was concerned the Fuller-Brent combine was dissolved. He didn't demand anything of her except, in the end, loyalty. He was not going to say what loyalty, from her to him, would be; that was a thing for her to decide. He would prefer that she, too, stop seeing Brent; but he would not argue that it proved anything if she didn't.

"Only I was through with him," Fuller said. "I didn't like him. I figured he was a bad actor, about women and, probably everything else. I thought he'd done wrong by his Claire—all that sort of thing. I thought he would make a mess of things for Jane, if she'd let him, and I didn't see how to stop her letting him. I couldn't pull the heavy husband, you see that. And it would have spoiled something, anyway, if I'd tried it. With Jane—it—well, it wasn't on our cards. D'you see what I mean?"

"Yes," Weigand said. "I think so. What did she do?"

Jane had, it seemed, seen Brent occasionally, quite openly. "At first because she wanted to," Fuller thought. "Then because she had started and had no clear, sharp reason for stopping. Then—oh, God knows. Because of some strange, perverted kindness. That was after Claire—" He stopped, suddenly.

"Yes?" Weigand said.

Fuller wasn't going on with that, he said. It was enough to tell all that about themselves. Suppose they said, merely, that Claire got fed up with it, as she might well. Right?

"Right," said Weigand. "I can't press you."

Well, then, they would stick to the main issue. Brent discovered that Jane would, other things being equal, rather not be with him. "That it was—well, call it momentum" alone that was maintaining their relationship. But relationship wasn't the word, if it meant anything in particular to Weigand. "There wasn't anything of that in it," Fuller said. "There was no question of it. Both Jane and I knew that." He paused. "You'll think I was fooled about it," he said. "The husband is the last person—all that sort of thing. But I wasn't fooled; I knew. Can you see that? If there had been anything of that I'd have known the first time I looked at her."

Weigand nodded. It could be that way. And, all right, Fuller could have been fooled.

Then, Fuller said, Brent realized that he didn't mean anything to Jane, and wasn't going to, but at first he did nothing. Kept on inviting her to lunch, taking her to the theater now and then. Being very cordial when they met at parties. Then he—

"Look," Fuller said. "This is all intangible. Anyway I say it, it sounds like nothing at all. As if I were jealous and imagining things. I don't know—"

"Well," said Weigand, "have a shot at it. I'm a cop, of course, but have a shot at it."

Fuller leaned back, smoking. Then he ground out his cigarette. All right, they could take it this way:

"We ran into each other rather often," he said. "You can understand that—it was inevitable, unless we all changed our habits. And people don't. We would go places and the Brents would be there; or Brent would be there alone. And then—well, say that he began to be pointedly solicitous of Jane. That doesn't phrase it, but nearly. He'd get her little things and light her cigarettes, d'you see? He'd touch her shoulder with his hand as if—well, as if it was an accustomed gesture, or the beginning of an accustomed gesture. As if—"

He paused again, and said that there was, really, nothing you could put your finger on. But it was in everything he said to her and about her, and in everything he did when he was near her. It was in the way he treated Fuller.

"There is," Fuller said, "something about the way men and women behave when they are together, even when they intend to be careful, that gives them away if they're lovers. It's in their voices and their hands, and their choice of words to each other, and if you know about people you can tell. Well, most of the people we meet know about people. And Brent is—was—clever, remember." He paused again.

"Yes?" Weigand said.

"So everything he did made it seem to everyone who saw them that Jane was his mistress," Fuller said. "That's blunt enough for you. It yelled itself at you—he was smug and attentive and—well, damn it all—satisfied. And the devilish thing about it was that it was all an act, and an act you couldn't put a finger on. It wasn't even anything you could object to; nothing Jane could object to, or I could. And he knew all the time what he was about; it was quite conscious and deliberate. Every now and then he would look at me and let me see that he knew I knew what he was up to, and that he knew there wasn't a thing I could do. Sweet, wasn't it?"

"Very," Weigand said. "Very sweet. He must have been a swell guy."

Fuller nodded.

"A perfectly swell guy," he said. "All right, you can see what I meant when I said I had a motive for killing him. I didn't kill him, but I tried to knock his block off, once. You heard about that?"

Weigand nodded.

"And you heard my wife was his mistress?"

"Gossip," Weigand said. "Some people think so, certainly. You can see how they might—on your own story."

"Sure," Fuller said. "That was the idea—the big Brent idea. All right, I've got a temper. You know that. So there you are."

There, Weigand agreed inwardly, he was. It sounded perfectly all right as Fuller said it; Fuller sounded entirely straightforward and honest. It was clear that Brent had something coming to him. It was also clear that whatever Brent had had coming had come. It could all be entirely true, except for one sentence. "I didn't kill him." That obviously didn't have to be true.

And if Fuller's story left Fuller in it, so did his account of his actions on Monday afternoon. He had left his office—he was an importer, running successfully the successful business left him by his father—at about 3 o'clock. He had gone out with a customer of his, and also an old acquaintance of his, for a drink or two before the customer went back to Chicago on the Century. They had had the drink or two and the customer had gone on to his hotel to pick up his bag. Fuller had walked part-way downtown to stretch his legs and taken a taxicab the rest of the way, getting home a little after four. The customer had, presumably, caught the Century. He was, at any rate, back in Chicago. What time had Fuller and the customer, a man named Raymond Crowley, parted?

Fuller couldn't put an hour and minute to it. It hadn't been long. Crowley had remembered, in the middle of the second drink, that he had promised his wife to give a message to a decorator for her, and leave some samples, and, being a dutiful husband, had dashed back to the hotel to get the samples out of his bag and drop them on his way to the station. It might have been three-thirty when they parted; it might have been three-twenty, or a quarter of four.

It wasn't, certainly, iron-clad. From the bar in Forty-second Street which Fuller and Crowley visited to 95 Greenwich Place might not be more than a quarter of an hour; a few minutes one way or another on the various times, none of which was exact, might make it possible for Fuller to get to the Buano house and give Brent what he had coming. There was, to be sure, the evidence that the engagement had been made in advance, and according to Fuller's story he was alone between three and four only by chance, and Crowley's memory. But that, evidently, was not conclusive; Fuller might have remembered an errand if Crowley hadn't. If you took everybody at his word, nobody had killed Brent; Brent was still alive. And Brent wasn't alive.

Weigand said yes, he saw. And was Mrs. Fuller in? Mrs. Fuller wasn't, but would be, if Weigand wanted to wait. He looked at his watch, found it was after seven, and decided another time would do. There were only a few questions. Where she was Monday afternoon. Things like that. Routine, really.

"Well," said Fuller, "I can tell you where she was. She was shop-

ping. She came home a few minutes after I got in and the taxi driver
had to help carry her packages. There were more the next day, too, by
truck. That's where she was."

"Right," said Weigand, thinking that it told him precisely nothing.
He said that, in that case, he would get along. He might, later, think of
some other questions. Fuller would be around? Fuller grinned, without
enjoyment. He would be around, all right.

"We'll both be around," he said. "Drop in any time."

Fuller was an attractive sort of a person, Weigand thought, as he
went out looking for dinner. Very attractive in his way. It was unfortu-
nate that murderers were not always unattractive people one could
enjoy arresting.

• 9 •

Weigand found dinner, walked across town to the B.M.T., and rode down to Headquarters. Mullins, comfortable with his feet on a desk, was waiting. He took his feet off the desk and said that the more he saw of the case the screwier it got. Yes, he had sent the slip to the Research Bureau in Brooklyn and they had promised a full report by morning. Also he had seen Edwards, the laundryman. William Edwards.

"He says no," Mullins said.

"No what?" Weigand wanted to know.

"No, he didn't commit the murder," Mullins explained, as if it should have been easy. Mullins was patient about it. "He knew Brent and he didn't like him much, but he didn't kill him. 'Over a shirt I should kill people?' he said."

"This is Edwards?" Weigand wanted to know. "Bill Edwards. Over-a-shirt-he-should-kill-people Edwards?"

Mullins nodded.

"It's just a name," he said. "It goes with the laundry. Every time a new man takes over the laundry he's William Edwards. He might have been a Chinaman."

93

"But he wasn't," Weigand said. "What about the shirt?"

Brent had, it developed, accused Edwards of destroying a new and custom made shirt of great value. Edwards had insisted that (a) he had not destroyed it, (b) it was not new, anyhow, and (c) anybody should pay fifteen dollars for a shirt, and did Brent think he was a greenhorn? So relations had been strained. But Edwards was up in the Bronx seeing his mother on Monday afternoon and he could prove it by "mama."

"He could probably, too," Mullins thought. "But he didn't like Brent. Nobody liked this guy Brent, much, did they?"

"Well," Weigand said, "lots of people didn't, apparently. But maybe some did—maybe his wife did."

"Maybe," Mullins said. "And maybe it was an act. Maybe she thought somebody had a swell idea. Maybe she had the swell idea herself. What does the Doc say? Could a woman have bashed him?"

Weigand had been over that, and it was, the doctor thought, possible. It would, naturally, depend on the weight of the weapon and, at least as much, on the strength of the woman. A weapon with a handle, weighted and balanced—with such a weapon almost any reasonably strong woman could have done it, particularly counting in the thinness of Brent's skull.

"The North dame?" Mullins wanted to know. Weigand nodded his head, but doubtfully.

"Physically—yes, with the proper weapon. But I don't think she did. I don't think she goes around bashing people." He waited for Mullins, who thought it over. Mullins might be interesting on the point. Mullins shook his head.

"Neither do I, somehow," he said. "She's too screwy and, oh—what the hell? It's not in the picture, Loot."

Two hunches didn't make a fact, Weigand thought. On the other hand, two hunches might be better than one.

"How about the Brent dame?" Mullins wanted to know. "She looked sort of hefty, somehow."

There wasn't, Weigand thought, much doubt that the Brent dame could have killed her husband as he was killed, if she had wanted to.

She was, well, "lithe" was the word. Then he remembered something Fuller had said.

"She had a good overhead smash," he said. Mullins looked puzzled and then said that somebody, sure enough, had had a good overhead smash. Weigand explained.

"In tennis," he said. "She was pretty good a few years ago. She was particularly good at hitting the ball when it was in the air, over the head. She reached up and came down on it. Anyway, that's what Fuller says."

"Oh," said Mullins, "tennis. A tennis ball ain't a man's head."

"Get under a good overhead smash some time," Weigand said. "Even with a racquet, and not anything heavy—like a mallet. You'd see things. Or maybe you wouldn't see anything."

Mullins didn't think much of the idea, it was clear; he thought tennis was something you played in white pants. But he let it go, in favor of something else.

"Parkes called up," he said. "Remember Parkes—Sergeant Parkes, assigned to the D.A.'s office?"

Weigand nodded.

"He said he thought we ought to know," Mullins said. "He thought we ought to know Brent had an appointment with one of the assistants for Tuesday. With an assistant named Cummings. They don't know what about and they sort of wondered why he didn't show up. Then one of them sort of thought to look in the paper and there, sure enough, it was. Even those boys could dope out why he didn't show up after they saw the papers."

Weigand was interested; very much interested.

"They didn't know what he wanted?" he said.

Mullins said that was it. He called up and said he wanted to give some information and they put him onto Cummings. He said he wanted to come around and see Cummings personally and made an appointment for Tuesday—the next day.

"It was Monday when he called, then?" Weigand said. "What time Monday?"

"Monday afternoon about one o'clock," Mullins said. "They made a note of it. Bright guys up there. About an hour ago they got to thinking we might be interested."

The District Attorney's office, it developed, was leaving the matter entirely to the Department, although in promising cases it often assigned detectives from the staff detailed to aid its investigations. Just now, however, its staff was busy on rackets.

"Parkes says they've got some hot stuff," Mullins reported, interestedly. "He says they're going to blow things open."

"Well," Weigand said. "That will be swell. What things?"

Parkes hadn't said. Just things.

"What about the other end?" Weigand said. "Brent's office? Did the boys turn up anything?"

Mullins hadn't heard and Weigand sent him to find out if Sergeant Auerbach, in charge of investigations at the law offices, had reported in. Auerbach had, and came along. He had been, he said, writing up his report to send along to the Inspector, but he could give Weigand the gist of it. They had interviewed everybody at the office and nobody knew anything of importance. "You'll get it all," Auerbach said. "But I don't think there's anything in it." They had checked Brent's bank account and income. His balance was not large, but large enough and his income was substantial and steady, running, apparently, around fifteen or twenty thousand a year. There was nothing irregular about it; no large unexplained deposits, no unaccountable withdrawals.

"They spent about all he made," Auerbach said. "But there was always more coming along."

The Brents had had a joint account, and Brent had had another in his own name. The bills from various charge accounts went to his office and were paid from there, apparently after reasonable lapses of time. At the time of his death he owed rather over a thousand, which was, Auerbach said, probably about average for his income.

"It doesn't show us anything that I can see," Auerbach said. "The details are all in the reports."

They had got a list of the firm's clients, on pledge that the information would go no further, and the cases especially assigned to Brent were checked.

The law firm had, Weigand discovered, a good many imposing clients, many of them corporations. Consolidated Foods was on the list, and the Framingham Steel Corporation and something called, rather oddly, Recording Industries, Inc., along with many others. These apparently were permanent clients, and a few of them were checked. There were also a number of individual clients assigned to Brent, and Weigand ran through them without finding any familiar names until he came to "Berex, Louis." He pointed to the name.

"Any correspondence from this man?" he wanted to know.

Auerbach thought there was; he went back to his desk to look and returned with two letters, which he tossed to Weigand. Both bore Berex's name printed at the top. One merely confirmed an appointment at Brent's office for a Friday in late September. The other, written a fortnight earlier, asked for information.

"Will you let me know," Berex had written, "what progress you are making in the Edwards matter? And what attitude he and his lawyers are showing? I appreciate that these things cannot be made to move rapidly, and that you are doing all that can be done. But you will appreciate, also, my anxiety to get the matter settled."

Clipped on was a carbon of Brent's answer, which said, in effect, that he hoped to have progress to report within a week or two, and that he did appreciate Berex's desire for a favorable conclusion of the matter. Both letters were direct and formal; neither showed that the relation between the two men was more than that of client and counsel. Weigand read them quickly and continued to stare at them. After a while he said, "Um," thoughtfully.

"Anything else?" he wanted to know.

"There were several notes from dames," Auerbach said. "Nice, friendly notes. I've got the boys checking them. Brent seems to have gotten around quite a bit."

"Anything from a Mrs. Fuller?" Weigand asked. "A Jane Fuller?"

They hadn't, Auerbach said, found anything. There was a note from Myrtle—"My God," Weigand said—and one signed "Honey" and another signed merely "Love, K." But the most recent of these, it developed, had been written almost three years earlier.

"What," Weigand said, "do you suppose they keep them for?"

Auerbach hadn't, he said, any idea. Mullins said that maybe they just liked to remember.

"Well," Weigand said, "they'll be fun for the boys to check. Let me know what they find, will you?"

"Sure," Auerbach promised. "It will be about Christmas, but I'll let you know. If you still want to know."

"Right," Weigand said. Then he said, "Thanks," and Auerbach went back to his report. Now, Weigand wondered, where were they? He looked at his watch and discovered, rather to his surprise, that it was almost eleven. He was tired and his head ached and Inspector O'Malley had gone home a long time before. Weigand checked, mentally. Brent's clothes were being looked for, diligently but without much hope. The Salvation Army had been checked, but had no record of receiving a man's complete outfit. The Post Office Department had been notified of the chance that the clothes worn by Brent might be jogging somewhere in the mails, bound for heaven knew what imaginary addressee.

A couple of men were checking the parcel rooms at the Pennsylvania and Grand Central Stations, and the railroad ferries. As fast as unredeemed bundles were removed from the lock boxes on the subway stations, from which they are taken after a stipulated twenty-four hours has elapsed, they were checked. But the clothes might just as well never turn up. If anybody wanted to go to the trouble, and sacrifice, say, a flatiron, there were always convenient rivers.

The slip Mrs. North found in the fourth-floor mailbox was being examined by modern science in Brooklyn. An eye was being kept on possible suspects. Weigand couldn't see O'Malley until tomorrow, unless something broke. Berex was the next man to see, but that could wait until tomorrow; would have to wait until tomorrow, when the mailbox slip had been fingerprinted and otherwise examined. Hmmm—

Weigand decided that there was nothing which prevented him from going home and sleeping a while. It was an agreeable thought. Mullins could drive him up in a Department car. He told Mullins as much, and Mullins said, "O.K., Loot."

It was turning cooler out, Weigand noticed, as they drove uptown. Weigand was stern about the red lights and the siren, this time; there was nothing to identify the car as belonging to the police except, of course, Mullins behind the wheel. Weigand was half asleep when they reached his apartment house in the West Fifties, three-quarters when he fell into bed.

· 10 ·

Weigand had gone to bed Wednesday evening with a feeling of tired satisfaction; he awoke Thursday in a mood of angry impatience which nature abetted by providing him with a mild hangover. He got up filled with smoldering indignation, directed chiefly against himself and for slightly intangible reasons; he bathed and shaved irritably, and the whirring of the razor tightened his nerves. He was at Headquarters a little after eight, and angrily in quest of Mullins. Before nine he was smouldering on the telephone to Brooklyn, inquiring bitterly for a report on the slip of paper he had sent over the evening before. Mullins, when he came, was snapped into motion, telephoning Louis Berex to make an appointment for eleven; checking on the progress of the search for Brent's clothing; arranging another interview to follow immediately with Edwards; finding out from the watchers' reports what Mrs. Brent, Fuller and the Norths had been doing the evening and night before.

None of them had, it developed, been doing anything out of the way. The Norths and their guests had gone to a motion picture theater around the corner and seen a mystery film, which Detective Cohen, rousted from his comfort at the bar across the street, had also seen and enjoyed. He was willing to tell Mullins the plot, but Mullins, feeling hostile eyes on the back of his head, demurred. Edwards had gone to a formal dinner in one of the East Seventies and his accompanying detective had had a dull time on the sidewalk.

Fuller had stayed at home with, it was presumed, Mrs. Fuller, who had arrived shortly after Weigand left. A man identified as Berex by the doorman of the apartment house near the East River, where Berex lived, had come home about ten and, apparently, stayed home, although, since there were several possible exits to the house, nobody could be quite sure, and if Headquarters really wanted him watched, two men would be necessary, at least. Mullins relayed this information to Weigand, who was frosty. This morning, Mullins decided, the Loot suspected everybody.

There was, Mullins knew by experience, a time in every case when the Loot began to suspect everybody. It came when things got too screwy even for the Loot, who could take things a lot screwier than Mullins could. Mullins suffered through this period, but he understood it. In his idle moments—never as numerous as Mullins would have liked—he experimented with crossword puzzles, and they were always too much for him at a certain point. Then, he had long since decided, the way he felt must be about the way the Loot felt now. He looked at Weigand warily, but with understanding.

Then the report from Brooklyn arrived, in an official Department envelope, and Weigand ripped it open. Mullins rallied around.

The Research Bureau had discovered several things. The slip was, to be exact, one and seven-eighths inches by five-eighths; it had been snipped from a good grade of bond paper with, the bureau believed, curved manicure scissors. The paper was of a type widely used and it was, the Research Bureau assured the Homicide Bureau, highly improbable that it could be traced, although the manufacturer's name could, no doubt, be established. From other indications, the slip apparently had been cut from a printed letterhead.

The marks on the narrow edge of the back of the slip led, the

Bureau reported, to this conclusion. In cutting the slip, the person who had prepared it had cut into what probably was the name printed on the letterhead, leaving on the slip a part of one of the letters. The letter was, the Bureau had satisfied itself by examination under magnification, an X or, if a K, the only other alternative, a K from a specially cast type font. The angle of the marks, together with the lengths of the serifs on the two marks, made it almost certain, however, that X was the letter cut. It might be either the first or the last letter of the name—the Bureau suggested, for what it was worth, that the letterhead might have been printed for a man whose first name was Xavier, that being the name which first came to the mind of Detective Sergeant Kelly, who had dictated the report. It might, in time, be possible to trace the identity of the owner of the letterhead by canvassing print shops. The printing was by a special method which gave a raised surface to the printed words, simulating engraving. The name had not, however, been engraved.

There were two fingerprints on the slip, one on each of the opposing surfaces. The prints had been developed, photographed, enlarged and compared with the records. They were not the prints of anyone on record in the New York Police Department and had been, duly, dispatched to Washington for comparison there. Since the prints had been removed, indexed and filed, the Research Bureau had applied a fixative to the originals on the slip so that detectives working on the case might study the positions. The Bureau also supplied technical details as to the weight of the paper stock, the grade and probably manufacturer of the ink and added that slight traces of ink of a different grade, presumably from a typewriter ribbon, were present in the thumb print—see exhibit—which indicated that the owner of the thumb was also owner of a typewriter.

Weigand, whose digestion was quieting somewhat, saw exhibit, with a good deal of interest. The two prints stood out, now, clearly. The face and the reverse of the slip now had this appearance:

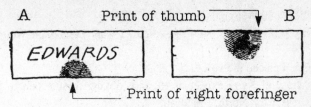

A   Print of thumb   B

Print of right forefinger

Weigand had picked up the fingerprints of both the Norths after Mrs. North had found the slip, and a glance was enough to show him that the prints on the slip were not theirs. Prints of Edwards had been developed overnight from the detective's watch—which was now scrupulously polished again and back in his pocket—and at first Weigand thought he saw a resemblance. Then he looked again and doubted it. Mullins was directed to have the prints from the slip and those of Edwards compared and get the answer. Mullins wrestled with the telephone a moment, and then announced he'd better go and see about it himself.

"Get them compared with Brent's, too," Weigand directed, "or do I have to tell you everything? And with anybody else's we've got on this." Mullins went to see about it.

Weigand stared at the slip and thought about Berex. The coincidence was, obviously, too great to be merely a coincidence; it was safe betting that the men whose names ended or began in X were few enough so that the chance of there being two in any one case was faint. Then he remembered something, and telephoned Detective Auerbach, who brought in one of the letters Berex had written Brent. The letterhead bore only the name of Louis Berex, and one glance at it pretty well clinched matters. He laid a piece of paper over Berex's letterhead so that the edge bisected the final letter. There was no doubt at all. He was less than ever surprised, therefore, when Mullins returned from the Identification Bureau to report that nobody so far printed in the case, beginning with the victim himself, had prints matching those on the slip.

It left the next step clear enough, and Weigand rose to take it. Then the telephone on his desk rang. He reached for it.

"And new binding on both edges," the voice said. "And see if you can't find the belt to—"

"Hello," said Weigand.

"—my brown dress," said the voice. "I want Lieutenant Weigand, please."

Weigand placed the voice.

"If," he said, "you expect us to start looking for the belt to your brown dress, Mrs. North, I'm afraid—"

Mrs. North's laugh came through the receiver and then was cut off suddenly. Apparently she had remembered something.

"It's terrible, isn't it?" she said. "Did you read about it?"

"Listen," said Weigand. "I don't get this. What's so terrible about a belt? Why should I read about it?"

Mrs. North said, "Oh, that," and that he should forget it.

"That was the boy from the cleaner's," she said. "They lost it, only really they just forgot to send it back. No, I mean it's terrible about poor old Timothy, who was sweet."

"Timothy?" Weigand said. It was, as far as he could remember, a new one on him.

"Barnes," Mrs. North said. "Timothy Barnes. The postman; the man who delivers the mail."

Weigand remembered something about a man named Barnes who delivered mail—oh, yes, who had helped Mrs. North extract the slip from the mailbox.

He said he remembered. What about Mr. Barnes?

"He's dead!" Mrs. North said. "Murdered. It's in the papers on the front page, only it doesn't say he was. But he was, of course."

Weigand jumped, sat down on the end of the desk and said, with something like excitement in his voice:

"What!" Then he said: "Listen, what paper?"

Mrs. North told him.

"It says an accident or suicide," Mrs. North said. "But it wasn't, of course. It was because he found the slip. The murderer got him."

Excitement ran through the real regret in Mrs. North's voice. Weigand thought quickly, and decided that it was odd, all right. Coincidence, maybe—but still.

"Are you sure it's the same man?" he asked. Mrs. North was; it was the same name. And the man was a mail-carrier, too; it was even in the neighborhood.

"And listen," she said. "Jerry and I were talking it over, and he was going *down* town. And he lived *up* town. And we thought he was going to Headquarters to tell you something and the murderer knew it and pushed him off."

It was muddled, Weigand decided. And then, with a rather chilly feeling, he realized there was something in it. It was too much of a coincidence; too hard to take unless there was something in it. Then he thought of something else. If the murderer was that kind of a murderer—the kind out to clean up loose ends, ruthlessly—there were others who weren't in too healthy a position.

Mrs. North said, "Hello? Are you still there?"

Weigand said he was, and then talked crisply. The Norths, he thought, had better stay in and be careful whom they let in and he would send Mullins up to stick around.

"If he's after people," he explained, "you and Mr. North are in line, perhaps. We don't know, but we'll play it safe."

"Oh!" said Mrs. North, in the tone of a person who hadn't thought of that before. "You think—?"

If you put it that way, Weigand said, no, he didn't. But there was a chance, particularly if the slip was at the bottom of it. He'd come up later and they'd talk it over; meanwhile Mullins would be around and stick close.

"And not too much rye for him," he added, for the benefit also of Mullins, who was listening. Mullins said, indignantly, "Now, listen here, Loot!" and Weigand waved him to silence. Mrs. North promised they would wait in for Mullins.

"The slip must be important, then," she said. "If it is the slip."

Weigand said that it began to look as if it might be, and that now he had things to do. "I'll be around," he said. "Sit tight."

Mullins already had his hat on when Weigand cradled the telephone. He said, "Listen, Loot," and Weigand waved him on. "Only if I find you boiled—" he warned. Mullins looked grieved, and went on. Weigand got hold of a paper. On the front page, Mrs. North had

said. It took him a minute to find the story. It wasn't a long story. It
read:

SUBWAY DEATH HALTS TRAFFIC

———

Elderly Mail-Carrier Ends Life in the City Subway.

———

Timothy Barnes, 57 years old, a mail-carrier, fell or jumped from
the downtown platform of the Independent Subway at the Fourth
Street station late yesterday, dying under the wheels of a Brooklyn-
bound express train. Traffic on the express track was tied up for
more than an hour and it was necessary to route express trains on
the local track below Fourteenth Street until the body was removed.

Police recorded the case as probably suicide, although Barnes'
wife, Mrs. Elizabeth Barnes, who lived with her husband at 643
East 172nd Street, the Bronx, said she knew of no reason why he
should take his life. He was, according to Mrs. Barnes, in apparent
good spirits when he left home yesterday morning. His health had
been good and he was looking forward to his imminent retirement.
He had been a Post Office carrier for twenty-four years, and would
have been eligible for a pension in August, next year.

Weigand called Charles Street Station, and got the lieutenant in
charge of the Sixth Precinct detectives on the wire. Rapidly he
sketched the situation and Lieutenant Sullivan at the other end figura-
tively threw up his hands.

"Could he have been pushed?" Sullivan repeated. "Sure he could
have been pushed. He could have got dizzy and fallen; he could have
jumped; he could have slipped on a banana peel. We'll never know."

The platform was, Sullivan explained, moderately crowded, and
there were half a dozen people, perhaps more, within arm's length of
Barnes before he fell. Some of them were still there when the police
arrived; some of them weren't. There was no way of telling. Nobody
saw Barnes pushed, if that helped—yes, they had asked, as a matter of

routine. Nobody saw that he wasn't pushed. A man nearby had reached
out in, apparently, an effort to grab Barnes, and had missed him. A
woman on the other side had, according to one witness, actually
clutched at Barnes' coatsleeve, and it had been torn from her fingers.
Neither the man nor the woman was among the witnesses the police
had found to question, which proved nothing.

"People go sort of crazy when something like that happens," Sullivan said. "Some crowd around; others run off. Some faint, and some
just gloat. If somebody pushed him, we'll never know it—we'll never
know either way."

"He was going downtown?" Weigand said. "Right?"

He was, Sullivan said. Yes, they had noticed that he lived in the
Bronx and that, normally, it was an hour when he would have been
going home. All right, Sullivan said, mark it "suspicious" and there you
were. It was going to stay suspicious, he thought. But he would send
Weigand copies of all the reports, for what they were worth.

· 11 ·

THURSDAY
10:45 A.M. TO NOON

Weigand tucked the slip of paper which had invited Stanley Brent to his death into a fresh envelope, holding both slip and envelope carefully by the edges, and dropped the envelope into a pocket. He started out, thought better of it and went to the door of the squad room. He beckoned Detective Stein, a tall, dark young man, to come along. Stein came along, pleased, but a little curious. Weigand answered the inquiry in his face by saying that Mullins was on another job, and that they were going uptown to talk to a man, not about a dog. Stein said, "Right," and Weigand grinned at him.

The appointment was at Berex's office, in a tall, rather old office building on Broadway, near Madison Square. It was, Weigand saw, a building of no special character—the directory listed men and firms in a variety of businesses. The white letters opposite Room 714 spelled out the name of Louis Berex and stopped, noncommittal as to the nature of Mr. Berex's activities. The detectives rode up to the seventh floor in an elevator which was in no hurry, and found Room 714 in the rear. Only one door gave entrance into it and black lettering on the door merely repeated Berex's name. Furthermore, the door was locked.

"What the hell?" Weigand said. He looked at his watch and discovered that they were a few minutes early. Then they heard the elevator stop again at the floor and a thin, wiry, sandy man came along the corridor. He stopped when he came up to them.

"Looking for me?" he said.

"Are you Berex?" Weigand said. The wiry man nodded and said he was sorry if he was late. It dawned on Weigand that Berex had come to the office solely to meet detectives.

Berex pushed open the door and waved Weigand and Detective Stein into an almost bare room. There was a desk, bare, too, and a steel filing cabinet and by the window there was a drawing-board. There were a couple of chairs, not inviting to repose. There was nobody in the office until the three went in, and Berex closed the door behind them. It was a bright day, but the room was dim and Berex switched on a shaded light hanging over the drawing-board. He sat down on the desk and motioned the detectives to chairs.

"So," he said, "the police."

"Right," Weigand told him. "We want to ask you some questions. You've read about the Brent case?"

"Brent?" Berex said. "No, I don't think so. Somebody—your man, I suppose—said Lieutenant Weigand wanted to talk to me and I could set a place or come to Headquarters. He didn't say why."

"And you just came?" Weigand said, not too believingly.

Berex looked at him and said: "Of course.

"I thought it might be something about my car," he said. "I always think of the police and cars together, for some reason. But you say it's about a man named Brent?"

He was, Weigand decided, a singularly casual man; a singularly casual young man, he thought a moment later, realizing that Berex could hardly be over thirty.

"Stanley Brent," Weigand said. "You ought to know him; he was your lawyer. He's been murdered."

"Well," said Berex, still quite casually. "Has he? Then I'll have to get a new lawyer, when I need a lawyer."

He didn't seem much interested, or much surprised or, so far as

Weigand could tell, much anything. He swung a leg as he perched on the desk and looked at Weigand, waiting for Weigand to go on.

"I gather he wasn't a friend of yours, particularly?" Weigand said.

Berex shook his head.

"No," he said. "He was just my lawyer in a case. And now there isn't any case, or any lawyer." He paused, and thought it over. "Claire's a friend of mine, of course," he said. "Was it something about Claire you wanted to ask? She's a very fine girl, Claire."

He was dispassionate about that, too. Weigand backed out, mentally, and decided to go back to the beginning. The beginning seemed to be Berex's occupation. Berex appeared rather more interested, and said he was an inventor.

"Well," said Weigand. "What do you invent?"

Berex didn't seem to feel that Weigand would understand even if he were told. He looked very doubtful about Weigand, and asked whether he knew about the transmission of telephotos. "Pictures," he explained. "You see them in the papers, sometimes. Very smudgy, usually."

Weigand said he had seen them.

"Well," Berex said, "that's what I am working on right now. Make them better, see?" He looked at Weigand still more doubtfully. "Electricity?" he said, as if he wondered whether Weigand had heard of it. "I've done some work in radio and television, too."

"Right," Weigand said. "I see. And it was in connection with your invention that you hired Brent?"

Berex looked rather astonished, and shook his head. He said of course not.

"I have a patent lawyer," he said. "Naturally. Brent isn't a patent lawyer. He was representing me in quite another matter."

"Something to do with a man named Edwards, wasn't it?" Weigand said. "You were going to sue Edwards?"

Berex nodded and then shook his head. He didn't seem interested in learning where the detective got his information.

"It had to do with Edwards," Berex said. "But I am not going to sue. It's all been fixed up." He seemed to regard the matter as closed, and moved as if he were about to get down from the desk and go away. But

Weigand shook his head and said there was a lot more. There was, it developed, but it took a lot of questions.

Berex, still vaguely puzzled that anybody should be interested, but not at all resentful, explained in a series of answers, with each of which the conversation seemed, as far as he was concerned, to die. It had to do, it turned out, with a trust fund. "An uncle," Berex said. "He thought I wouldn't know what to do with it, so he left it in trust. He was quite right, too." Edwards was the trustee; Berex seemed to feel vaguely that there had been another, who had died and not, as yet, been replaced. The amount of the trust was around two hundred thousand dollars.

For the past year or two, Berex went on, as Weigand dug it out, the income had mysteriously dwindled. Edwards had said that all incomes were dwindling, these days, but Berex had not been satisfied. He did not suppose, for a long time, that there was anything he could do about it, but then somebody told him he could ask Edwards for an accounting and find out where the money was and perhaps learn what was happening to the income. So he had written Edwards a couple of times asking for an accounting.

"He kept promising," Berex said. "But I didn't get it. He just sort of slid around it, somehow, and gave me a long rigmarole. It was annoying."

Berex finally, it appeared, got annoyed enough to do something about it, the something being the employment of Brent. Brent was to look around and see what went on. Then, if he couldn't get the accounting, he would take the matter into court and sue for it, petitioning to have Edwards removed as trustee.

"I was really very annoyed," Berex said. "There were certain experiments which were costing money and I wanted to find out where I stood. I have a laboratory out in New Jersey to keep running. But it's all right now."

Weigand wanted to know how that was.

"A week or so ago," Berex said, "I got the accounting from Edwards and it's all shipshape. I showed it to a banker I know and he said it was a very good list. That, I took it, meant that the securities were all per-

fectly good securities, and that my income was all right. So I don't
need Brent, after all."

"Well," Weigand said, "that's just as well."

Berex nodded, with rather the air of one who discovers a happy
coincidence.

"And that was all you had to do with Brent?" Weigand asked. "Or
Edwards?"

Berex said it was—with Brent, anyway. Edwards had once or twice
represented him as agent in the sale of an invention.

"A year or so ago," Berex said, "before this trust fund business
came up. I went abroad and left Edwards power of attorney to sell a
device I'd patented—a radio device."

"And did he sell it?" Weigand wanted to know, as long as they were
on the subject.

He had, Berex said. Very satisfactorily, on a royalty basis.

"I make a very decent thing out of it," Berex said. "And what has it
to do with Brent's murder?"

Weigand said he couldn't think.

There was, however, the slip of paper from the vestibule of the
Buano house. Weigand took it out, still in its envelope, and handed it to
Berex.

"Have a look at that," Weigand said. "And tell me about it. It's been
photographed, so you can handle it."

Berex drew the slip of paper out of the envelope and looked at it. He
turned it in his fingers and shook his head.

"It looks as if it came out of a mailbox or something," he said. "In
one of the old houses. Mr. Edwards'?"

"You tell me," Weigand said. "What do you know about it?"

Berex looked to be, in an incurious way, somewhat astonished.

"Me?" he said. "What would I know about it?"

"Well," Weigand said, "I think you've seen it before. I think you cut
it off the top of a letterhead of your own, and wrote Edwards' name on
it and stuck it beside a bell at 95 Greenwich Place. And that was where
Brent was killed."

Berex did not seem at all alarmed. He smiled and shook his head.

"No," he said. "I never saw it before. Why should I do any of those things?" He paused, and looked at Weigand more sharply. "You're not, by any chance, thinking I killed Brent, are you?" he said.

"I think you prepared that slip of paper," Weigand said. "I think it was cut off the top of one of your letterheads—a letterhead sheet like this." He took out of his pocket Berex's letter to Edwards. He took the slip from Berex and laid it near the name at the top of the full sheet. He pointed to the little mark at the edge of the slip, and to the X in Berex's name.

"And I think you slipped up," he said. "I think you signed it, without knowing it."

"No," Berex said. "I never saw it before. I see what you mean, and it's funny, but I never saw it before. I think you've slipped up, somewhere, yourself. I think if you try to prove I knew anything about Brent's murder you're working yourself into trouble."

His voice was rather hard, now.

"I haven't," Weigand said, "said anything about murder. I'm talking about a slip of paper."

"The hell you are," Berex said, but his voice was still unexcited. "I don't know how it works in, of course, but you think the murderer wrote the name of Edwards on this slip of paper and used it somehow in killing Brent. Maybe he did, for all I know. But I'm not the murderer; I never saw this slip before. So what do you do next?"

There were, Weigand told him, several things he might do. "Like taking you down to Headquarters," he said. But that could wait a while.

"You'll be around," Weigand said, without inquiry. "We'll know where to find you if we want you."

Berex said he would be around, but that they wouldn't want him.

"Right," Weigand said. "Let's hope you're right." He started for the door. "But," he said, "I wouldn't be so sure you won't need a lawyer. I wouldn't be sure at all if I were you."

Berex sat on the desk, swinging a foot, and merely looked at him. His right hand, Weigand noticed, was stroking the handset telephone on the desk. The detectives went through the office door and closed it. Weigand stood outside the door for a moment, listening. He could hear the faint whirr of the dialing mechanism of a telephone inside the office. On impulse, he bent so that his ear was near the mailslot in the door.

After a moment, Berex's voice came to him, no longer level or bored.

"Claire," he heard Berex say. "Claire—we've got to talk . . . "

Weigand straightened up a minute later, knowing that Louis Berex had invited "Claire" to lunch with him at some place called "Charles," and gathering that the invitation had been accepted. It was interesting, Weigand decided, as he and Stein walked to the elevator.

Going down in the elevator, Weigand wheedled the slip of paper out of the envelope, still holding the envelope by the edges, and gave the envelope to Stein.

"And give me a ring as soon as they bring the prints up," he directed the detective. "I'll be at Mr. Gerald North's."

Weigand remembered the telephone number and Stein jotted it down. Stein went toward Centre Street in the squad car and Weigand walked south, turning down Fifth Avenue. Maybe, he thought, he was beginning to see a pattern in it.

Last name: **WIL**

First name: **AL**

Phone number: **1577**

Title: **The Norths meet murder**

Hold until: **Tue May 23 2023**

Pickup   Nelson Memorial

• 12 •

Both the Norths were home, and Mullins was in the midst of them. Any apprehension which Mr. North might have left from the last interview had, Weigand noticed, evaporated. The detective was rather surprised to find the male North, and looked at him inquiringly.

"I've stayed home to read a manuscript," Mr. North explained.

There was, however, nó sign of a manuscript. Mr. and Mrs. North had apparently been sitting in the living-room talking to Mullins. It was a very comfortable-looking party, Weigand decided. Mr. North said how about a drink? and Mullins' face went up. Mrs. North said not for her, so early, and Weigand felt the same. Mr. North and Mullins had ryes. Mrs. North looked admiringly at Mullins while he drank.

"And without a gun!" she said. "Or was it without a rod?"

It was past Weigand, but neither Mr. North nor Mullins seemed at sea, although Mullins looked slightly taken aback. He said it wasn't anything.

"But *four gangsters,*" Mrs. North said. "In a hallway! It sounds to me like a good deal."

Mr. North nodded.

115

116 FRANCES & RICHARD LOCKRIDGE

"It certainly sounds like a good deal," he agreed.

Mullins looked at him quickly, but saw nothing to support any suspicion.

"Wasn't he brave?" Mrs. North said to Weigand. "Four of them, with machine-guns, and he went right in!"

Mullins looked at Weigand, hopefully.

"Very," Lieutenant Weigand agreed. "We call him Mighty Mullins down at Centre Street. He's historic."

Mullins said: "Now listen, Loot."

"But it was such a lovely story," Mrs. North said. "Full of action. I like them to be full of action, don't you?"

"Well," Weigand said, "in real life it's different. Four gangsters, now—with machine-guns. It means a good deal of action, I should think. I never ran into anything like that, myself. I always sent Mullins."

"Now, Loot, listen—" Mullins said, aggrieved.

Weigand grinned at him. The odd thing about it was that Mullins had, or thereabouts. There had been four of them, all right, and automatics, if no machine-guns. Mullins had had a gun, too, and had gone in shooting. But the fact remained that he had gone in, and, eventually, came out, rather nicked but with a couple of his men. A third of them wasn't going anywhere, any more, and the fourth had gone, very rapidly. Of course, it needed the breaks; but there had been four of them, all right.

Mrs. North watched Weigand's face, and nodded.

"I knew he had," she said. "He *is* brave, I mean."

Mullins said: "Listen, Mrs. North—"

"Well," Weigand said, "nothing's been going on here, I gather. No alarms or excursions?"

Mr. North shook his head.

"It was Timothy?" Mrs. North said, sobered.

Weigand nodded, and said it was.

"Why?" said Mr. North. "Was it the slip?"

It brought up a point, Weigand said, about which he had been wondering. Assuming that the mail-carrier had been killed, as they would have trouble proving, and assuming it hooked up with the Brent case—

"But it does," Mrs. North said. "You *know* it does."

Weigand nodded and said that he thought it did, certainly.

"But it's a little hard to see how it can hang on his finding the slip," he said. "Because I think we were supposed to find the slip, if we found the body."

Mrs. North looked puzzled and Mr. North nodded.

"How—" said Mrs. North, and then stopped. "Or he would just have thrown it away," she said. "Not put it in the box. Of course, how silly of me!"

Both Mr. North and Lieutenant Weigand looked at her approvingly. Mullins looked at his glass.

"Precisely," Mr. North said. "I've been wondering about that."

"But why?" Mrs. North said. "It points to him."

Weigand and Mr. North shook their heads and so, still looking at his glass, did Mullins. Mr. North said, "Have another?" abstractedly, and Mullins nodded.

"If we were supposed to find it, it doesn't point to him," Mr. North said. "But it points to somebody else. Only why point at all?"

He and Weigand looked at each other, and shook their heads.

"Especially," Weigand said, "as we weren't supposed to find the body—not right away, anyhow. We weren't supposed to find it until— that is—" He seemed doubtful, and looked at Mrs. North.

"That's all right," she said. "They do. Even women have heard about that. 'Dust to dust,' only not immediately."

"Two closed doors and the ventilator in the bathroom," Weigand said. "And the apartment at the top of the house. It might have been a long time, particularly with the people on the floor above you not at home. It was sheer chance that it was found so soon."

"If I hadn't been going to give a party—" Mrs. North said.

Weigand said, "Right," and pointed out something else. The murderer had, apparently, made allowance for such a chance. That was where the slip of paper came in.

"The chances are," he said, "that, if the murder hadn't made us look around, we would never have found the slip—you wouldn't have found it, Mrs. North. Or, if somebody had come across it, the chances are it would have meant nothing. But if we did find the body, the murderer must have realized that we would probably find the slip; if we found the body he *wanted* us to find the slip."

"Why?" said Mrs. North.

"That," Mr. North said, "is where we came in."

Weigand nodded. They looked at one another and nobody had any suggestions.

"It was something on the slip," Mr. North said. "That's obvious."

Weigand nodded.

"And what is on it is pretty obvious," he said, and stopped. The Norths waited.

"Well," he said, "this is damned irregular, but here it is."

He told them of the evidence connecting the mark on the back of the slip with Berex. He told them about the fingerprints; he brought the slip out and showed them the prints. They both looked at them.

"But—" Mr. North said. Then, with almost absurd timeliness, the telephone rang. It was Detective Stein for Lieutenant Weigand. Weigand said, "Yes" and "Um" and "I thought so." Then he said, "Thanks," cradled the telephone and sat thinking. The Norths looked at him with hopeful interest.

"Well," he said, "I may as well tell you. Those are Berex's prints. I had him handle an envelope and the detective who just telephoned took it down to Identification. The prints match those on the slip, all right."

"But—" said Mr. North. He was worried about something, and took the slip up to examine it again. What he saw confirmed his suspicion.

"They're in the wrong place," he said. "They ought to be the other way round."

"Let me see," Mrs. North commanded. She saw and said: "Oh, yes." Then both of them looked at Weigand.

"The prints are upside-down," Mrs. North said, "aren't they?"

Weigand nodded and said it looked that way to him.

"I wanted to see whether I was right," he said. "We'll go down and try."

They went down to the vestibule, but a glance was enough to show them that the prints were in the wrong place. The slotted container which held the slip opened at the top. The thumb and forefinger which had held the slip, and left identifying marks upon it, had held it from the bottom; they had, moreover, held it in such a way that, with any likely position of the hand, the name on the face of the slip would have been innermost, assuming that it could have been got in at all. Whenever Berex had left his prints on the slip, it was not when he had put the slip in the slot opposite the fourth-floor bell.

Furthermore, if the slip had ever been in the slot at all, it had been put in by somebody who had left no prints while doing it, because there were no other prints on the slip.

"Damn," said Weigand.

"Gloves?" said Mrs. North.

Mr. North shook his head. It would, he pointed out, be hard to handle the tiny slip of paper, inserting it in the narrow slot, while wearing gloves; it would, he thought, be impossible to do it with any speed. It must have been held in something.

"Like pincers," Mrs. North said. "Manicure pincers."

Weigand said, "Huh?" and what were manicure pincers? Mrs. North looked a little flustered. She said they were things women used. She was evidently willing to let it go at that.

"If they have a hair on the chin," Mr. North said. "To pull it out. Manicure tweezers, she means."

"Well," said Weigand. Then he added that the slip had apparently been cut out with manicure scissors.

"Then it's a woman," Mrs. North said. "It's a *Mrs*. Edwards. Or married man, of course."

They went back upstairs, thinking it over. Mrs. North went back to the beginning. She said it didn't explain about poor Timothy.

"And that," she said, "was terrible. I knew Timothy, and it was wrong to kill him. When it was only Brent it was just a story, but now it means something. People can't kill people like Timothy."

She was firm about it. Then Mr. North could see an idea growing, and reflecting in her eyes. She said she bet she knew what it was.

"It wasn't the slip at all," she said. "It was when he was delivering!"

"Huh?" said Weigand. "I mean—what?"

"When he was delivering," she said. "The last time. He saw her."

"Her?" Weigand said.

"Mrs. Edwards," Mrs. North said. "When she was coming out. Or Mr. Edwards, if he was married. X, I mean—The murderer."

Mr. North nodded, quickly.

"It could be, you know," he said, to Weigand. "The time would have been about right—sometime between three-thirty and four is the last delivery. He might have seen somebody coming out with a suitcase and got to thinking about it. Brent's clothes would have been in a suitcase, wouldn't they? And maybe there was blood or something."

It might, Weigand thought as he nodded slowly, very well be. Assuming Timothy Barnes to have been delivering his mail at the Buano house at the right time, somebody might have brushed past him, carrying a suitcase, anxious to get away from there. Barnes and the person with the suitcase, who just then rather desperately wanted not to be seen, would have noticed each other. And, later, Barnes might have been able to describe the man or the woman. Or the murderer might have feared he could, and taken no chances. It would, probably, have been easy to find out what time the carrier left the branch post-office; easy to follow him to the subway station. There would be no risk in following him to the downtown platform; hardly any in working through the crowd to stand behind him; to give a quick push and then to seem to be attempting to save a life instead of destroy one. A man and a woman had reached for the falling man in gray-blue, Weigand remembered. It was an ugly way to do it, but efficient. Their murderer looked like being efficient, and not minding ugliness.

He would, he realized, have to recheck those who had so far come into the case as possible suspects, determining where they were at the time Barnes had plunged from the platform. It had happened, he realized now, suddenly, while he was having another martini in Goody's Bar. The crowd around the station exits in Sixth Avenue had, after all, been part of his case. And then where were all these people?

The Norths, anyway, had been at home. That much he remembered from the report of their guardian detective. Edwards and Mrs. Brent?

"Damn it all," Weigand said, remembering that he had directed that they be kept under observation so late that the observation could not possibly have been begun until half an hour or so after Barnes had been killed. There was no report that Mrs. Brent had left her apartment house, but the uniformed men assigned to hold the reporters and the curious in check would not necessarily have noticed if she had gone out; might not even have known her. And she could have gone out through a service exit, if need be. The situation was no clearer as it concerned Edwards. Benjamin Fuller would have had time to kill Barnes and reach his home before Weigand got there; it had, judging by the already arrived ambulances, been at least ten minutes, probably a quarter of an hour, after the Barnes killing that the detective had left the bar and noticed the excitement down the street. Where Berex was at that time he hadn't, naturally, the faintest idea, because at that time Berex was only an element postulated by the evidence, and not yet visible.

"We were home," Mrs. North said. "At home with bacardis."

"I know you were," Weigand said. "That is—"

Mrs. North looked at him with widening eyes.

"Darling!" she said, to Mr. North. "We are being tailed! We're *really* suspects."

Mr. North nodded, without elation. It was, he thought, really very foolish for a grown man to go out walking in Central Park in the middle of the afternoon.

Mr. North joined Mullins in a short one and Pete, the cat, walked in from the bedroom. Pete sat down in the center of the group and started to wash his chest earnestly. Then he stopped washing, with the abruptness of a cat, and looked around at the humans inquiringly. He looked at Mr. North and at Mullins and made a small sound, neither quite a mew nor quite a purr. Then he walked over to the coffee-table and put his forepaws on it, so he could examine its top. His nose quivered with the intensity of his examination and then he looked around at Mrs. North and said, rather indignantly, "Miaow."

"No little fishes, Pete," Mrs. North said.

"He thinks there ought to be little fishes because we're drinking," Mrs. North explained to Weigand. "We have canapes with cocktails and sometimes there is fish on them. So whenever he sees us drinking he looks for fish."

Pete got down, looked around reproachfully and went to sit with his back to everyone. He swished his tail at them.

"Nice Pete," Mrs. North said. He swished his tail more vigorously, but did not turn. "And to think he knows who did it and can't tell us." They all thought about it for a moment. Then Weigand sighed. It was too bad Pete couldn't, but he couldn't.

"Fish reminds me," Weigand said. "That lobster recipe. Perhaps I'd better have it, after all, if you don't mind."

Mrs. North didn't, and got it. It was typed on a sheet of paper, and Weigand read it over. It seemed very complicated.

"You use as many lobsters as you want, of course," Mrs. North said. "And step it all up accordingly."

Weigand nodded.

"How many, say, for—oh, twenty people."

Mrs. North thought a minute, and said she thought ten, anyway.

"Only," she said, "not, of course, if he was serving other things, too. Just if it was only lobster. With other things, maybe six."

Weigand studied the recipe. It looked, certainly, as if it would take a long time. Starting with even six lobsters, cracking them and taking out the meat; boiling the shells down, straining, adding other ingredients, boiling again—it was complicated enough.

"An hour, anyway," Mrs. North said. "Probably longer, unless you were very good with lobsters."

Weigand nodded, and said it looked very likely. It was, he thought, an odd thing for an alibi to hang on, but the alibi apparently hung, pending further checkup. It was, however, time for a further checkup, because if there was anything phoney about it, it would be very helpful. Just one phoney alibi, he thought, would fix him up fine; it was aggravating, in a way, that so few of the possibilities had any alibis at all.

"Well—" he said, tentatively. He had, he decided, better start on and start others on. He looked at Mullins speculatively. Mullins could check alibis for the time of Timothy Barnes' death, and also see what

Berex had to say about Monday afternoon. He told Mullins as much, and Mullins said, "O.K., Loot." His eyes brightened a little.

"Except Edwards," Weigand said. "I'll be dropping in on Edwards myself."

Mullins rose to get on with it, and Weigand also got up. So did the Norths. Mr. North said they might as well go and have some lunch. Mrs. North said where and Mr. North said, oh, he didn't know, what did she think?

"Charles," Mrs. North said. "And the lieutenant with us. And Mr. Mullins, of course. Mighty Mullins."

Mullins looked reproachfully at her and said he'd have to be getting along, like the Loot said. Weigand started to shake his head, and then something pricked his mind. "Charles." He hesitated a moment, weighing it, and said it would be fine, if this Charles place wasn't too far. It wasn't, they assured him; only around the corner. They all went down together. Mullins stemmed off toward Grove Street and Fuller; the Norths and Weigand went up Sixth Avenue to a large, bright restaurant with a circular bar. Mrs. North led the way to the bar and the men followed her. They had a round of martinis, and peanuts, and found a table. Mrs. North decided, after internal debate, on frogs legs *au beurre noir.* Mr. North and Weigand had omelets. Mrs. North said it was a fine restaurant, and that it was a shame to waste it on omelets.

"We always come here when we're not at home," Mrs. North said.

"Well," Mr. North said, "when we're eating, that is."

Weigand said nothing, because he had just caught sight of Berex at a side table. Berex and Claire Brent had their heads together and were talking engrossedly. There was, Weigand thought, an air of very good friendship about them.

"There's Berex," he told the Norths, nodding his head in the right direction. "Berex and the Widow Brent." The Norths looked at them and Mrs. North said, "Well!" The men looked at her.

"So *that's* who they are," she said.

"Who *who* are?" Mr. North said. "I mean, he says there's Berex and Mrs. Brent but you sound like they were somebody else, too."

Mrs. North looked at her husband a little impatiently. She said that he knew, or didn't he ever see *anybody?* He shook his head.

"Why," Mrs. North said, "we've seen them here often, and I wondered who she was because of her hats. Very *nice* hats."

"Well—" said Weigand. It was interesting, he thought. Then the omelet came, and Mrs. North's frogs legs. The lieutenant glanced at Berex and Mrs. Brent now and then and wished he knew what they were saying.

· 13 ·

Weigand left the Norths outside the restaurant; left them discussing, amiably, whether they would go uptown and look at a new dress Mrs. North thought was becoming, but wasn't sure about, or whether they should go home so that Mr. North could really read the manuscript. Weigand walked along and in a moment the Norths passed him in a taxicab, going uptown. Mrs. North waved at him from the window of the cab and he realized, with a qualm, that everybody had forgotten about protecting them, or even seeing where they went. It wasn't, he decided, important, and walked on to see Mr. Edwards.

But Mr. Edwards was not at home, Kumi, the Japanese, assured him, holding the door inhospitably a foot open. He was at his office. Kumi was unloquacious about it and started to close the door, and Weigand, for the first time in a long while, had to put his foot in a door. He said that Kumi would do, for the moment, and pushed his way in. Kumi backed away, bowing defensively, and saying: "I know nothings, pliss."

"All right, Mr. Moto," Weigand said. "We'll just talk it over, anyway."

"Kumi," Kumi said. "I know nothings, pliss."

125

It was hard to get him started. When Weigand said, "Suppose you tell me about Monday," Kumi shook his black head. He remembered, pliss, nothings whatever about Monday. "Monday?" Kumi seemed to doubt that there had ever been a Monday.

"Mr. Edwards had a dinner party," Weigand said. "Lots of people. You remember—Monday."

"Oh, *Monday?*" Kumi said, with the air of one who sees through cryptic mysteries to the heart of truth. Weigand nodded.

"Tell me what happened," he directed.

"I don't remember, pliss," Kumi said, helpfully. "I just work. Clean up. Put away. Serve the guests."

It came slowly. On Monday morning, knowing that his employer would be still in the country, Kumi had arrived rather later than usual; perhaps about ten o'clock. He had decided to defrost the refrigerator and turned off the power so that the heavy hoarfrost on the freezing unit would thaw. "Then it freeze faster later," Kumi explained. He had taken advantage of the opportunity to clear out the icebox. Edwards had left a list of things for him to order from the market and he had ordered them by telephone.

"Lobsters?" Weigand inquired.

Kumi remembered the lobsters, because he was to tell the market they must be delivered as soon as possible and, in any case, not later than three o'clock; the other things could come later, on the regular delivery around four. Kumi had so instructed the market, which promised—and, as it developed, performed. Then Kumi had— Weigand told him to wait a minute.

"When you cleaned out the icebox," he said, "what was in it then?"

Kumi looked bewildered for a moment, then painfully thought. "Eggs," he said. "Butter, maybe. Milk." He struggled, "Beer!" he reported, triumphantly. "Maybe cheese—not much anything."

"No lobster?" Weigand said.

Kumi looked astonished.

"I just tell," he said. "Lobster not come until later—maybe three o'clock, I think. No lobster then."

Weigand said, "Right."

So then Kumi had cleaned the lower floor. Mr. Edwards had come home, changed and gone out. Kumi had turned on the refrigerator again. Then Mr. Edwards had come home again, early in the afternoon. Then the lobster had come.

"Yes?" said Weigand.

Kumi had been upstairs, cleaning, when the bell rang and he had gone down to let in the boy from the market. That was shortly after his employer came home. Kumi had led the boy in through the service door, near the kitchen, and Mr. Edwards had looked out to see what it was, looked at his watch and told the delivery boy he was ten minutes late. He had not been cross about it, however, but said it was near enough. Then Mr. Edwards took the lobsters, six of them, already boiled, into the kitchen and Kumi went back to clean the second floor. It had taken him about an hour and a half.

"So you didn't see Mr. Edwards between a little after three and about four-thirty?" Weigand said. Kumi looked surprised.

"He was in kitchen," he said. "I never go in kitchen when he there. Mr. Edwards not like I go in kitchen when he working there."

So— Then he came back down and opened the kitchen door and looked in to see whether his employer had finished. He was just finishing. Then the other things came from the market and Kumi let them in. It was about four-thirty, then. How had he known the time? When the boy from the market came on the second trip, Mr. Edwards had thought the kitchen clock was wrong, and had asked Kumi to "ask the telephone."

"Ask the telephone?" Weigand repeated.

"One two, one two," Kumi explained. That was the number of the telephone company's time service. He had called only a minute or two after he came down, and the time was thirty-two minutes and forty seconds after four o'clock, Eastern Standard Time.

"And was the clock wrong?" Weigand wanted to know.

The clock was wrong, it turned out; it was about five minutes fast. He had set it. Mr. Edwards had told him the lobster was all ready and showed him the big pot of Spanish lobster on the back of the stove, ready to be put in a chafing-dish and heated when the guests came. It was still warm from its preparation, then, but Mr. Edwards said it would, of course, have to be reheated. It smelled very good, Kumi reported, and, when Mr. Edwards had taken off his apron and gone to the front of the house to arrange the flowers, Kumi tasted it. It was very good.

There were, the servant said, when Weigand questioned him, no shells left around and everything was tidy. Weigand jumped at that. No debris in the garbage pail? Kumi looked a little shocked at the suggestion.

"We have incinerator," he said, a little loftily. "All in and down to burn."

There was, Weigand gathered, nothing unusual about Edwards' having disposed of the shells himself; there would have been, he realized, a good many, taking up a good deal of room in a small kitchen, where Kumi still had considerable other, less special, food to prepare. It was only a step from the kitchen to the service hall and the incinerator opening. There was, so far as he could see, nothing irregular about any of it. While Brent was being killed, Edwards had been at housewifely pursuits, preparing dinner for company. He could see no way around it and the only way through it was through Kumi, who would be a stumbling-block. Only through Kumi, and, he realized, the boy who had actually delivered lobsters at 3:10 or thereabouts and, apparently, seen Edwards. If it ever came to a showdown, Weigand decided, the two stories, together with Edwards' own, would go a long way; would go further than he could, at the moment, go in rebuttal.

Nor, Weigand realized, did he disbelieve the story himself. The Edwards angle was, he was about ready to believe, a side angle, not germane. No motive; fair alibi. Probably he was wasting time. The information, duly extracted from Kumi, that Mr. Edwards had been at a cocktail party with friends the afternoon before, during a period which apparently included the time of Barnes' murder, neither confirmed nor lessened the detective's belief. Cocktail parties with guests coming and going and in constant motion, did not, to be sure, provide much in the way of alibis. But if Edwards had gone to the trouble of preparing an alibi for the first murder, he may be expected to do as much for the second. The inference was in his favor.

It was hardly, Weigand thought, worth looking over the apartment, especially since he did not know what he was looking for, but he did look. It was all very neat, now, and comfortably furnished; the kitchen, which interested him particularly, was small but convenient, with shining aluminum pans hanging along above the stove, flanked at one end by a coffee-grinder, fixed to the wall, and at the other by a chromium device which was, Kumi told him, for crushing ice. In addition to the large refrigerator there was, next to it, a small one intended, he realized, solely for freezing ice cubes. Weigand, thinking how ice cubes ran out under normal circumstances, looked at it with cupidity and thought, again, that Edwards, for a bachelor, did himself very well. Then he told Kumi that he would see Mr. Edwards at his office and went along.

Out on the sidewalk, it hardly seemed worth while to make a trip down to the financial district to talk to Edwards, and he hesitated whether to go there, or to return to Headquarters and wait for returns from Mullins and the rest. He thought that, if he went to Headquarters, Inspector O'Malley would be after him for his report, and decided that, perhaps, he had better see Edwards after all. He went down on the subway to Wall Street and found Edwards' office.

The offices of Clinton Edwards & Company, Investments, on the second floor of a corner building, were fairly numerous, and sedately busy. Edwards' own office, when Lieutenant Weigand was permitted to enter it, was the corner office, large and light and comfortable. Mr. Edwards was large and comfortable himself, if not light, and half rose from behind an expansive desk as he verbally assisted the detective to a chair. It was, he reported deeply, a pleasure to see Inspector Weigand again, and it would be another if he might, should he say, be of service in any particular.

"Lieutenant," Weigand said. "Not inspector. Just lieutenant. I've been talking to your man, Kumi."

"Ah?" said Edwards.

Weigand confirmed Mr. Edwards' impression. He had been talking to Kumi. And now he wondered whether Mr. Edwards himself would, as a formality merely, give a more detailed story of the preparation of the lobster on the Monday afternoon of Brent's death.

"Ah," said Edwards, "it is very sad, don't you find? On thinking it over, it seems to me very sad that Brent should die so." There was nothing in his voice to suggest that it was keeping him awake nights. And the lobsters? It was, did not Lieutenant Weigand think, strangely ironic that the death of a man, and a man so young and vigorous, should come to be concerned, even remotely, with the preparation of lobsters. Did not Lieutenant Weigand find that oddly, disturbingly, ironic?

"Right," said Weigand. "And about the lobsters—"

Well, the lobsters had been delivered a little, Edwards believed, after three o'clock and Kumi took them from the delivery boy. Then Kumi had gone back upstairs to carry on the cleaning, and—The rest of the story agreed with that of the Japanese, and Weigand said as much. Edwards smiled.

"It should," he said, "since we are discussing the same events. I am, although you will think it odd, no doubt, a little surprised it does. Kumi is so very forgetful, so often gets things tangled. I am a little surprised, indeed, that he remembered anything precisely. I am really *quite* surprised. He often forgets things which are, shall we say, much more immediate; he has even, on occasion, forgotten to serve half my dinner after he had cooked it." He paused and smiled reminiscently. "But in other respects he is a most satisfactory servant for one of my simple needs," he added. "And a very courteous little man."

Edwards seemed to be in a mood to run on about Kumi, Weigand noticed. The detective guided him back to the lobsters.

"Ah, yes," Edwards said. "It is the tangible things which are important, is it not?" He would tell about the lobsters, as he remembered it. Naturally, since he had no idea the lobsters would prove to be, in the end, so ironically entangled with the death of a man—But he must confine himself to the tangible things, must he not?

The lobsters had come a little after three, Kumi had received them and given them to Edwards and Edwards had taken them into the kitchen. Then he had cracked the shells and removed the meat. How long had it taken? It had, certainly, taken some time. Half an hour, should he say? Perhaps longer. It must, he thought, have been nearly four when he finished. Say ten minutes of four. Then he had broken the shells and put them on to boil and meanwhile diced the lobster meat and added the other ingredients. Then he had removed the shells from the broth and added it to the meat, added more ingredients and finished a little after four. Then he had looked at the clock to see how the time was going and seen it was almost twenty of five.

It had occurred to him that it would be well, should he say, to have the clock accurate and, when Kumi came in a moment later, he had had the Japanese telephone for the exact time. It had been about four-thirty, in reality, and Kumi had set the clock. Then Edwards had left the kitchen to his servant, who could be trusted to prepare the other dishes for the buffet supper, and had gone into the living-room to see about the flowers. And then—

"Right," Weigand said, since the essential time was covered and his interest in the rest of the afternoon was negligible. "I think you've covered it. *You* have an admirable memory, Mr. Edwards."

Edwards nodded and smiled, indicating that he thought so himself. And was there anything else? He was anxious to assist in any way possible. Weigand thought a moment. There didn't seem to be—oh, yes. It was, perhaps, a rather delicate thing to ask, but Mr. Edwards would understand that the police could not be too definite.

"Berex," he said, "and Mrs. Brent. Have you heard them mentioned together? Someone has hinted that they were—well, friends."

Edwards' expression became judicially reluctant and he shook his head a little wryly. One was to understand that such matters pained him very much.

"I fear," he said, "that I have already been indiscreet in mentioning the friendship between Brent and Mrs. Fuller. I had hoped—it all puts me, as you will understand, in a rather difficult position. I am greatly afraid, my dear Lieutenant, that I would much rather, shall we say, not answer this last question. I would not like to play the part of, if I may use the term, a male gossip. You will understand? Particularly in view of my relationship with Louis."

He did understand, Weigand decided. He was, he thought, intended to understand. Mr. Edwards' conversation was full of things which Mr. Edwards, being a gentleman, could not say. Mr. Edwards dripped discretion—and implications. Weigand half smiled his recognition of reticence and got up to go.

Edwards half rose from his chair, and, with grave gestures, assisted the detective to discover the door. Lieutenant Weigand discovered it. He returned to Headquarters.

At Headquarters several things awaited his notice, including Mullins, who had nothing very helpful to report about alibis. He had found both Fuller and Mrs. Fuller, who was quite a dame.

"Right," said Weigand.

Fuller had been, Fuller supposed, on his way home from his office at the time of Barnes' death, but he knew of no way of proving it. He had come downtown on the Interborough West Side line, more convenient for his purposes than the Independent System's Eighth Avenue, and had, as a result, seen nothing of the excitement at the Fourth Street station. He had got in a little before Weigand had called to see him. Mrs. Fuller had been having her hair done at Saks and could, Mullins guessed, be accounted for if it became necessary. He hadn't checked at Saks, but could, if desired. Berex had been, again, alone in his office working on drawings, and nobody could prove it. Edwards, the laundryman, had been out delivering the wash to customers in the neighborhood, and had seen the police cars and ambulances outside the station. He had continued to deliver the wash.

"Was it my business?" he had asked Mullins.

"I said I hoped not, for his sake," Mullins said, with the air of one who has committed a quip too good to waste.

Mrs. Brent had been out when Mullins called.

"Yes, I know about that," Weigand interrupted and Mullins said, "O.K., Loot."

Mullins had talked to Mrs. Brent's maid, who had told him Mrs. Brent was alone in her room with the door closed all that afternoon and evening. "Grieving," the maid had told Mullins, who passed the word on without any conviction of his own.

"So it could have been anybody, except maybe Mrs. Fuller," Weigand summed up.

Mullins thought that was about it. Weigand said, "Well—" and turned his attention to other things. The report of the fingerprint men who had gone over the room at 95 Greenwich Place had come through. They had found a lot of prints, several of both Norths and a great many more, unidentified, but presumably of the past tenants of the apartment. There were also various smudges, including several on the knobs of the outer and bathroom doors. "Gloves," said Mullins. Weigand thought he was probably right. There were no prints of any of the persons who could be catalogued as suspects.

"Nobody that's in the records," Mullins said, glumly. "It's—"

Weigand said yes, he knew.

There was a report that Western Union had sent no messenger to 95 Greenwich Place on Monday, and carried on no search for a Mr. Shavely. So that theory was confirmed. There were reports from two detectives who were familiar with, and had acquaintances in, the financial district. They had tuned their ears to gossip, but heard little. Edwards' firm was substantial and sound, so far as gossip knew.

Gossip had a little more to say about Benjamin Fuller's importing house. The Fuller firm had had considerable dealings with Germany and the animosity to Hitlerism, translated by thousands into a boycott, had been a fairly damaging blow. But everybody, quite openly, was certain that the Fuller firm could take even harder blows, if it had to, and beat the count.

It had been difficult, for a time, to come on trace of Louis Berex as an inventor, but digging had done it. In a small circle he was well enough known; his contribution to the development of cabled and wireless pictures had been small, but important. He was generally believed, now, to be working on television, and making progress. One or two were pretty sure he was on to something. It was possible, some thought, that he might be short of funds to carry on his research, since he stubbornly refused to tie up with one of the several companies which would have been glad to provide him with equipment and a salary—in exchange, of course, for a majority interest in anything he discovered.

He had made reasonable money from one or two inventions, but might very well have sunk it all in his work on television. Everybody thought he was able and nobody had anything against him. And the detectives, necessarily getting what they could in a hurry, had found nobody who could profess to being a close friend of Berex's.

Weigand had got so far when the telephone rang, and a report came through from one of the detectives who had been trying to find Brent's clothes. It was a conclusive report; Brent's clothes had been found.

They had turned up at the offices of the Dime-a-lock Company, which had its public lockers scattered on subway platforms, in the railway stations and ferry buildings and wherever some burdened person might come upon them and for ten cents relieve himself of his burden. Anyone with a parcel to dispose of, temporarily, could do it in any of the lockers for a dime, which opened a steel lock-box, and released a key which the checker could take along. If he came back within twenty-four hours, his key would open the box again and make his parcel available.

But if he did not come within twenty-four hours, the Dime-a-lock Company would remove his parcel itself, and, in a manner of speaking, reset the trap. The parcel would then go to the company's office, where it would remain for fifty days, pending a claim. If no claim was made, the contents of the parcel would be sold to cover storage. The offices of the company were one of the first places the police visited when looking for stray, portable objects.

They had found Brent's clothing there, after a little search through parcels which had overstayed their welcome in lock-boxes. The clothes were in a cheap, brown suitcase and had been easy to identify because Brent's name was in the inner pocket of the suit jacket, where Brent's tailor had put it. It was a good suit, fairly new and such as a prosperous lawyer might wear; the other garments were of suitable quality. And it was, when the clothes had been brought in and Weigand had examined them, a little hard to tell where the clothes helped them to get. They would, neatly labeled as they were, have been useful in establishing identity, but identity had already been established.

Brent's wallet was gone, assuming he had had one, but his keys, watch and loose change remained. A silver cigarette-case, half-full of cigarettes, remained also. Everything Brent would have been likely to have in his clothes remained, Weigand realized, except things that would burn. Or, of course, bills, which wouldn't need burning.

It would be nice, Weigand thought, if the murderer had left finger-prints on the suitcase, or on the cigarette-case, or anywhere. That would be fine, but it wasn't likely. Without them the find seemed to lead them back to Brent, where they had been already, and not much forward toward Brent's murderer. Weigand sighed and directed that case and clothes be sent to Brooklyn and the Research Bureau. He was keeping a lot of the boys busy, anyway.

Weigand went in to see Inspector O'Malley. He told O'Malley where he was, and promised a full report. O'Malley nodded and made impatient sounds and said it looked to him as if Weigand certainly had enough stuff. Weigand said the trouble really was that he had too much. O'Malley said, "Well, get on with it. Crack it open." O'Malley seemed to be giving the matter only about half his mind.

"Listen, Bill," he said, unbending suddenly, "what do you hear about this racket investigation of the D.A.'s? What do you hear, huh?"

Weigand said he hadn't heard anything. O'Malley sighed, and said the hell of it was you couldn't tell where the so-and-so's might decide to go next. "Under his hat," O'Malley said, angrily. "That's where he keeps it. The so-and-so."

Weigand expressed such sympathy as becomes a lieutenant who is confronted by the woes of an inspector, and then went quietly out, leaving the inspector to his grief. He wondered if the D.A. was threatening to get something on O'Malley, and hoped not. O'Malley was all right, in his way; an honest cop, within reason.

Weigand got back to his desk just as the telephone started ringing. He said, "Hello," and the telephone assured him, with uncharacteristic clarity, that this was Pam North.

"I'm into something," Mrs. North said.

"Huh?" said Weigand. "I mean—what?"

"*On* to," Mrs. North corrected herself. "Can you come up?"

"Well—" Weigand said. "Is it important?"

"Well," said Mrs. North, "sort of, I think. And bacardis, anyway. Jerry and I think maybe it's important."

Weigand said he would try to make it.

"Or martinis if you'd rather," Mrs. North said.

Weigand said he was pretty sure he could make it.

· 14 ·

THURSDAY
4:30 P.M. TO 5:30 P.M.

Weigand made it, and sat comfortably before the little fire in the
Norths' living-room. It had turned enough cooler to make the fire just
possible.

"If you open all the windows," Mrs. North said. "So we did. And we
left that chair so you could sit by it."

"Both," Mr. North said, "being roasted ourselves."

Weigand said it was nice of them. And what—?

"He's going to make cocktails," Mrs. North said. "You can have
martinis, though."

Mr. North went out to the kitchen, and made several trips back with
his hands full of bottles, shakers, ice containers and lime-juice.

"Why not there?" Mrs. North said.

"Martha," Mr. North said. "We bumped."

He dumped the ice from the container into a canvas bag, picked up a
short wooden mallet and, laying the bag on the hearth, began to beat it.
Weigand watched him idly. Then Weigand stiffened suddenly, and
stared. Mrs. North watched him and Mr. North looked up.

"Well," said Weigand, "I'll be damned!"

137

Mr. North nodded and Mrs. North said she had thought he would. Mr. North waved the ice mallet and then handed it to Weigand, who balanced it in his hand.

"Right?" said Mr. North.

Weigand nodded, slowly. Then he looked at the Norths with a new expression, and Mrs. North gave a little gasp.

"Oh," she said. "I never thought! Of course he would."

Mr. North nodded and said it was inevitable.

"Only," Mr. North said, "we still didn't. Weapon or no, we didn't. And I was in Central Park. But it could have been a mallet like this, couldn't it? Not necessarily a croquet-mallet? We thought so, but we wanted to see what you thought. It's heavy enough?"

"Quite," Weigand said. "Quite heavy enough. If you didn't know."

The Norths looked at each other, and Mr. North stood up.

"Listen, Weigand," he said. "It's up to you. You're a cop. We've understood that all along. If you suspect either of us, we'll go along on that basis, and you can prove and be damned. If you've any doubts—"

Mr. North's voice had a timbre which Weigand had not expected to hear in it. He stood up, too, and then Mrs. North stood up. The moment stiffened, and both the Norths waited for Weigand. Mrs. North's expression was expectant, waiting, and Weigand looked slowly at her, and steadily. She stood very erect and slim and challenging. Weigand turned from her and looked at Mr. North, whose expression waited, too. There was hardness in Mr. North's gaze, when it met the detective's. Weigand, all at once, felt rather silly.

"Hell," Weigand said, rather helplessly. He hesitated a moment and said: "Right." It didn't mean much of anything, as he said it. Then he noticed that a smile was beginning on Mrs. North's lips.

"Oh," Weigand said, "all right. Take it as said. I don't—that is, *I* don't. The cop—well, we'll skip the cop, for a while. Right?"

He looked at Mr. North.

"Right, North?" he said.

Mr. North looked at him a moment.

"Well," Mr. North said, "do you want a drink? Or don't you?"

"Sure," Weigand said. They both sat down, and Mr. North took back the mallet, which Weigand had been holding, and returned to pounding ice. Then he mixed the drinks, while nobody said anything. He poured a martini for Weigand, and bacardis for Mrs. North and himself. He was, he thought, probably making an issue, but it was an issue curiously hard to break.

"Well," he said, and lifted the glass. He waited for Mrs. North to lift hers, and then both waited for Weigand. Weigand picked his glass up, quickly, and drank half the martini. "Maybe I'm a fool," he thought. But he didn't, he decided, really think he was a fool.

"As a matter of fact," Mr. North said, after a sip or two, "there are a lot of these mallets about. It's the simplest way to break ice. Almost everybody we know has a mallet like this around somewhere. Somebody found them in Macy's basement, and passed the word along. The Fullers, Edwards—I suppose the Brents and this fellow Berex, if he has an apartment and makes cocktails, Pam's mother—hell, they're a lot more prevalent than croquet-mallets, if you were looking for croquet-mallets. They're pretty handy, if you want to bash people."

"But what we wondered," Mrs. North said, "was whether they would be heavy enough to bash? I mean, to kill—as Brent was killed? You think they would?"

Weigand lifted the mallet again and balanced it. He said he thought so. He would get expert advice from the Medical Examiner's office. He would pick one up at Macy's and have it looked at.

"Or," said Mr. North, "you can borrow this one, if you like. And if you'll bring it back."

Weigand said it was an idea. Then he said he thought he would just pick one up. Mr. North poured him another cocktail.

"Was," Weigand said, "this what you people called up about?"

Mr. North looked at Mrs. North, who said part of it.

"The rest," she said, "is Mrs. Brent and Berex. And what Jane told me about them."

"Yes?" Weigand said.

The Norths had, it developed, run into Jane Fuller as they were leaving the store after looking at the dress Mrs. North thought she might buy. "He didn't like it, though," Mrs. North said. "He said it bunched."

They had met on the ground floor, near the door, and Mrs. Fuller had said wasn't it awful about Stan Brent. "And you *found* him," Mrs. Fuller had said, and the Norths had told her something about finding him.

"And then," Mrs. North said, "I said wasn't it terrible for his wife, and Jane looked kind of funny and said, 'Yes, of course,' as if she didn't think it was so very terrible.

"I looked at her," Mrs. North said, "and she said, 'Well, there was always Louis, you know—Louis Berex.' She said he and Claire were in love, and had been for months, and everybody expected her to get a divorce. She said one saw them together everywhere; that she had seen them together only last night."

"Last night?" Weigand said.

Mrs. North nodded, and said she thought that was interesting.

"She said it was around six o'clock," Mrs. North said. "And that they were walking together through Ninth Street, toward Fifth Avenue, and she was holding his arm and looked very white and tired."

"Well," said Weigand. "Hmmm."

"So we thought we wouldn't say anything," Mrs. North said, "and then we thought we ought to. And it fitted in with the lunch today and everything. And then we thought of the mallet, too, and decided to find out whether you had thought about mallets. So we had bacardis, because we always crush the ice for them, although the lime-juice isn't good for me."

"About six?" Weigand said. Mrs. North looked surprised.

"Oh," she said, "that. Yes, but that was just one time; she said they were together lots of times and that everybody knew they were that way. It might have been any time, like today at lunch; last night is just an *example.*"

Weigand looked at Mr. North and waited, but Mr. North shook his head. It was just an example to him. Weigand had something else in mind, though—then it came to Mr. North and he nodded suddenly.

"Barnes!" Mr. North said. "About that time and they were within a few blocks. Yes, I see."

Mrs. North said, "Oh," and looked worried.

"Maybe we shouldn't have," she said. "You know I thought maybe we shouldn't."

Weigand said they had, on the contrary, been right to tell him.

"You see," he said, "they gave us to understand they weren't there. Berex was in his office, he said, and Mrs. Brent was home. At least her maid thought she was at home. It's interesting."

Mrs. North nodded, interestedly. Then she thought of something, and it worried her.

"And Jane," she said. "Jane when she saw them? Was she home too?"

"No," Weigand said. "She wasn't home. She was uptown having her hair curled."

The Norths looked at each other. There didn't seem to be anything to say. After a while Mrs. North spoke, and her tone cut Weigand out.

"You know what?" she said.

"Yes," Mr. North said. "I know what."

"I wish I hadn't ever found it," Mrs. North said. "That's what I wish. It makes you do things you wish you hadn't."

Mr. North nodded.

"But we couldn't help it," he said. "It just happened. It was just the party. And, after all, you can't let murderers just—well, run loose. You have to think of that."

Mrs. North said she was thinking of it.

"But that is theoretical," she said. "Just 'murderers.' But people you know aren't just murderers." She paused, and thought. "Even if they are," she said.

There was a little pause. Then Mr. North said that all the glasses seemed to be empty. He asked how Weigand had happened to become a cop and Weigand, after saying it wasn't interesting, said he hadn't planned to. He said he was going to be a lawyer, but the money ran out while he was in school, so he decided suddenly to be a policeman and went to the Police College. He was a patrolman for a long time, he said, and then a detective and finally a lieutenant of detectives.

"And you'll be a captain, and then whatever is next—an inspector or something—won't you?" Mrs. North said.

Weigand started to say one thing, and found himself saying another.
"Well," he said, "yes, as a matter of fact. I probably will."

Mrs. North nodded. She said it would be nice to know an inspector.
"Or a Police Commissioner," she said. "For parking by fire-plugs."

Weigand dashed her hopes, on that. He said commissioners were
different. He didn't, he said, expect ever to be a commissioner. But
then, he added, inspectors were all right, too, for parking by fire-plugs.

· 15 ·

THURSDAY
5:30 P.M. TO 8 P.M.

Weigand had a qualm or two, as he left the Norths and, as he went down the stairs to the street, heard Mrs. North's voice faintly through the apartment door behind him. "I think he's nice," he heard Mrs. North say, "and not at all—" Then he had gone out through the downstairs door and left the voice behind. "Not at all like a policeman," he supposed she had finished, and he had an uneasy feeling that she had summed it rather too accurately. A policeman ought not, he thought, be disarmed by people merely because he could not imagine them doing anything so aggressive as murder. He had as good as told them that he took their word for things and that they were no longer on his books as suspects, and that was going further than a good policeman should go. He thought of Inspector O'Malley and had a third qualm. O'Malley would not approve fraternization with suspects. When O'Malley was going up, he was definitely a rubber-hose cop.

"But definitely," Weigand said to himself, thinking of Edwards. But Edwards was in the clear as far as evidence went, and still on the books; the Norths had opportunity in plenty, perhaps motive, and were not on them. Weigand damned all hunches and found himself a new idea, and a telephone. Mullins was standing by at Headquarters to answer Weigand's call and say, "O.K., Loot." He would get from the District Attorney's office a list of the cases Brent had handled during the brief period when he was an assistant district attorney, and check it over for familiar names.

"Before you eat," Weigand directed. Mullins sighed, said, "But listen, Loot," and then, when the telephone receiver stiffened in his ear, lapsed into formality and said: "Yes, sir."

Weigand left the booth and the cigar-store which housed it, and stood on the sidewalk, thinking. He thought of all that he knew about the case, and had a hunch that he knew most of it, and that what else he had to know was somewhere near at hand if he could put a finger on it. Then he could crack down and really break it; once he knew where to crack, it would be easy. Somewhere in what he had already discovered, and heard, there was, he felt, a weak spot, if he could find it. But the trouble was that, as a policeman, you had to know first. You knew, and then you proved; once in a great while you knew, but couldn't prove. But evidence was raw, scattered stuff until you could shape it with knowledge.

You got to know from some fact, perhaps a very small fact, which did not fit with other facts. Or from something about character which you caught in an inflection, or a twist of expression or a breath drawn quickly or slowly. Once you really knew the people who might have done what had been done, you knew which of them had done it. The trouble was now, apparently, that he did not really know the people. He had missed something, or something had been well hidden. He ran over, in his mind, the people who had been about Brent when Brent was alive, and then realized that one face was missing entirely. He hadn't yet so much as set eyes on Jane Fuller, who had a long, red-headed husband with a quick temper, and who had not been having her hair done at Saks when Barnes was pushed off the subway platform.

Weigand crossed Sixth Avenue and went toward the Fuller house. A maid let him in; a maid would see if Mrs. Fuller could be seen. The maid returned to report that Mrs. Fuller could, in the upstairs living-room. Weigand went up, with the maid ahead of him, and into a large, low room with glass brick in front in place of windows. Mrs. Fuller stood up.

She was a slight, vividly colored young woman, perhaps around twenty-five, and she was wearing rust-colored slacks and a soft, silken white shirt, with a design which looked like a monogram, but turned out not to be, embroidered on a pocket. She had black hair swept up at the back, and a heart-shaped face. She said, "Yes, Lieutenant?" She did not say anything about sitting down, so Weigand stood up. He said there were just one or two things. He said he understood that she knew something about Berex and Mrs. Brent that he should know.

"And," she said, "who told you that?"

"It doesn't matter," Weigand said.

"No," said Mrs. Fuller, "because of course I know anyway. It was Pam North, wasn't it? And she said you were very attractive."

Mrs. Fuller did not say whether she agreed with Mrs. North on this point, but she looked Weigand over.

"Sit down, why don't you?" she said, and sat down herself. The chairs on the second floor, like those on the first, were modern, but they gave a greater impression of lightness. Weigand sat down.

"Well," Mrs. Fuller said, "if Pam thought you ought to know, all right. Louis Berex and Claire Brent are that way. They've been that way for months. Everybody knew about it."

Including, Weigand wanted to know, Brent? Mrs. Fuller nodded her head vigorously.

"From the first, I think," she said. "He told me about it weeks ago, anyway; asked if I had noticed anything. I said anything what? And he said I needn't stall, so I didn't. He said it was all right with him as long—" She stopped, suddenly.

"As long—?" Weigand inquired.

"Listen," Jane Fuller said, "what do you know—about Stan and me, I mean? What did Ben tell you."

"A good deal," Weigand said. "From his point of view, naturally."

"From *our* point of view," Mrs. Fuller said. "Absolutely from *our* point of view. We didn't agree about what to do about it, but we agreed about where we wanted to get." She paused. "In case you were thinking otherwise," she said, "I wasn't in love with Stan Brent. In case you wanted to know."

"Right," Weigand said. He said that that was what he gathered. So Brent had said as long as—?

"As long as I was around," Mrs. Fuller said. "But I wasn't. I don't know whether he even thought I ever would be, or just pretended to. He was—oh, well, say he was hard to get. I mean to understand, to know about." She paused again, and tucked one foot under the other knee. "Part of it was just to annoy Ben," she said. "Stan thought it was fun to make Ben flare. I told him not to, often enough; I told him it mightn't stay so much fun." She stopped then and drew her breath quickly. Then she smiled suddenly.

"That," she said, "was a silly thing to say, particularly to a policeman. I didn't mean anything, really. Except that Ben might—well, try to beat him up." She paused, with a reflective look in her eyes. "And Ben could have," she said reminiscently. "But not *with* anything, except his fists. Ben wouldn't *use* anything—I mean, Ben wouldn't go around hitting people with blunt instruments. So if you've been thinking that—?"

Weigand said he wasn't thinking anything, in particular. Just finding out. He said that they were wandering, anyway, from Louis Berex and Mrs. Brent. He wanted what she knew about them.

They had, she told him, met at a party somewhere. "Probably at that Edwards man's," she said. And had started, almost at once, running around together, not making any great effort at concealment. Everybody, she said, knew about it.

"And it didn't make any difference to anybody?" Weigand wanted to know.

Mrs. Fuller looked surprised.

"No," she said, "of course not. Why should it? It was obviously their business."

"You think they were—that is, lovers?" Weigand asked.

"Oh, yes, of course." Mrs. Fuller seemed to have no doubt.

Weigand let the point go, for the time, and raised another. "About last night," he said.

"Last night?" Jane Fuller echoed. "Oh, my seeing them. Well, I just did. They were walking through Ninth Street, probably going to her place. She looked white and tired, I thought."

"And Berex?" Weigand said. "How did he look?"

He hadn't, Mrs. Fuller said, looked anyway that she'd noticed. He just looked like Louis Berex.

"Rather tight," she said. "And quick, as he always does. I mean nervously tight, not alcoholically."

Weigand said that that brought up a point, as perhaps she had noticed. She looked inquiring.

"Well," he said, "you told Mullins you were having your hair curled, or something. Anyway, that you were uptown until after six last evening. And it appears you weren't."

"Oh," Mrs. Fuller said, "that! Was it important?"

"Well," Weigand said, "we thought so. Or we wouldn't have asked. And we're investigating a murder."

"But the murder was Monday," Mrs. Fuller said. "Anyway, it was silly. I said that because Ben was there, and it had to fit what I'd already told him. You see, I'd told him I'd surely be in by five-thirty yesterday, and I wasn't."

"No," Weigand said. "I gathered you weren't. You were down here in the neighborhood. Well?"

"Well," Mrs. Fuller said, "it's simple, really. Saturday's Ben's birthday and I'm giving him a party; a party he doesn't know about. It's going to be at Charles, and I wanted a special table, with flowers and everything, and a special menu. So I stopped by to see Charles and talk about it, but I didn't want to tell Ben where I'd been, and it took longer than I thought it would. That was all. You can ask Charles."

"Thanks," Weigand said. "I probably will."

Mrs. Fuller nodded approvingly. She said she would, certainly, if she were a policeman.

"And Monday?" Weigand said. "Just to fill in the record, were you really shopping Monday, as your husband said?"

Mrs. Fuller nodded, and said that was it.

"But I don't know who you can ask about that," she said. "I was at a

good many places, and I couldn't say what time I was at any of them."
She named four or five stores in any one of which she might have
been. She thought that the charges might show, if they noted the time
on charge purchases when they came through, a matter about which
she didn't have the least idea.

"And," she said, "also for the record, I didn't kill Stan. I can see you
might think I might want to, but I didn't even want to. I liked him less
than I used to, but I still liked him. I certainly didn't want him dead."

"Right," said Weigand. "I'll put it on the record."

Nobody, apparently, wanted Brent dead; nobody was, so far as he
could see, particularly regretful at his taking off. Mrs. Brent, to be sure,
had acted as if she were, but he was beginning to believe—to be fairly
certain—that shock, rather than grief, had affected her. And there were,
he reminded himself, a number of ways in which a person could under-
go a shock. Hitting a head with a mallet, and feeling the skull give,
would probably be a rather shocking experience, particularly for one
whose life had known nothing more violent than, say, the competition
of a tennis match.

"Listen," Mrs. Fuller said, "one reason I'm glad you've come is
because I wanted to ask you something. Ben and I were going away for
a couple of weeks after the dinner Saturday. Will it still be all right?"

Weigand shook his head and said he was sorry, but it wouldn't. Not
as things stood.

"Not unless we break it," he said. "I'm sorry, but you'll have to put
it off."

Mrs. Fuller said, "Oh," in rather a hurt tone.

"It's like that, is it?" she said.

"Not necessarily," Weigand said, getting up. "Call it a matter of routine. Say you might be needed to give evidence, or might remember
something to tell us. But I'll have to ask you to stay in town for a
while, anyway."

Mrs. Fuller looked rebellious. She also, Weigand decided, looked
very appetizing. But he shook his head, just the same, and said he was
sorry, but he really meant it.

She wasn't, Weigand decided as he was politely shown out by the maid, really his type. He was, however, getting to see some attractive women in this case. He smiled as he thought of Mrs. Fuller and thought of Mrs. Brent, also, with pleasure. Then he thought of Mrs. North, and chuckled. They were all nice girls, in their various ways, he thought. He hoped nothing would have to happen to any of them. That would be too bad.

He hesitated which way to go; and decided to combine business and nutriment. At Charles they told him that, quite truly, Mrs. Benjamin Fuller had made arrangements for a special dinner, for eight, on Saturday evening, and that she had talked over the menu and wines the evening before. And at Charles they served him mignonettes of beef with Sauce Bernaise which were, he decided, precisely the kind of hamburgers he had been wanting to find all his life.

He had coffee afterward and then, because the mignonettes seemed to deserve it, a small cognac. After all, he was going to have a long evening at Headquarters.

• 16 •

THURSDAY
8 P.M. TO 9:55 P.M.

Mullins had moved fast. Both he and the list were on hand when Weigand reached Headquarters. Mullins had already gone over the list of cases handled by Brent, and was able to assure the lieutenant that it didn't add up to anything. He mentioned, also, that he was getting pretty hungry, and how about it? Weigand waved him out, told him to hurry back, and picked up the list himself. It was not a long list; Brent's service in the District Attorney's office had, the detective noticed, lasted a little less than a year. Then he had seen a chance to go into a law firm, then Strahan, Mahoney and Butler, which became Strahan, Mahoney and Brent several years later.

The cases on Brent's list were all old cases now, buried at the District Attorney's office under the steady pouring of crime, great and small, which keeps the prosecutor's office of New York County an ever-filled reservoir, always slightly overflowing. Weigand ran down the names—varied offenders against the law, guilty or not convicted of various offenses. Forgeries were numerous, conversion of the securities of others frequent; shoplifters scattered here and there. Brent had prosecuted a band of young holdup men for first degree murder after a

shoe-store robbery, and accepted second degree pleas from three of
them. The fourth had been shot while resisting arrest. The surviving
three insisted that they were unarmed, had embarked on robbery as a
lark, and were more surprised than anyone else when their companion
had shot the store clerk. There were manslaughter cases and a burglary
or two—burglary wasn't, Weigand realized anew, what it had been in
the old days—and the rather engaging case of a man who had bought
two acres of Central Park from a persuasive stranger and been very surprised when he was unable to take possession. Brent had prepared
extradition papers in a couple of cases.

The names of the offenders reflected the tangled population of the
city. Cohens and Murphys rubbed shoulders on the docket; a Mr.
Brown and a Mr. Kumiatchi were neighbors in offense against the law.
Isaac Rotovitch and Hans Bremer had, against all Herr Hitler's pre-
cepts, entered into concord to rob a store and Mr. Sing Wu had, in a fit
of Oriental petulance, slashed at a throat. Abraham Washington Jones,
colored, had, on a jealous night in 1931, bashed his sweetheart, Amanda, over the head, inflicting contusions and letting himself in for a felonious assault charge, but Amanda, on recovering consciousness, insisted that she had fallen downstairs, and let him out of it. A lot of things
happened in New York, but none of them, so far as Weigand could see,
was subject to connection with what had happened Monday afternoon
at 95 Greenwich Place. It hadn't, he decided, been much of an idea, but
worth just about the time it was getting.

He ran his eye down the list once more, and something ticked in his
mind. One of the names rose up from the others and he stared at it.
Kumiatchi—Kensuke Kumiatchi, manslaughter, conv., five to ten
before Judge Greenberg in General Sessions. Weigand said "Hmm" to
himself. It occurred to him that, if he had a servant named Kumiatchi,
he would be inclined to call him Kumi and let it go at that. And it
occurred to him that, if he were an Oriental named Kumi, or Kumiatchi, he might cherish some resentment at the assistant district attorney who got him sent to Sing Sing for—for, he noted, on reading the
attached record, merely using a knife in a fight which began, and continued, on a purely personal basis.

He pondered over it, and figured times. Sent up on a five to ten years' sentence in 1931, getting time off for good behavior, one could be out and around quite easily in 1939. One would even have had time to get a satisfactory job as personal servant, and become a fixture at it. Nor was the period too long to harbor resentment, if one were going to harbor resentment. It would do with looking into.

Mullins returned, appropriately, from dinner. He kept his hat and coat on, and went forth again, to bring in Kumi, even if he were still washing the dinner dishes. Kumi would be looked into.

Weigand returned to other reports. The detectives searching for the girls who had written so affectionately to Stanley Brent were able to report no progress whatever, although they were industriously visiting night clubs on off chances and accumulating agreeable expense accounts. Detectives had attended Brent's funeral, held inconspicuously that morning, and reported no untoward incident. The financial district men had spent another day combing out the gossip about Fuller, Edwards and Berex, and had found nothing to contradict, and but little to strengthen, their previous reports. Specific information could, they concluded, be obtained only if office records were subpoenaed, which they judged was not yet on the cards. Weigand, rather regretfully, acquiesced in their judgment.

No claim had yet been made on Brent's insurance policy, and the company would agree not to rush the payment through when the claim was made, but would not consent to any long delay, unless definite evidence of irregularity was uncovered. If there was suspicion of irregularity, however, they would be glad to have their own operatives cooperate.

The Research Bureau had completed a minute examination of the recovered clothing and was able to assure Weigand, from a comparison of dust particles, that the one-time wearer had spent at least a short period in a room which had dust similar to that recovered from the fourth floor of 95 Greenwich Place. The Bureau would be glad to identify other places the wearer had been, if the Homicide Bureau would get them more dust for comparison. The Research Bureau suggested dust from the Brent apartment, for a starter. Weigand made a note of it;

such information might be useful in court, if and when they got to court; and if and when the defense, the still very shadowy defense, chose to question the identification of the garments, for whatever strange reason of its own. Defense counsel were quite capable of raising such a question, only to annoy, because they knew it teased.

There were, the Research Bureau further reported, no fingerprints of any kind to be found anywhere on the suitcase, or the belongings which had accompanied the clothes. This the Research Bureau regarded as rather strange, and indicating that everything had been carefully wiped—with a linen cloth, apparently, since a thread of cloth was caught on one of the keys. The Research Bureau suggested the use of a handkerchief by a person or persons unknown. Well—

The Police Department of Danbury, Connecticut, in response to a request for assistance teletyped from Manhattan, reported—Weigand gave a low whistle, and said he *would* be damned. The Danbury police reported that they had been able to discover no exhibitors or others who had seen a woman answering the description given of Mrs. Stanley Brent at the Danbury Fair on Monday, the twenty-fourth instant. This did not surprise the Danbury police, because the fair had closed on Sunday, the twenty-third instant, and was in the process of being carted away on Monday. No members of the public had been allowed entrance. The Danbury police hoped this information would be of service.

Weigand leaned back in his chair and thought that one over. And he had thought he knew all the elements! Well, it only proved . . .

So the supple, light-haired Claire Brent was a liar, apparently, to boot. Her alibi was a clumsy fake, not worth the trouble she had gone to—not much, evidently—to invent it. She was a liar and probably a violator of her marriage vows and stood to pick up a hundred grand if something violent happened to Mr. Brent. And in the time missing from the sequence of her activities, she could, without too much hurrying, have driven in from near Carmel, New York, to 95 Greenwich Place, and struck Mr. Brent sharply on the back of the head with a mallet more conventionally used for crushing ice. She could have stripped him, stowed his clothing in a suitcase, checked the case in a lock-box at a nearby subway station and driven back to Carmel, none the worse except for a mild fatigue, probably hardly noticeable to a young woman in such evidently excellent physical condition.

"Hmmm," said Weigand. "Well!"

He would have to see Mrs. Brent again. He could still go up this evening, if— But he remembered the imminent arrival of Kumi, no doubt even now clutching wildly at projections inside the police car which, with red lights blinking and siren wailing in the night, was coming down to Centre Street. Well, Mrs. Brent would keep until next day, and tell her story then. It would, Weigand decided, have to be a good story.

There was a thudding sound in the passage outside, presaging the arrival of Detective Mullins. But Kumi shot through the door, first, evidently propelled. Mullins, a new contentment on his face, followed.

"Here's your man," Mullins said. There was also a new contentment in his voice.

Weigand nodded and went on looking at papers. Mullins sat Kumi down where the light was best. Kumi looked alarmed and resentful and started to speak. Mullins told him to wait until he was spoken to, huh?

"Your name is really Kumiatchi, isn't it?" Weigand said sharply, indifferently.

Kumi blinked.

"Yes, pliss," Kumi said.

Mullins made a low, menacing sound, the inarticulate symbol for "now-we've-got-you-fella."

"Pliss, Kumi is easier for Americans," Kumi said. "Everybody call me Kumi because it is easier."

Mullins started a snort of derision, but stopped it when he saw that Weigand was nodding.

"Yes," Weigand said. "So we found out. You're Kensuke Kumiatchi. In 1931 you were sent to Sing Sing for killing a man with a knife. Right?"

Weigand's "Right" was barely a question. Merely a pause to permit Kumi to admit the inevitable. But Kumi shook his head.

"No, pliss," he said. "I not go to prison. I never go to prison. I never kill a man."

Weigand looked coldly disapproving and Mullins completed his snort of derision, judging the time for it had come.

"Lying won't do you any good," Weigand said. "We know about it, see? We find out things here. We know all about you. And you decided to get Mr. Brent when you came out. Right?"

Again there was no question in the voice. Again Kumi shook his head.

"Not Kensuke," he said. "Not Kensuke. Atoke. I Atoke."

"What?" said Weigand.

"Kumiatchi," Kumi said. "All right. Atoke Kumiatchi. Not Kensuke Kumiatchi. Lots of Kumiatchis."

"No," Weigand said. "Kensuke Kumiatchi. Just one Kumiatchi—you. You tricked Mr. Brent into going to the apartment. You used Edwards' name. Then you hit him. Right?"

"No," said Kumi. "No, pliss. I kill no mans."

"Huh," said Mullins. "We'll work over him, huh, Loot?"

Weigand shook his head.

"Not yet," he said. "He'll tell us. There's no reason he shouldn't tell us. We know, anyway."

But Kumi shook his head.

"Not Kensuke," he said. "Atoke. Not Kensuke."

He was, Weigand decided, going to stick to it, unless Mullins— Then he thought of something.

"Right," he said. "You're Atoke. Who is Kensuke?"

There was the faintest of changes in Kumi's face; perhaps not a change at all. It was hard to tell what was in the faces of unfamiliar races. A flicker of something in Kumi's?

"Your father, wasn't he?" Weigand said, suddenly. "It was your father killed a man in a fight and went to prison. And you revenged him. Right?"

"No," Kumi said. "No, pliss. Not father." He paused. "Brother," he said. "Kensuke my brother. But I not kill anybody."

"Now," Weigand said, "we're getting places. Kensuke was your brother and when he got sent to prison it made you mad, didn't it? Angry? You wanted to get the man who put him there? Right? And that man was Mr. Brent."

"No," Kumi said. "I not kill anybody."

Mullins offered again to give him a going over, with a couple of the other boys. "Not a hand on him, Loot," he said. "Not a hand. Just a little light and a few questions for a while."

It might, Weigand thought, have to come to that. But perhaps—

"Well, Kumi," he said, "we'll say it was your brother. Were you fond of your brother?"

Kumi nodded.

"Tried to help him when he got in trouble?" Weigand asked.

Kumi nodded again.

"Yes, pliss," Kumi said.

"Of course," Weigand said. "And you got him a lawyer, probably. Helped him get a lawyer?"

Kumi said yes.

"And you thought he got a dirty break when he was convicted?"

"Pliss?"

"You thought—you thought it was unfair to send him to prison because he got in a fight and killed a man who was after him?"

Kumi shook his head.

"He break law," he said. "Man who break law should be punished."

He said it simply, and Weigand had an uneasy suspicion that he meant it. But you couldn't tell about men; particularly about men of another race. He started to nod to Mullins, surrendering Kumi to a going over, and then stopped. They might, of course, break him down. They might get admissions; they probably would get admissions. But perhaps they could get along without it, and perhaps they had now all they were going to get, except by digging. And Kumi looked rather small, beside Mullins, and—

"You know jiu-jitsu?" he said to Kumi.

Kumi shook his head.

"No, pliss," he said. "I am not athlete. I quiet man."

He certainly, sitting there under the light, looked a quiet man. But then, probably, his brother had looked a quiet man, too. Weigand shook his head.

"I don't know," he said. "I think probably you're lying to me. If you are you're in bad trouble. But maybe you're not."

"I not lying," Kumi said, eagerly. "I kill nobody."

That, Weigand told him, was what he said.

"We'll look into it," he said. "We'll find out if you are lying, and if you are, you're in bad trouble. But now I'm going to let you go home. But we'll be watching you all the time. We'll know everything you do, everybody you meet. If you killed Mr. Brent we'll find out. Don't think you're getting away with anything."

"No, pliss," Kumi said. "I not get away with anything."

Weigand nodded at Mullins.

"Right," he said. "Mr. Mullins will take you out, and you can get a subway uptown. Don't try to run."

Kumi shook his head. Kumi would not run, pliss. He looked scared. But he did not look very scared.

"All right," Weigand said, to Mullins. "Let him out. Keep an eye on him."

Mullins led him out and returned in a few minutes, looking much less contented.

"All right," he said. "There's a man on him. But listen, Loot. You'd ought to have let me work on him."

"Yes," Weigand said. "Perhaps I ought. Perhaps in a day or so, I will. Meanwhile, you might have a look at that." Weigand tossed over the report from the Danbury police. Mullins said that he'd be damned.

"Maybe they all did it," Mullins said. "Sort of a gang, huh? They got this guy on the spot and—"

Weigand said that he didn't think so.

"It's a funny one, all right," he said. "A very funny one." He looked at his watch. It was a little short of ten o'clock. "Come on," he said.

"The Brent dame's?" Mullins said.

"Right," said Weigand. "And maybe the Berex guy's," he added.

· 17 ·

Mrs. Brent's manner was not cordial. She said, "Really, Lieutenant," with inflection. But Weigand was not cordial, either. He looked at her and ignored the evidence that, under the thin hostess gown, there was the attraction of rounded suppleness.

"Sit down, please, Mrs. Brent," he said. She hesitated, looked at him, and sat down. Weigand and Mullins, who glowered, remained standing.

"Well," Weigand said, "I tried to make it easy. I tried to be nice and a little gentleman. Maybe that gave you wrong ideas?"

His voice was not high or bullying, but it was not friendly. Mrs. Brent looked inquiring.

"Is there," she said, "something wrong? Something new wrong?"

Weigand said you could call it that.

"I'll give you another chance," he said. "What did you do Monday afternoon? You can leave out the painting, the Danbury Fair."

"I don't understand," Mrs. Brent said. "It was like—"

Weigand said no, it wasn't like she had said. Not at all like she had said.

158

"You missed something," he assured her. "People who lie often miss something. The fair closed Sunday."

Mrs. Brent said, "Oh," with a little gasp.

"That does make me look pretty silly," she said. "I didn't know. I thought it had just begun Saturday."

Weigand told her she was a week off, and waited.

"Well," she said, "I really meant to go to the fair. But not alone. I may as well tell you."

"Right," Weigand said. "You may as well. And don't make it fancy, this time."

It wasn't fancy. She had, she said, planned to go to the fair, as she had told her maid, but she had planned to take Louis Berex with her. He had never been to the fair, and she thought he would like it. "Lots of people go up from New York," she pointed out. Weigand nodded. The plan had been that she would meet Louis Berex at the railroad station in Brewster and drive over to Danbury, see the fair, and drop him at the station again afterward. But they hadn't done that.

"We started to," she said. "But it was a lovely day, you remember. Like summer, but full of color. And we decided we didn't want to be in a crowd."

So, after driving a few miles toward Danbury, they had turned off onto a side road, and then onto another side road and finally, miles from anywhere on a one-lane road near the top of a hill from which they could look down the Croton valley, they had stopped the car. They had pulled to the side of the road and got out and walked up to the very top of the hill and sat there in the warm sun, looking out over the valley and at the bright hills.

"And time just passed," Claire Brent said. "We sat there, and there was nobody near and time passed. We talked and—"

"And?" Weigand said.

"Just talked," Claire Brent said. "It was a lovely afternoon."

"And why," Weigand wanted to know, "did you tell me this other yarn? About the picture and scraping the canvas, and all that?"

She looked at him.

"Really, Lieutenant Weigand," she said. "Why should I? I was alone, far from anybody, with a man not my husband. Why should I—shout it? It made no difference to you, really; I was just as far from town as I would have been at the fair. It would have looked bad, in the newspapers. People would have talked about us, and suggested all sorts of things. After all, Lieutenant, why squander a reputation?"

She gave, Weigand thought, every indication of being entirely naive about it. He wondered whether it was possible she did not know how much people were talking, or what they were saying, about her and Louis Berex. He decided that it was, of course, possible. Still—

"As a matter of fact," he said, and felt cruel as he said it, "as a matter of fact, Berex is your lover, isn't he?"

Claire Brent stood up in one rhythmic movement.

"Lieutenant Weigand!" she said. She stared at him. He stared back.

"Listen," he said, "I don't give a damn. Your habits are nothing to me, you know. I'm a cop. I have things to find out. You're just another fact to me."

"What has that got to do with it?" she said.

He continued to stare at her. He said he thought she could figure it out, if she tried. She was still and cold, and after a moment she nodded.

"You'd have to prove it, wouldn't you?" she said. "You couldn't just guess about it, could you?"

"Maybe I can prove it, if I have to," Weigand told her.

She nodded, and said she couldn't stop him trying.

"But," she said, "I can get you out of here and I can stop answering questions. And I can get a lawyer and find out what right you have to ask questions, can't I?"

"Yes," Weigand said. "Sure."

"All right," Claire Brent said. *"Now suppose you get out of here!"*

There was hard anger in her voice, finally. Weigand said, right, if that was the way it was going to be, that was the way it was going to be. He gathered Mullins, who looked darkly on Mrs. Brent, and got out.

"Wow," said Mullins, when they were out. "You've sure got a way with dames, Loot."

Weigand told him to shut up. They went in search of Berex, but

Berex was not at home. Nor was he at his office. Mullins said how would it be if they called it a day? Weigand frowned on him and took him back to Headquarters. It was time, Weigand decided, to do a bit of thinking.

"You can just sit," he told Mullins, unkindly. Mullins said, "Hey, listen, Loot."

At Headquarters, Weigand tossed a full package of cigarettes to his desk, switched on a hooded light and pulled off his necktie. Mullins recognized symptoms of thought, and sighed. Weigand took a pile of yellow paper from a drawer of his desk and put it in front of him. He lighted a cigarette and stared at the paper.

"O.K." said Mullins, "the Brent dame."

"Claire Brent," Weigand wrote at the top of the first sheet.

"Could she of?" Mullins said.

"Have," said Weigand. "Could she have."

"That's what I say," Mullins said. "Could she of?"

Weigand leaned back.

"Physically," he said, "yes. She's a strong girl, in good condition. She knows how to hit; probably has a free swing, at least for a woman, and is accustomed to reaching up and hitting down from her tennis. She could move fast if she had to, probably faster than Brent, who was no athlete. With an ice-mallet, or something like that, she could do plenty of damage. Probably, with a little effort, she could have dragged Brent into the bathroom after she knocked him out, and hit him a couple more times."

"Yeh," said Mullins, "I think so. Yeh."

He paused.

"Was she there?" he said.

Weigand said wait a minute, and noted down a summary of what he had just said. Under Claire Brent's name he wrote the summary in two words, "Strong enough."

"Was she there?" he repeated then. "We don't know. We know what she says—what she said first and what she said the second time. She was in the country, either at the Danbury Fair, which had closed the day before, or on the top of a hill, looking at the pretty scenery with Berex. Berex will say she was with him, and she will say he was with her. But she was away from the house, and as far as we know, nobody but Berex saw her from a little after lunchtime until about six. She says herself she can drive in from Carmel to her apartment in town, which is about the same distance as to the Buano house, in two hours at the outside. She can, too; I've had it checked. She could do it in an hour and forty minutes, if she hurried. She could have driven in, killed her husband, and driven out again. It's just about the right interval of time. But we haven't proved anything yet, and it would be hard to prove anything."

"Yeh," Mullins said, "it's what I think. She could of."

Weigand jotted down, under "Strong enough," the words: "Opportunity? Maybe."

"Weapon?" Mullins said. "You want to think about the weapon?"

"We can't," Weigand said, "prove anything about that, one way or another. If it was an ice-mallet, anybody could have bought one and thrown it away afterward. It's the kind of weapon anybody could get, use and destroy or throw away. Maybe drop down an incinerator. Is there an incinerator at No. 34?"

"Sure," said Mullins. "In the service hall. Sure."

"And probably she had a mallet in the country," Weigand said. "Or she might have had a croquet-mallet in the country, and brought it in and thrown it away, anywhere, going back out. Or not thrown it away, but just wiped it off and banged it in the dirt a few times. She is, incidentally, the only person we've run across who might have had a croquet-mallet handy. And there's another thing. She's been hitting things all her life—tennis balls, anyway. If she wanted to kill, she might naturally think of doing it by hitting."

"Yeh," Mullins said. "I'd been thinking that."

Weigand wrote: "Weapon—available" on the sheet of paper. Mullins opened his mouth, but Weigand waved it shut.

"We could show a motive," he said. "We could, really, show several. She's in love with Berex, whatever she says. Maybe she thought it was the simplest way of getting rid of a husband who is in the way. Although why not divorce, I wouldn't know."

"They do, though," Mullins said. "Mrs. Snyder, for instance. The sash-weight lady."

"Yes," Weigand said, "they do. But Mrs. Brent might have had a stronger motive—a couple of stronger motives. Maybe, in spite of Berex, she still loved Brent; maybe Berex was just revenge for Brent's playing around. And maybe she got desperate, after a while, at Brent's two-timing her and decided to bash him. That's happened too."

Mullins said it had, sure enough.

"But the most likely motive," Weigand said, "would be the insurance. That would combine with the first motive, too—explain why it was better to kill than get a divorce. If she killed and got away with it, she'd collect a hundred grand and she and Berex could spend it. That's a nice motive, all right."

"Mrs. Snyder and Judd Gray," Mullins said. "Like I was saying." He thought a moment.

"Listen, Loot," he said, "I think we've got it. I think we ought to pick her up."

Weigand wrote down "Motive—plenty," and leaned back in his chair. He crushed out his cigarette, and then lighted another. "Maybe," he said. "We'll look at the others, though. Take Berex."

Weigand leaned forward and wrote "Louis Berex" on the sheet of yellow paper. Mullins sighed.

"O.K., Loot, if you want to," he said. "Could he of?"

Physically, Weigand said, it was hard to say. Berex was slight, slighter than Brent. But he was wiry and moved vigorously. Making allowance for the difference in strength natural between men and women, he was probably as strong as Claire Brent, although he was not so strong for a man as she for a woman. Probably, on grounds of physical ability, he would have to be counted in. Mullins nodded and said, "Yeh, I guess so." Opportunity? So far as Weigand could see, Berex's was identical with Mrs. Brent's, equally hard to prove or disprove, equally certain to be supported by one person and by no more—and that one person obviously a prejudiced witness. He could have left Mrs. Brent sitting on the hill, looking at the pretty autumn leaves, borrowed her car, driven to New York, killed, driven her car back to the country and returned it to her, been driven by her to the railroad station in Brewster, caught a train back to New York.

But, and here was a point, if he were to be counted in on opportunity, did it not necessarily imply that he and Mrs. Brent were in it together, at least to the extent that she would countenance murder and provide an alibi for the murderer?

Mullins nodded, and said it sure looked like it.

It did, Weigand agreed, but it might be got around. Berex might have invented some urgent and hidden errand—such as a secret meeting somewhere near about one of his inventions—and have sold her on the story, particularly if she were in love with him, and ready to believe. He could, for example, have invented an important meeting with the engineers of the big United Electric plant a few miles outside Danbury. Her belief in such a story would, incidentally, explain more satisfactorily why she had lied in her first account. She wanted to keep Berex out of it entirely, not so much for the sake of her reputation, as to lessen any chance that his secret might be exposed.

"It could be that way," Weigand said. "With a little time, anyone could invent a perfectly satisfactory story for Berex to tell her."

In that event, of course, she would give an alibi to Berex to prevent anyone's suspicion that he was, really, engaged in secret negotiations—or whatever he had said he was engaged in. "That's just one story he might have told, of course," Weigand said. "It might be any of a dozen others."

Mullins said, "Yeh," but rather doubtfully.

"If you ask me, they were both in it," he said.

The weapon, Weigand went on, rubbing his ideas against Mullins, was still one that anybody might have had.

"Suppose," he said, "we figure that anybody we suspect could have got the weapon, or, for that matter, anybody we don't suspect. Right?"

Mullins said it was O.K. with him.

Then, Weigand said, they came to motive, and there they were all right, again, assuming Berex and Claire Brent to be in love. It might have been, although Weigand doubted it, chivalry—avenging the marital betrayal of his beloved on the betrayer.

"Hooey!" said Mullins. "That don't sound right."

Weigand agreed that it didn't, although he could, he assured Mullins, give him cases in which murder had resulted from such a situation—when a hotheaded lover had avenged bloodily a slight to his mistress.

"Yeh?" said Mullins.

Weigand said, O.K., they could skip that, for the time being. There was a better motive—the hundred grand.

"Like I said," Mullins said. "They were in it together."

That, Weigand pointed out, was not necessarily true. They might have been. On the other hand, Berex might have been in it alone, figuring that if he killed Brent he would get Mrs. Brent and the hundred thousand along with her. Or, possibly, even without the hundred thousand—just eliminate the husband and marry the wife. Perhaps Mrs. Brent, for some reason, would not try to get a divorce, and Berex, with or without the hundred thousand in mind, in addition to his desire for the lady, might have decided on the shortcut.

"That's happened, all right," Weigand said.

Mullins agreed that that had happened, all right.

"Listen, Loot," he said, "I think it was the two of them together. That's how I think it was."

"Then why," Weigand said, "would Berex leave in the mailbox the slip of paper with Edwards' name on it—and with his own fingerprints on it? And with enough of the letter X on it to lead us to him? Why did he do that, Mr. Bones-Mullins?"

Mullins wrinkled his brows, sighed deeply, and then brightened.

"To lay it on Edwards," he said. "The piece of the letter he didn't cut off was just an accident and he forgot about the fingerprints. He was trying to lay it on Edwards, because he had it in for Edwards."

"Did he?" Weigand said.

Mullins said he didn't know.

"I dunno," Mullins said. "He could of had. Or maybe he just had to use some name that Brent would know, and picked on Edwards', not caring much either way what happened to Edwards."

"Then why didn't he destroy it afterward?" Weigand said. They looked at each other, and Weigand looked almost as much pained as Mullins.

"He must have wanted to pin it on Edwards," Mullins said. "That's the only way it makes sense."

Weigand nodded, and said it looked like it. But why the finger-prints? Mullins said that Berex probably just didn't think of them.

"Then why," Weigand said, "were they upside-down?"

Mullins said, "Jeez, Loot."

"Well," Weigand said, "it might be this way. Berex might have got the prints on the paper at some other time, perhaps when he was pulling a sheet of paper from the pile. Perhaps sometime he pulled a sheet out, and decided not to use it for some reason, and shoved it back, leaving his prints. Then, by accident, he used that particular sheet when it came to cutting out the slip, but when he was actually cutting it he was very careful about prints, and when he slipped it into the slot at the Buano house, he was still careful and used tweezers or some such instrument, never dreaming his prints were already there."

"It could be," Mullins said.

Then, Weigand went on, say Berex decided on murder, either with or without Claire Brent, and prepared the slip of paper the day before, went to the country, telephoned Brent from there and made an appoint-ment with Brent in the name of Edwards, met Brent at the scene of the appointment—the Buano house—and killed him, left the slip to lay a false trail to Edwards and then drove back to the country, completing his alibi. Mullins said it could be. Then Mullins thought of something else.

"That slip," he said. "Doesn't it count Claire Brent out, figuring her as having done it by herself? Wouldn't she have thought it would lead to Berex, who she's sweet on?"

Weigand pondered, and agreed that it was a point. But she might merely have clipped the piece from a letter Berex had written her, not noticed that she clipped a bit of the X onto the slip and never thought of his prints being on it.

"She couldn't see them, of course, until they were brought up," Weigand added.

"Yeh," Mullins said. "I guess they did it, all right."

"Both of them?" Weigand said. "Or just Berex? Or just Mrs. Brent?"

Mullins shook his head, and said Weigand had got him there, all right. Then he thought of something else.

"How about the postman?" he said. "The guy Barnes, who was pushed. Did they push him, too?"

Weigand figured, he said, that whoever killed Brent killed Barnes, and he also figured that they would never prove anything about Barnes until he proved everything about Brent. Certainly, Berex and Mrs. Brent were in the neighborhood at the time, and certainly both had told stories which put them somewhere else.

"But we'll never prove anything about Barnes," Weigand said. "We'll stick to Brent. Only if we get the right person for the Brent killing, he has to have been able to kill Barnes, too."

"Listen, Loot, you're making this sort of hard, ain't you?" Mullins said. "It's screwy, anyway."

Weigand agreed, but not that he was making it hard. Somebody else had made it hard. He was just trying to soften it up. So—

"D'y want to go on to the others, Loot?" Mullins asked. "It looks to me like we got 'em already."

Weigand said he thought they had better look at the others, too.

· 18 ·

FRIDAY
MIDNIGHT TO 2 A.M.

They looked at Edwards. He was a big man, and if he was also a soft man it would take no great hardness of body to hit an unsuspecting man over the head and not too much more to drag him from one room to another and hit him again. Say, Weigand and Mullins agreed, he could do it. He could have secured a weapon with no difficulty. But—

"Why?" Weigand asked Mullins, who said, "Yeh, why?"

Weigand turned up a copy of the report of the auditors who had, at Edwards' so generous invitation, been looking over the records of the Berex trust fund; the fund which had, to start with, been a frail enough thread to tie the expansive party giver to the murder of a man who was, inconveniently, not Berex at all. The report left the thread more frayed than ever. The accountants had not, to be sure, entirely finished, but so far as they had gone, could find nothing in the accounts which gave any ground for suspicion. Edwards had, apparently, managed well, and paid over income regularly. Nothing which resembled a motive for murder of Brent by Edwards had turned up.

And could he have been at the place of murder at the time fixed? Apparently not; Edwards was, by all accounts, and by all evidence, wrist-deep in lobsters at the moment. There was also the slip of paper with Edwards' name on it, obviously left so that it would be found.

It had seemed to point to Edwards, but, looked at more closely, as they now looked at it, it pointed away from him. It had brought him at once into an investigation from which he might, otherwise, have been omitted altogether, or reached only casually. Weigand remembered Mrs. North's happy assumption that the murderer had left his name, and grinned over it. Murderers didn't, in his experience, leave their names. Certainly not intentionally; certainly not if they were men as astute as he suspected Edwards to be.

"We can wash him out," Weigand said. "Right?"

Mullins nodded sagely, if a little sleepily, and said, "Yeh." Then he brightened a little.

"There's that guy Kumi," Mullins said. "He's something to think about." Mullins' tone turned that duty over to his superior. Weigand looked at him, blinked and suggested that he send somebody for some coffee. Mullins looked relieved and went to find somebody, while Weigand thought of Kumi. Perhaps he could have done it; he was a solid, vigorous little man, who might, in spite of his denials, know jiu-jitsu. He could have got a mallet.

"Hell," Weigand said to himself, "who couldn't?"

Could he have been on hand? Weigand thought it over, and nodded. Perhaps he could have been, at that. With Edwards husking his lobsters, enthralled by cookery, Kumi might very easily have left the apartment, done his spot of murdering, and returned without Edwards' being the wiser. Motive? He picked out Kumi's statement from a pile of papers and skimmed through it. He nodded to himself. Taking into account everything—racial pride, Kumi's alien psychology, perhaps other things which had not yet come to the surface—and you could give him a motive.

Weigand let a cigarette burn into the edge of his desk, and thought about Kumi. He sighed and picked the cigarette up and inhaled varnish. He ground it out, angrily, and started another.

He also started the Fullers, and things brightened. There was no need to ask whether Benjamin Fuller was up to the task; that, from one glance at him, was clear. He also had, Weigand suspected, the glowing, angry temper which would make the thing psychologically possible. A quick uppercut to the chin would be more likely, perhaps. He was not a man to lay long plans. But "long" was a relative word; all preparations for, and the accomplishment of, Brent's death might have come within one not too long period of anger. And Fuller had cause enough for anger; cause enough to hate Brent, who was making him appear, among other things, a complaisant fool; who was making life difficult for the slim, alive young woman to whom Fuller had so evidently given his smoldering devotion.

The weapon, again, was nothing. The time? Weigand picked Fuller's statement out of the pile and checked it over. There was an alibi of sorts. Clipped to the statement was a report from Chicago. Crowley, Fuller's temporary companion on Monday afternoon, had remembered and confirmed. He thought, however, that he and Fuller had separated nearer three o'clock than any other time. Weigand pulled his chin and nodded. That made a vague alibi vaguer. He wrote Fuller's name on his sheet of paper and drew a line under it. Then he drew another line. Mullins came back, with coffee, and they had coffee. Weigand tried to fit Mrs. Fuller into the picture. He conjured up, with amazingly little trouble, a picture of Jane Fuller herself—a vivid picture of a girl in rust-colored slacks, with a heart-shaped face.

It was a very agreeable picture, and Weigand caught himself regarding it with agreeable sensations. He reminded himself, hurriedly, that he was a cop, looking for somebody to send to the electric chair. But, in a moment, he decided that Mrs. Fuller would hardly fit the role. She, among all the possibles, seemed unlikely to have the necessary physical strength. Possibly she had a motive—sheer annoyance at Brent's peculiar pursuit, and indignation at the false position in which Brent had put her—but it was not too strong. She didn't, to be sure, have an alibi, or anything approaching one. From the point of opportunity, she was more likely than anybody except, possibly, Mrs. North. But there must have been, in the city, several millions with opportunity, and without alibis. Weigand drank coffee, wearily, and hoped his murderer was not, unsuspected, among those millions.

He thought of the Norths, and felt obscure guilt. Tacitly, he had promised that he would not think of the Norths as murderers. Had he made a mistake in that promise? He thought them over, recalled Mr. North's motive and grinned over it; his lack of alibi, and grinned again. He finished his coffee and stared at Mullins, who was nodding over his empty cup. Weigand shook his head, sadly, and set his own cup down hard on the desk. Mullins jumped and looked indignant.

"Listen, Loot," he said. Weigand grinned at him and held out his cup for more coffee. Mullins poured from the cardboard container.

Weigand drew a fresh sheet of paper toward him, and made himself a little list. He paused over it, now and then; interrupted himself for more coffee; now and then scratched out one word and wrote another. When he finished he had this:

Suspects	Motive?	Physical ability?	Alibi?	Opportunity to kill Barnes?
Mrs. Brent	jealousy—greed	yes	weak	apparently
Berex	love—greed	yes	weak	apparently
Mrs. Brent and Berex	combination of above	yes	none	yes
Fuller	jealousy and anger	yes	fair	probably
Mrs. Fuller	weak	improbable	none	probably
Kumi	revenge(?)	probably	none—really	probably
Edwards	none known	yes	fair	probably
Mr. North	faint	yes	none	probably
Mrs. North	none known	no	none	probably

He looked it over, and felt rather sad about it. It seemed to rule out almost nobody. It left Mrs. Brent and Berex, together or singly; Ben-

jamin Fuller and Kumi well up; Edwards and Mrs. Fuller and the
Norths, lower down and in about that order. Weigand drew a line
through it; then crumpled the sheet and threw it on the floor. He took
another sheet and wrote at the top: "Funny questions?" He filled it in,
with the aid of more cigarettes and many fits of staring at the ceiling.
When he finished, it read:

1) Why leave a slip of paper with Edwards' name and Berex's fingerprints on it? Why was Edwards' name used?

2) Why did Mrs. Brent lie about the Danbury Fair?

3) Where were Berex and Mrs. Brent going when Jane Fuller saw
them?

4) What did the postman know? Could he identify the murderer?

5) Why pick the empty apartment at the Buano house?

6) Why was the window of the apartment left open, so that the cat
got in? Air to dissipate odor of decomposition?

7) What is the racket the District Attorney's office is investigating?

8) What was the purpose of Brent's proposed visit to the D.A.'s
office? Why didn't one of them up there ask him?

9) Were Brent and Jane Fuller really lovers, whatever Fuller
thought? And, on that point, was Fuller really saying what he thought?

10) Is Berex really an inventor, and has he ever invented anything
of importance? And how badly does he need money?

11) Since Brent knew where Edwards lived, why was he not suspicious when invited, as he apparently had been, to meet Edwards in an
apartment he appeared to occupy in the Buano house?

12) Is my man really on this list, and if he is, how am I ever going
to hang it on him?

Weigand looked at his list and shuddered slightly. A few of the
questions were probably extraneous, including, he gloomily decided,
all to which he could guess the answers.

Number 11, for example, was easy. Brent had not been at Edwards' apartment for several months. Whoever invited him to the Buano house had merely to tell him Edwards had recently moved. None of the answers he could guess seemed to get him much nearer an answer to the final question, or, at any rate, to the latter half of the final question. Hunch told him the answer to the first half, but not very firmly. The man or woman was, hunch told him, on his list. He picked up the crumpled paper from the floor and looked at the list again. No name glowed red. Suddenly Weigand thought of a fine thing to do.

"Well," he said. "I'm going home. I'm going home and sleep on it. What do you think of that, Mullins?"

But Mullins was already asleep, and his answer was an annoyed murmur.

· 19 ·

FRIDAY
8 A.M. TO 1:30 P.M.

Weigand slept and, when his mind returned to him Friday morning, scanned it eagerly for signs of new perception. It disappointed him; things looked much as they had the night before. He went back to Headquarters and brooded over his tabulation of suspects, and sighed. No hunch pointed. He looked at his questions and closed his eyes. Perhaps he was asking the wrong questions; perhaps he had, even, the wrong suspects. His telephone rang and he went in and explained matters to Inspector O'Malley, who was grumpy about them and wanted to know what he was to tell the reporters.

"Listen," he said, "it's going to be off the front page in another day if we don't liven it up." O'Malley slapped his desk. "Break it!" he commanded. "Break it!"

Weigand went sadly back to his office and looked at the list again, although he had it by heart. He called Mullins in and was severe with him, and Mullins angrily ordered the latest reports from a uniformed clerk, who had nobody to be cross with. The reports came, and showed nothing much. Investigations were still in progress into Brent's professional and extraprofessional life. The State police were cooperating in

174

an effort to find somebody who might have noticed Berex and Mrs. Brent in their wanderings in Putnam County, assuming they had really wandered in Putnam County. A New York Central conductor had, from a picture, identified Berex as a man who might have been on the 11:05 train out of Grand Central for Chatham, and might have alighted at Brewster.

The precinct reported that it was continuing its efforts to find a witness to Barnes' death who could remember, and be sure about, what he had witnessed, and thought perhaps it had a lead. It would amplify its report later. The tailor who made Brent's clothes had identified them as the clothes he made for Brent. Everything that did not particularly matter clicked comfortably into place. Uptown, a detective had, by chance and knowledge of a good many people, found one of the girls who had written affectionately to Brent, and had got out of her a sufficiently vivid account of a trip to Atlantic City two years before. It had rained heavily in Atlantic City that week-end. And Brent had been a fine boyfriend, for the duration.

Weigand shook his head over these reports, and others as illuminating. He left Mullins to keep in touch and went uptown to visit Berex.

Berex was at his office, and at the drawing-board. He swung around lithely when Weigand entered and ran pencil-darkened hands through his sandy hair. He said he had been expecting Lieutenant Weigand to call, and grinned slantingly.

"We sort of made a mistake about the fair," he said, before Weigand asked him. And, before Weigand asked him, he told a story identical with that of Mrs. Brent. He told it cockily, with assurance, and his eyebrows challenged the detective to make more of it than he was told of it. Berex denied that he and Mrs. Brent had been apart at any time during the afternoon; he denied any implications as to their relationship.

"And if you don't believe me, prove different," he suggested. "Meanwhile, I've got work to do."

Weigand said, as darkly as he could manage, that maybe he would, but he did not convince himself and he was not sure he convinced Berex. At any rate, Berex's rather impudent smile did not falter, and he nodded satirical encouragement.

"Luck to you," he said, brightly, and Weigand was aware that he glowered. Berex seemed to be gaining, rather than losing, confidence as time went on, which was not a thing Weigand liked to see in suspects.

Weigand looked as forbiddingly as he could manage at Berex, nodded with what he hoped might, if Berex were guilty of anything, be taken as emanating from a fund of inner knowledge, and went along. What he needed to do, he decided, was to go some place and think. He looked at his watch and was astonished to discover that it was almost lunch-time. He toyed with the thought of a drink or two, to lubricate thought, tried to convince himself that it was time to be sternly about a policeman's duties, and walked downtown. A little walk would help, he thought. It had not helped, noticeably, when he discovered that he was in front of Charles Restaurant. His feet turned with comforting independence and carried him in. He sat at the bar and ordered a martini.

Weigand had found his stool automatically, with most of his mind buried, and he was astonished when a familiar voice spoke from the next one.

"Personally," the voice said, "I don't think people ought to drink this early, do you? Except if it's special, of course."

He pivoted and observed Mrs. North fishing for the olive in the bottom of her glass.

"I," she said, "just come for the olives. Don't they give you fine, big olives, here?"

"Well," said Weigand, and looked to see. "Yes," he said. He seemed to amuse Mrs. North, who showed it.

"Detective," she said, and nodded to herself. "Even has to verify olives. Who did it?"

"What?" said Weigand.

"Mr. Brent," Mrs. North said. "Who did him? Or don't you know yet?"

The last was in a disappointed and slightly chiding tone.

"Oh," said Weigand. "Well, the fact is, we expect—" He looked at Mrs. North. "No," he said. "I don't know who did for Mr. Brent. Do you, by any chance?"

Mrs. North looked surprised, and said of course she did.

"He left his name," she said. "Didn't you know?" Weigand smiled and shook his head. He said he had told her it wasn't that easy. She sobered and nodded and said all right.

"I know," she said. "No, I don't know who did it. Sometimes I suspect somebody and then I suspect somebody else, but I thought detectives didn't do it that way."

Weigand sighed and said he wished they didn't, but that sometimes they did. He asked Mrs. North if she had had lunch, having an uneasy feeling that a cocktail wouldn't prove anything about that, either way. She would say, likely as not, that she always had an olive for dessert. But she had not had lunch, and would be delighted to eat it with him, although Mr. North might be along and join them.

"But he won't mind," she said, leaving Weigand to wonder what Mr. North wouldn't mind.

They were led to a table by a captain who beamed on Mrs. North, and assured her that another place could easily be set for Mr. North. Mrs. North had waffles and sausage and Weigand wondered about her digestion. He had broiled sea bass, and wondered a little about his. After a few minutes Mr. North did come, groaned openly over the choices of the other two, and ordered a green salad. Mr. North had passed wondering about his digestion; he knew.

Before he realized it, Weigand found himself telling the Norths about the case, to date, omitting very little and conveying his own puzzlement. Mr. North looked puzzled, too, and nodded glumly.

"What do you do next?" Mr. North said, and Weigand, unguarded, said he wished he knew. Mrs. North speared a piece of sausage, consumed it happily and said she had an idea.

"It just came to me," she said. "Out of the blue."

"Or," said Mr. North, "out of the martini. I doubt whether Weigand—" But Weigand stopped him, and said you never could tell.

"Frankly," he said, "I'd like an idea; something to break the jam. And if she got one out of a martini she's one up on me."

"Well," said Mrs. North, "it comes out of books, really. Get them all together and spring it on them."

"Spring," said Mr. North, "what?"

"Right," said Weigand. "Spring what?"

"The solution," Mrs. North said. "That's what the detective always does. He gets them all together and tells the man who did it that he knows he did it and then he confesses. And there are discrepancies, usually."

"Discrepancies?" said Mr. North. "You mean between what the detective thinks and what happens?"

Mrs. North shook her head. She said she meant in the stories.

"And when they're all together, they all come out," she said. "It always happens, in books."

"Well," said Weigand, "this is the New York Police Department. We don't get them together, usually. We more often keep them apart."

"But," said Mrs. North, "they are apart. And so's your solution. And I could give my party."

"Listen," said Mr. North, and Weigand looked at him hopefully. Mrs. North beamed at both of them.

"The party I was going to give, except for the body," she said. "Only in our own apartment, of course, except that people can look if they want to, and you don't mind. A suspect party."

"A what?" said Weigand, fascinated.

"A suspect party," Mrs. North repeated. "All the suspects, and maybe some other people—people I owe to—and you can come and discover the murderer."

Mr. North ran a hand through his hair. Weigand, bowing to superior experience, ran a hand through his hair.

"Listen," both men said together. Mr. North waved Weigand on.

"Well," said Weigand, "let's see if I've got this straight. You want to give a party for the suspects? Right?"

"Yes, and some other people I owe to," Mrs. North said. "People we've been to since they've been to us. But mostly for suspects."

"Yes," said Weigand. "A party for the suspects. And I'm to get them all talking and find out which one did it? Right?"

Mrs. North nodded.

"Only," she said, "you couldn't arrest them there. Salt."

"What?" said Mr. North, looking at his wife rather anxiously.

"They'd have eaten it," Mrs. North said. "So you couldn't arrest them until they got out. But it won't be our best friends, so it won't matter a great deal."

Weigand shook his head. He reminded Mrs. North that the Fullers, for example, were still on that list. And Edwards. Mrs. North paused a moment, thoughtfully, and then brightened. She said she was sure, really, it wouldn't be their best friends, and if it were why, after all, they had killed somebody under their roof and weren't really friends any longer. Also, and what was more important, she said, they had killed Mr. Barnes, who had been sweet and harmless.

"And we'll borrow Kumi to help serve," she said. "Then we'll have everybody, only I don't know Berex or Mrs. Brent. So maybe they wouldn't come."

That, Weigand told her, might be managed. As he spoke, he realized he was beginning to take the plan seriously. It would, he thought, be interesting to get them all together, and see what happened; what sparks flew.

"Sunday," Mrs. North said. "Sunday evening, and a buffet supper."

"Well," said Weigand, and turned to Mr. North. "How about you?" he said. "What do you think of it?"

Mr. North thought of it, his face reflecting thought.

"If you think it might help," he said, "I'd be willing. It might, at that."

Weigand nodded, slowly. Then he nodded more confidently. With any luck he would have the case broken by Sunday; if he did not, he would be willing to take any reasonable chance to break it. He needn't mention it to O'Malley, unless it worked, of course.

"Right," he said, when he decided. "I'll take you up on it."

"And I'll send out invitations," Mrs. North said, "and mark them 'R.S.V.P. Lieutenant Weigand.' How would that be?"

Mr. North looked at the lieutenant a little helplessly, and Weigand grinned over his coffee.

"Invite your friends," he said. "The ones you know. I'll see the rest are there, if the case isn't broken by then."

"And some other people?" Mrs. North said. "Some people who aren't suspects at all, but sort of fit in? Would that be all right?"

Weigand could see nothing against it, and said so. He also arranged that he would come rather late, after people had had time for a few drinks and introductions; possibly even after dinner. It occurred to him that coming, cold sober, to a crowd which had already had several drinks might be helpful, and illuminating.

They called it settled and finished coffee and cigarettes. Then they parted—Mr. North to his office, Mrs. North to have her hair done, Weigand to Headquarters, where Mullins, detecting an odor of cocktails, looked at him reproachfully. Weigand, by that time, had decided that he was letting himself in for a rather foolish plan, and settled down grimly to routine, determined to break the case before Sunday night. All he needed, he told himself, was routine and a hunch. Any time, now, he told himself, a hunch might come.

· 20 ·

Weigand worried his mind, and went over things, and waited for a hunch. He waited for the hunch all Friday afternoon and evening. He slept on it Friday night and went to Headquarters grimly on Saturday. Things seemed to have stopped entirely. Even routine was running low. By noon the audit of Berex's account with Edwards was finished and the accountants could report, finally, that everything was in order, so far as records showed. Mullins confided his opinion that it was a screwy case and inquired what they did next.

"We wait for a break," Weigand said, as confidently as he could. "There's always a break, sometime."

There always was, too, he assured himself. Digging and a hunch and luck—that summed it up, for a detective. Somebody did a thing which didn't fit, or made a break or got nervous and tried to run for it. Or somebody finally decided, for motives of his own, to tell a thing he knew and the whole structure was knocked down by the loosening of one foundation stone of falsehood. Hard work and logic were fine things, and hunches when you got them, and just enough luck to serve as a binder. And you always, sooner or later, got the luck.

It was fine and reassuring and, even as Weigand tried to convince himself, he knew it was not true. "It ain't necessarily so," the refrain from a Gershwin song hummed maddeningly in his mind. "It ain't necessarily so." Because, sometimes, the luck never came. There were plenty of such cases, some in Weigand's own experience, although he had been, for the most part, lucky. The stub of a Pullman ticket in the Snyder-Gray case had been luck for the detectives on the case. But luck had never come in the Elwell case. Nor had the stumbling investigators of the Hall-Mills murders stumbled, by chance, on the good fortune they needed. It was fine to argue that murderers always made mistakes, and sometimes they did. And sometimes they didn't, and there you were. There you were, often enough, nowhere at all; perhaps without even a hunch to help. All men die, and some are murdered, and many who die quietly may have been helped to death. And many who die as unquietly as Brent had died are not, if luck fails, avenged. There was, whatever it was convenient to tell the public, no assurance in the matter. Among those about Brent in life, one, or at most two, had killed him, and the group was not too large. But it was too large to accuse en masse. A needle may be hidden as well in a small, neat folder of needles.

There was no luck Saturday morning, and no hunch. There was no luck that night and Weigand slept on it again. He regarded the approach of the North suspect party with misgiving, and wondered why he had ever agreed to it. Then he wondered what he would have done if he hadn't, and sighed. Headquarters was not dead on Sunday; it is never dead. But it was dozing. Routine had congealed to be resumed Monday, if Weigand could, by then, think of a use for routine. He sent Mullins home, telling him to show up at the Norths in the middle of the evening.

Rather guiltily, Weigand went to a movie. It was a mystery film, full of guns and violent action in the dark, and the murderer conveniently confessed. Weigand snorted and went out and had a drink. Then he had another drink and went home. He sat in his small living-room and stared across it, and decided he had made a mistake in going on the cops. He sat staring for a long time, and then, moodily, he dressed for the party.

It was still early when he finished and he thought for a moment of abandoning his plan to arrive late. A few drinks and a few people would help, he thought and by taking a taxi downtown he would arrive near the beginning. Then he abandoned the notion, as he was about to lift a hand at a passing cab, and decided to stick to the original plan. He would walk downtown, and perhaps it would clear his mind.

Weigand walked from his apartment in the West Fifties across town to Sixth Avenue, and turned down it, walking slowly and looking around. He would, he thought vaguely, fill his mind with trivia; let it rest, empty of thoughts of the case. Perhaps, then, something would come bursting into it. He walked south. It was night and Sunday, but men were working on the new subway under flood-lights. Men in helmets which looked like pale brown derby hats emerged from the ground and crossed the street and submerged themselves in the ground again. A construction shack was a glare of light inside. Men were working on blue-prints, at drawing-boards like Berex's. Weigand walked on, looking in windows.

A pawnshop window displayed, in Sabbath semidarkness, and behind a netting, a tray of wedding rings and, farther along, a window so bright one could hardly look at it, presented bedroom suites and lamps dripping with fringe. Weigand shuddered at the fringe and passed a store where knickknacks filled a window. Leaning against the side of the building, trustfully, was a picket's sign, abandoned until Monday brought pickets back again. "Do Not Buy NAZI GOODS!" it commanded, illustrating its text with a picture of a lowering brute, swastika bedecked, planting a boot on a shrinking child. Weigand wondered what that sort of thing had done to Fuller's importing business, and how he felt about it.

The next window was full of radios and, a little further along, a tiny sporting goods store offered footballs and skates and a couple of tennis racquets left over from the summer. There was also equipment for paddle tennis, which a sign said was the new indoor game for winter, and a neat display of golf clubs. A golf club made an ugly weapon, Weigand thought, looking at one with a steel shaft and head. He wondered how many of his suspects played golf, and entered the section of

sewing-machines and wholesale florists. All the florists' windows
were bare.

It was hard, Weigand realized, to kill time merely by walking. He
pulled his muffler close to hide his white shirt and black tie and
stopped in a counter restaurant for a sandwich and coffee. The coffee,
pale with milk and already sweetish, came in a cup which seemed to
have been hollowed from a solid chunk of porcelain. It was too heavy
to lift comfortably; it would, Weigand realized, make a fine weapon.
He had another cup of coffee, black, and thought that lawyers lived a
good life, and paid twenty cents to a weary young man who leaned at
the far end of the counter in a not very clean white apron and read
Monday morning's *Daily News*. Weigand walked on south.

There were few people on the street in the Twenties. There were
more south of Twelfth Street, and drugstores and restaurants predomi-
nated along the sidewalks. Drugstores displayed cosmetics; restaurants
seemed, for the most part, to devote themselves to shellfish on beds of
ice. Posters in a travel agency invited him to abandon everything and
sail around the world. The United Cigar Store urged alarm-clocks, and
patented ash-trays, and special offers of shaving-cream and razor-
blades upon him. Weigand remembered that he still hadn't sent his
guarantee voucher to the manufacturer of the electric razor and thought
he had had a good hunch about that, anyway.

He passed the Jefferson Market Magistrate's Court, and the House
of Detention for Women, which looked so much like an apartment
house that strangers were always trying to rent flats in it. He wondered
if he would provide lodging, temporary and a prelude to something
worse, to any of the women who had known Brent. He thought of
Claire Brent and Jane Fuller and Pamela North and hoped that he
would have nothing to do with caging any of them there. But he did
not, he realized, want to cage anybody. He felt no animus, except for
his annoyance at being blocked.

It was a puzzle with pieces missing, and one is not annoyed at the
maker of a puzzle. The pieces were around somewhere. He passed a
used car lot and paused to look at the cars, deceptively shining. He
wondered about their gears, and what they were packed with to dis-

guise any inconvenient grinding, and whether any of them would make it from Carmel to downtown New York in, say, an hour and forty minutes. Most of them wouldn't, he decided, but he knew at least one that would—and knew who owned it. It would be helpful if cars could speak up and tell where they had been driven on Monday afternoon.

And if Berex's drawing-board could speak up and report on the words and thoughts of its owner; if the shops and windows he had passed could tell him whether Fuller had walked that way on Monday, and if so at what time, he would call them blessed. If even the fringed lampshades could break silence, he would forgive them their monstrosity and—

Suddenly Weigand stopped, because something was stirring in his mind. He waited, hardly breathing—something was coming, something was clicking into place—something he had seen had laid a train to—

"Well," Weigand said. "Well, I'll be damned. So *that's* it!"

He walked on toward the Norths, but now he was walking briskly, because for the first time he was pretty sure he knew where he was going.

Except for the quiet animosity with which Martha, in the kitchen, and Kumi, in charge, temporarily, of the rest of the apartment, regarded each other, Mrs. North could find nothing wrong with the preparations. She plumped a chair cushion, turned off a light and turned it on again and put folders of matches in all the ash-trays. Mr. North removed the matches and put them beside the ash-trays, thus completing the ritual. Mrs. North saw that all the cigarette-boxes were filled, and Mr. North reminded Martha to empty all the ice-containers into the ice-preserving-pan and fill them again. Then he filled the tallest martini mixer with gin and vermouth and reminded Martha to be sure that there were plenty of strips of lemon peel and cocktail olives in the silver dish sacred to their use. The Norths did a number of other things, most of them two and three times over, and sat down, almost completely exhausted, to wait for their guests. Mr. North got up and moved a chair and Mrs. North decided it was cool enough for a small fire if they opened the windows. Mr. North built the fire and Mrs. North went to the bedroom to see, for the fourth time, if she had really remembered to fill the glass dish with little powder puffs for the women, who would use their compacts anyway. Kumi, proper in his white coat, said how did he let people in, pliss? and Mr. North, for the third time, showed him the little button on the wall phone in the hall, and explained to him how to push it. Mrs. North rearranged a vase of flowers.

The Norths sat down, even more exhausted than before, and the guests began to arrive. They arrived very rapidly for several minutes, so that Kumi darted from hall to door and back to hall again, clicking madly, and small batches of guests stood around waiting to be digested. Then Mr. North brought ice in himself and added it to gin and vermouth, and all the guests looked relieved and hopeful. They drank and sighed, relaxedly, and the Norths had a chance to identify them.

Clinton Edwards had been among the first group, rather elegantly attired for Sunday evening, and for Sunday evening only in striped trousers. The rest of the men were in dinner clothes, except for one young man who had, years before, chosen gray tweeds and blue shirts as the garb for all occasions, and was sticking grimly to it. Edwards was talking, in an assured and easy rumble, to Ann Lambert, who sometimes painted pictures, and Edwards seemed to be telling her how to paint pictures. It was, so far as Mrs. North could see after a quick checkup, a perfectly normal party. Miles Sackett handed her a cocktail and smiled at her and said that he had been drinking daiquiris all afternoon, and might fall over at any time. It was a perfectly normal party and with, so far, only one suspect.

As was so often true of Mrs. North, one invitation had led to another and now, looking at the already comfortably full living-room, she wondered with something of a start how many, in all, she had invited. She tried to count, and ran over, first, the suspects themselves— "guests of honor," Mrs. North told herself. There was Edwards, whom she had invited herself, and the Fullers, only the Fullers were not there yet. There was Kumi, not so much invited as borrowed. There were the Norths themselves, if one wanted to count them. Mrs. North thought this over, impersonally and from the viewpoint of Weigand, and decided that one did. There would be, on invitation of Weigand, Mrs. Brent and Berex. That was the lot, and not so many; not enough to make more than a sprinkling among the non-suspects who were, Mrs. North began alarmedly to feel, myriad. She checked further—Ann Lambert, Ralph Birtman, Clarence Fitch, who did something on a magazine and spent a lot of time at Twenty-one, Miles Sackett, who came from Mr. North's office and was a tall, diffident man who wrote brisk, utterly undiffident books, and Henry Cordon, who spent most of his life explaining that his name was not, was really not, Gordon. "With his hands on his hips," Mrs. North thought. There was Harold Klingman, who wanted only to get a boat and spend his time floating off Florida, and who meanwhile built boats in which other people floated off Florida, and his wife, Loretta, who wanted to live in a penthouse in the East Seventies and go to all the first nights. "It's funny how people do," Mrs. North said to herself.

They knew a great many odd people, she told herself, thinking of Isaac Romenman, who, years before, had come around and invited them to a party and only told them, after they had accepted, that there would be a nominal charge of fifty cents for each person, and of how, someway, he was still around—and might even be there that evening, if he remembered about it—although neither of them was or, for that matter, ever had been, in the least interested in him. And there was Mary Brown, whom they both liked very much and almost never saw, and who was advertising manager of one of the big stores and had a breathless energy which seemed never to diminish. And there was Florence Sackett, wife of, but for the present unattached to, Miles Sackett. She seemed always to be asleep, and never really was, and was, it had turned out, an old and close friend of Claire Brent, although the Norths had never known it until recently.

Mrs. North gave up counting and decided it was time for her to receive guests. She received Isaac Romenman with great expressions of pleasure, and a dark, angry young woman whose name she did not get, and whose name, as it turned out, she never did get. And after her there was a graceful, blond young woman and Mrs. North found herself saying, "Mrs. Brent, so glad," to a suspect whose gracious politeness was not in the least marred by the evident fact that she was unobtrusively looking the party over for a face she did not see. The bell rang again, and Louis Berex came in with Ralph Birtman, both with the frozen friendliness of men who, not knowing one another, have met on their way to the same party, and need only hostess approval for acquaintance, but are rigidly obligated to await it before either can acknowledge the presence of the other. Mrs. North greeted Birtman, hesitated for a moment and guessed:

"Mr. Berex?" she said, with the hostess inflection, found she was right, and added: "So glad you could come."

"Are you?" said Berex. "Why?" But he said it very pleasantly.

"It will please the lieutenant so very much," Mrs. North said, sweetly. "Do you know Mrs. Brent?"

That, she figured, was catching up with them. She relented and introduced Birtman and Berex, who suddenly found themselves left together and moved, as one man, to Mr. North, who was dispensing drinks. Kumi arrived with canapes and set them down to let in the Fullers, who seemed very gay and had, Mrs. North realized, really been drinking something all afternoon. "But reasonably," Mrs. North decided, after a quick inspection.

The Fullers greeted Mrs. Brent, who had come back from removing her coat, and the three picked up Berex, and Birtman, who clung. Everybody seemed very comfortable and at ease, Mrs. North decided, although the suspects seemed to be drifting together.

Edwards rose from the sofa to give a seat to Florence Sackett and loomed within sight of the little suspect group, and bowed and smiled. They bowed and smiled back and he joined them, and Mrs. North was called away by Kumi, who touched her on the arm and made sounds which seemed to indicate that the supply of canapes was diminishing. Mrs. North said it couldn't be, had a martini to reinforce her, and went to see. There were plenty of canapes, but Martha was frowning above them and making grumbling sounds, indicative of little use for the small houseman. Mrs. North carried back a plate of canapes and entrusted them to Kumi, and went back to see that Martha did not forget to open the wine. Then she switched on the electric chafing-dish, looked at the watch hanging in its little silver ball around her neck, and counted the guests. Not all present, yet; time for another drink. Mrs. North circulated, keeping an eye on things. Mr. North had, by now, mixed a new batch of cocktails and turned bartending over to Kumi, who was circulating with a tray of drinks. Everything went fine. The Norths drifted together for a moment, toasted themselves and their party silently and swiftly, and drifted apart to host.

The room was full of smoke and talk, and the contented restlessness of people who are getting enough to drink. The party swirled and eddied around Mrs. North and she smiled at it, and was not disconcerted to discover that its edges were softening for her eyes. It was always odd and interesting to be a little changed by alcohol, but only enough to appreciate the change and relish it—to see how some faces came clear out of the crowd and others wavered; to feel that faint, indescribable fluidity which was a little akin to dizziness, but was not dizziness, but only a pleasant state to be maintained judiciously. "I can come clear out of it any time I want to," Mrs. North told herself, "only I must drink very slowly, now, and not hurry it."

She felt very good and it no longer seemed like a suspect party, or anything serious. The situation, even the murder itself, seemed less real than the pleasant, warm stir of the party; looking around at the suspects, who had scattered again, she realized that it was absurd to think of any of them as having actually killed Brent and decided that Weigand must have made a mistake. "It must have been a gangster," Mrs. North told herself. "That's what it was, a gangster."

She wished Weigand would come so she could tell him what she had discovered about its being a gangster, and then he could join the party and they could all have a fine time. And then—

"Feeling all right, kid?" Mr. North said, suddenly beside her with two cocktails, one for her. She smiled and nodded and started to tell Mr. North about its being a gangster after all, but then didn't. It would sound as if she had had too much to drink if she said it, because of course it wasn't true—not true in the different, outside, factual world which was not the party; not true yesterday and not true tomorrow, but only true at this moment, while she was thinking of it. She looked at

Mr. North and decided he was feeling fine too, only perhaps not quite so fine. He sat on the edge of her chair for a moment and, seeing him sit, Mrs. North realized how physically tired they both were, and that probably everybody needed food.

The conversation was a blur around her and she sipped her drink very slowly, because when she finished it, it would be time to start the serving of food and after that, she knew, she would not feel at all the same. After that she would not drink anything more, but only get soberer and soberer and after a long time, she knew, she would begin to wonder why people did not go. She could think all this and still enjoy the moment, and she did not want to break the moment with action. Then she looked at Mr. North and raised her eyebrows and nodded. Pam North stood up, completely herself again, and hoped that everything would be hot and that Kumi would manage the business of serving without too many hitches. She told Martha she could start, now, and touched the cover of the chafing-dish with wary fingers, and said "Uh!" She sought out Kumi, still serving drinks, and summoned him with an eye, and when he came, she began to fill plates. She put on each a spoon of lobster from the chafing-dish and a slice of ham and some of the salad and a small, hot buttered roll which had just come out of the oven. Mr. North poured cool wine into glasses and set them on a tray and everybody found, or tried to find, a place to sit. Most of the men found places on the floor.

Everything went without a hitch and, with everybody sitting and eating, the party seemed much smaller and more manageable. Berex and Mrs. Brent were sitting together on the floor and Berex was talking quickly and eagerly while Mrs. Brent leaned back against the wall and looked, smiling faintly, over the party and now and then nodded, or turned her head toward Berex. Edwards was still talking to Ann Lambert, and he was sunk a little more comfortably into the sofa, but still rumbled diligently. The Fullers had drifted into separate groups, but every now and then, Mrs. North noticed, each would look at the other and when their eyes met they would smile, as if in reassurance. Kumi brought Mrs. North a glass of wine, and made a little bow and said: "Wine, pliss?" She took a glass and tasted the food on her plate. She might find, when she tasted it, that she was too tired to eat.

They were all, Mrs. North thought, looking at them, nice people and she wished it could have been a gangster. Only now, of course, she knew it wasn't, and that Weigand was right. It was one of the people on his list, Mrs. North knew, looking at them one after another. It was Berex or Mrs. Brent or Clinton Edwards or Benjamin Fuller (or even Jane Fuller?) or Kumi, because it wasn't she, and it wasn't Jerry and—

She lifted her fork again and then, with no warning, it was as if some cold fluid were running through Mrs. North, or as if her blood had grown suddenly cool and shivered. It was not until some time afterward that she was able to define what had happened, and comprehend its cause, because now it was too frightening and cold. She had given, she saw, a little start, and some of the wine in her glass had slopped over and the surface was still agitated. That frightened her still more, because it might have been seen by the one who might, somehow, know it for what it was—know that Mrs. North now, as she lowered the fork from her lips, knew who had killed Stanley Brent, and that the person who had killed him was in the room.

"I mustn't show it," Mrs. North told herself, and arranged a smile on her lips again. "I mustn't show it. Oh, Jerry—*Jerry!*"

But Mr. North, from across the room, merely smiled back at her, and Mrs. North could see that he did not realize she was calling to him frantically.

· 21 ·

Mrs. North's lips ached with the smile, and her jaws ached with their pressure against food gone tasteless. And still, not knowing what else to do, she moved mechanically through the actions of a hostess; she caught Kumi's eye and indicated the empty plates; she rose, as in a nightmare, and poured coffee. She wanted to scream the name, and she wanted to run. She wanted to get Jerry by the hand and run to a quiet place where they could talk. She wanted Lieutenant Weigand to come, so that she could tell him what she knew and then get away until it was over. Desperately, she waited for the bell which would announce that Weigand had come, but the bell was silent. She set her mind hard and did not look at anybody who mattered, because her face might give her away; she looked stabbingly at the back of Mr. North's head, turned toward her as he talked, and the back of his head was impervious to her thrusting demands. Later, she knew that it would have been better if she screamed, better if she did almost anything but what she did. . . .

Empty cups were beside most of the guests, now, and there was that pause which comes in parties when one thing is ended and before the next begins. Anxiously, Mrs. North sought the words to break it; only in the party, in its warm segregation and unreality, was there safety. But before she could speak, she heard Mr. North speak.

"Why, yes," Mr. North said, "if you want to. But there's nothing to see and it—"

He was speaking, she saw, to Loretta Klingman, who was nodding eagerly.

Her voice was quick and eager in the comparative silence.

"But I *want* to see it," she said. "I *want* to. I love murderers—but I *love* them. If we can't, I'll *never* forgive you."

She turned swiftly to face the others.

"Listen, everybody," she said. "I want to see the place—oh."

She had realized, Mrs. North saw, that the audience she was addressing with such enthusiasm included the widow of the central figure in this so exciting and delightful murder. Mrs. North felt everything grow still inside her, and heard a small voice which no one else could hear crying "No! no!" And yet everything outside was suddenly clear and sharp; across the room she could see the symptoms of withdrawal and distaste which always appeared in Mr. North when he was discomfited, and at a loss.

But Mrs. Brent was smiling, in a rather fixed fashion, and saying words.

"But of course," Claire Brent was saying. "Why shouldn't you?" She picked a tiny glass of cognac from the mantel near her, and drank it quickly. "Why shouldn't we all," she said. "Sightseers. On your left, ladies and gentlemen, is the bathtub in which—" Her voice, Mrs. North realized, was close to hysteria. But before anybody could stop her she was at the door. "Come on," Claire Brent called, her voice high. "Come on, everybody!" She cupped one hand to her lips, and there was a high-pitched brittleness in her voice which Weigand would have recognized. Only Weigand wasn't there.

Mrs. Brent flung the door open, and the click of the released lock was loud in the room. There was a nervous uneasiness in the party, and a hesitancy. "In a moment somebody will scream," Mrs. North thought. Then she heard her husband's voice, desperately—but only she could hear the desperation—calm and matter of fact.

"Why, yes," he said. "Why not? There's nothing there, of course. Only empty rooms. But why not?"

There was a stir in the room; a kind of settling.

"We'll need candles," Mr. North said, moving to the mantel and picking lighted candles from the girandoles. He looked at Mrs. North, and she could tell that he read in her face something more than the general uneasiness. He nodded, almost imperceptibly. "Candles, Pam," he said. "We're going exploring." Mrs. North took a candle in its silver stick from the table.

And so, the Norths and some of the others with candles, they went exploring. It was confusing, crowded in the narrow stair hall, and Mrs. North had a vague impression that some did not go; some shrugged and turned back to drinks; some stood for a moment undecided, and there was a movement of two or three toward the front room, which could only be for hats and coats. There went the party, Mrs. North thought, in an odd, and entirely unexpected, return to hostess-ship. The explorers went up and along the third-floor hall and up to the door of the fourth-floor apartment, which was closed. Mr. North, leading, pressed against it and it opened. It was dark in the apartment, except where light came faintly in through the street windows, and the candles illuminated it flickeringly. Dark and, Mrs. North realized with a flooding relief, matter-of-fact.

Perhaps it was merely that there was, after all, nothing to see; perhaps it was that there were so many there to see it, that the basic artificiality of this mass search for the bizarre and exciting trampled excitement into powder. At any rate, once there, the party found very little to do about it.

There were a few gasps, which sounded a little theatrical, and several candles were poked into the bathroom, which was merely an empty, and immaculate, bathroom. A few wandered into the front living-room, and a few more looked out of the rear windows and down the fire-escape toward the dark yard. And nowhere was there anything to see. Interest and excitement seeped out, and there was the scuffling uncertainty of people who realized, all at once, that they are engaged in an escapade which has gone silly on them.

"Well," Mr. North said, in the flickering darkness. "This is it. I told you there would be nothing."

He moved toward the door.

"Everybody had enough?" he said. "If so, we may as well go down before we set something on fire."

He went out and started down, and the others followed him. Seeing his calm, and feeling the calm of the others, Mrs. North regained her own. She even spoke, assuring those nearest her that that was all there was; that she would hold the light until they were out and close the door behind them. Her previous excitement seemed, all at once, absurd. After all, she had only to wait for Lieutenant Weigand and tell him what she knew, and then the rest could be carried out quietly and in order, probably tomorrow. Now she ought to go down and save the party, if it could be saved.

"Although it was a fool thing to give," Mrs. North told herself, with her new-found clarity.

The rest filed out in front of her, and the stairs were confused in the half-light with people going down. She had her hand on the door to leave and close it after her, and her finger pressed the button which would set the snap-lock and end any chance for more thrill-seeking. But then something brushed against her feet, and moved softly on, and in the light from her candle and a few feet away toward the front of the apartment, two shining spots appeared.

"Pete!" said Mrs. North, to the two shining eyes of the cat which had passed her and turned to look back. "Come here, Pete!"

There was a soft, pleased cat sound from the darkness, and the eyes disappeared. There was the faint thud of a departing cat on bare boards, and the faint scratch of cat claws going away.

"Miaow," said Pete, interestedly, pleased by the new game.

"Pete!" said Mrs. North, sharply. The sound of retreat stopped and the eyes reappeared. Pete gave the small, excited cry of a cat which enjoys being chased, and departed toward the front of the house. Mrs. North commented to herself on the ways of cats, and followed, leaving the door ajar behind her. As she moved, the thud of retreat became a scamper, punctuated by tiny, excited cries. Pete disappeared into the large living-room, where there was plenty of space to run. Mrs. North, leaving another door ajar behind her, went after him. Inside the living-room door, she set her candlestick on the floor and watched for eyes. They were in the corner and she advanced cautiously. She could almost reach him when they vanished, and a black blur departed for another corner. Pete was having a lovely time.

But Mrs. North, also, knew a trick. Instead of following, she stooped down and became deeply interested in a spot of bare floor. Gently she scratched on the floor with her nails, and then she squatted and examined the floor even more intently. The eyes reflecting the candlelight moved a little. Mrs. North continued to scratch gently on the floor. A soft black blur came curiously forward, passed out of arm's-reach, hesitated and came on; suddenly was gathered up, struggling angrily for a moment, purring as fingers found the right place behind a furry ear. Pete held gently to Mrs. North's shoulder and looked over it as she started back toward the hall.

And then, from very close, Mrs. North heard the firm snap of a closing door. It was a little sound, but it snapped against her nerves and drew them taut. Feeling the difference in her body, Pete wriggled for a moment and, unconsciously, she let him drop to the floor. He did not run, but crouched against her ankles, and growled softly. Mrs. North found that terror made her cold and curiously ready. The candle a few feet away, on the floor—she must get the candle.

Then, beyond the candle, there was a dark shadow, and a foot came out, sharply, toward the little light. The candle went over and went out, and in a moment there was the penetrating scent of an extinguished wick, smoldering. The shadow came on into the half light of the front room, and boards creaked under weight. The light from the street shone faintly on the face Mrs. North, desperately, had known she would see. She made a little, gasping cry.

"So," said the voice, "I thought you did. You should learn not to show what you think, Mrs. North. You should have learned. When you could."

The voice was calm, unexcited, almost expressionless. That made it more terrible. There was not even anger in the voice; in the words there was only a change of tense. "Should learn"—"should have learned." It was a horrible difference to Mrs. North, backing slowly from the voice, with the black cat growling softly at her feet.

"But you can't—you can't!" she said, and her voice was low, too, and almost steady. "Everybody will know, this time—they're all around you."

"No," said the voice. "It is all very confused down there. Nobody knows where anybody is. And I've left, you see. I took my hat and coat after you came up here and left. There were several who saw me leave. And this will not be noisy. You can't scream, you see."

But she could scream; blindingly it came over Mrs. North that she could scream, and the people would run; that she should have screamed—that she had forgotten—

She backed away and a scream formed in her throat. Then there was sudden movement, and a hand was hardly, bruisingly over her mouth. Another hand was at her throat. She could scream—her hands went up, frantically, to the other hands—she could scream—

"Jerry!!" she screamed. "Jerry!"

But the scream died against the palm of the pressing hand, choked in the constricted throat.

"No," said the voice. "You can't scream. People die quite quietly. I know that, you see. I know—"

But they did not, Mrs. North knew. Now there was a beating sound in her ears; a rising, roaring sound, drowning the voice—drowning—they would hear it and come—they would—

Lieutenant Weigand walked along briskly, with the air of a man who knows where he is going. It would be simple, now; now that he had his hunch. A good deal was still obscure; he would have to recast some things, and look further. He would have to prove some things, too, but that would be easy, now that they knew what to look for. They could fill in after the arrest. He planned the arrest—a tap on a shoulder, a request for a moment's time, the formal words. It would be well, however, to have Mullins on hand in case of trouble. It was lucky he had told Mullins to wait for him outside so they could go in together. They could get it over with and hardly disturb Mrs. North's party.

Weigand smiled as he thought of the party, now so unnecessary. He wondered what he would have got out of it by questioning them all together, and what questions, half an hour before, he would have thought to ask. Weigand rounded the corner and neared the Buano house, looking in the light from the street lamps for Mullins. There was no Mullins, and Weigand made a remark or two to himself. Then he looked at his watch and withdrew the remarks. He had said about ten-thirty, and it was less than that by several minutes. He could go in, or he could wait. There was, he decided, no hurry. He lighted a cigarette and leaned against a railing across from the Buano house. Looking up, he could see lights in the windows of the North apartment; looking higher he was startled to see faint light in the top-floor apartment.

"What the—" he said. Then he guessed that some of them must have gone up to look at the scene of the crime. He smiled, amusedly. Well, they would do no harm—nor get much satisfaction; and down the street he saw a dark figure. The figure passed under a light, and he saw it was Mullins.

Weigand whistled softly and Mullins came across.

"O.K., Loot?" Mullins said.

"Right," said Weigand, enjoying it, and drawing deeply on his cigarette. "Right. It's broke."

Mullins said "Yeh?" in a delighted tone. Weigand drew again on his cigarette and tossed it away, almost reluctantly. They might as well finish it.

"Come along," he said.

Mr. North stood at the door of the apartment and greeted the detectives. He looked sharply at Weigand's face for a moment, and then he smiled slowly. Weigand realized that his face told the story.

"So?" Mr. North said. "So—you've got it?"

There was curiosity in his voice, and Weigand was pleased by it.

"I think so," he said. "Yes, I think so. I'm going to make a pinch, anyway. If—?" He paused. Perhaps the Norths would prefer that it finish somewhere else, and now that made no difference to him. "Is your wife around?" he said. "She ought to be in on it."

Mr. North said, "Yes, sure," and led the detectives into the living-room. There were fewer there, now, and they glanced quickly around. Mr. North's voice was puzzled when he spoke.

"She ought to be," he said. "She was just a minute ago—when we all came down." Then his voice became more doubtful. "Or was she?" he said. "Come to think of it—"

Weigand was looking quickly for another face—and not finding it, suddenly, hardly knowing why, he was worried. He spoke quickly and sharply, and Mullins, who knew the tone, looked at him with inquiry as quick and sharp. Mr. North swung on them.

"Yes?" he said. "What is it?"

"I don't know," Weigand said. "Did you all go upstairs?" Mr. North nodded. "And all come down?" the detective asked.

"I thought so," Mr. North said. "Some went out, though— I thought Pam—"

"Come on!" Weigand said. "We'll look. Come on!"

Turning, he stepped quickly toward the stairs, and North was quick after him. Mullins started to follow, checked himself and ran to a rear window of the apartment. He threw it open, jumped through and in a moment was running up the fire-escape. The men and women in the living-room swung, suddenly quiet, and stared after them. They heard the pounding steps of hurrying men on the stairs; a moment later the hollower pounding at a door.

The door was locked. Weigand flung his weight against it and it rattled but held. Together, he and Mr. North hurled themselves on it, and it threw them back. They hesitated a moment, and from inside there came the angry yowl of a frightened, furious cat, and the sound of scuffling movement. Frantically, the two men surged against the door. Weigand whirled angrily when he realized Mullins was missing; then whirled back as glass crashed inside.

"The fire-escape!" he said, grasping it. "Mullins—the window."

The two men raced downstairs, through the window Mullins had left open, and up the fire-stairs outside to the window of the fourth-floor apartment. Weigand's flashlight beam bit into the darkness, as, on North's heels, he hurled himself into the room.

But there was no need to hurry, any longer. The beam picked out Mullins, enormously tall and burly, with his shadow enormous behind him. Even as they ran across the room toward him he stooped over one of two figures lying at his feet, and there was a flash of metal and a click. Then he stood up again, turned to face the flashlight.

"O.K., Loot," he said. "Got him. Only—the lady—"

But Mr. North was already beside the other figure on the floor, and held its head in his hands and was saying, over and over, "Pam. Pam. Pam, kid!"

What had been black in front of Pam North's eyes began to eddy and whirl, and her hands went up to soothe a clutching burning at her throat. She fought to push hands away and the black swirled into gray, and then in the center of the gray, light broke through and she heard a voice saying: "Pam. Pam, kid!" She had to scream, she remembered—she had to scream. She had to scream and bring them and she had to tell them about the murderer.

The light space in the center grew, and she could see a face in it. It was not a face she knew, and below the face there was stiff whiteness, and a voice, which she didn't know, either, said:

"She'll do now, I think."

Then the lightness grew still larger and she could see Jerry, kneeling at her feet, and knew it was he who was calling her name. She smiled and tried to speak, and he nodded and smiled. He was terribly white, she thought, and she wondered if he was going to be drunk, because he looked like a person who was going to be drunk. She wanted to tell him that he should lie down a while and then there was another face, and it was the face of that detective—that detective?—Lieutenant Weigand, of course.

"It was—" she said. It was terribly hard to speak, but Weigand was nodding. "I told you he left his name," Mrs. North said. "From the first—"

The ambulance surgeon was shaking his head at her and telling her not to try to talk, but she could see Weigand nodding.

"Right," Weigand said. "You said that all along. Sure you did."

The ambulance surgeon was less gentle in restoring consciousness to Clinton Edwards, out from the effects of a blackjack laid with scientific precision behind his right ear. And when Edwards came to, he found that his wrists were cuffed together, and that Weigand was standing over him, looking down without expression. When Weigand saw Edwards' eyes open, he turned and nodded to Mullins.

"All right," he said. "You can take him along and book him. Felonious assault." He looked down at Edwards, who was trying to sit up. "Just for now, Mr. Edwards," he said. "Don't get any wrong ideas. We'll have something else for you in the morning." He stared down at Edwards. "We'll make it murder in the morning," he said. "And glad to."

• 22 •

WEDNESDAY, NOVEMBER 2

Mr. and Mrs. North finished their lunch in a little restaurant near the Criminal Courts Building, and finished their coffee and had more. Their waiter had begun to hover when finally Lieutenant Weigand came in the door and walked across to their table and looked down at them. He looked down and, after a moment, answered their unspoken inquiries with a nod.

"Yes," he said. "They voted the indictment. Murder in the first degree."

He sat down and ordered coffee.

"And that's that," he said. "Except for the trial, at which you'll both have to testify. But heaven knows when that will be. I hear he's hiring Verndorf, and Verndorf's good." He paused. "Verndorf will need to be," he said, rather grimly.

"Well," said Mr. North, a little uncertainly. "You don't think Verndorf can get him off?"

Weigand shook his head. He said he didn't think Clarence Darrow could get Clinton Edwards off, if Darrow were alive and willing to try. "As he wouldn't be," Weigand added. He sat brooding over his coffee, relaxed. The Norths waited hopefully, and finally Mrs. North spoke.

"There are still a lot of things I don't understand," she said. "Why he

did, and how you knew. You did know, didn't you—before he went
after me, that is?"

Weigand nodded.

"Only a little while before," he said. Then he looked at Mrs. North
with livening interest.

"What did you find out?" he asked. "I mean, what suddenly made
you dangerous to him, so that he had to try to get you out of the way?"

"Lobster," Mrs. North said. "When it didn't taste right." She paused.
"Or, really, when it did taste right," she said. "That made me remember."

Weigand felt he ought to be expert by now, but he had to shake his
head. Mrs. North explained.

"It was when I tasted our own lobster at the party," she said. "Tast-
ing it made me think of Edwards' and then I realized for the first time
that something had been troubling me all along about that. His wasn't
right; it wasn't the same thing at all. Just lobster, warmed up with
cream and butter, and probably a little chili-sauce, and all at once I realized it. But he had got the recipe from me specially and he had
described to you how he made Spanish lobster by the recipe and how
long it took. I realized he had told a lie about that, and so there must be
something about it—funny business. But if there was funny business,
then he was trying to hide something, so he had really done it." She
paused. "Of course," she added, "I said that from the first, you know."

Weigand smiled and nodded, and said he remembered.

"And when I found out," Mrs. North said, "I was startled and frightened and, I suppose, showed it. And he saw me show it, and guessed
what I had found out. Which was shrewd of him, wasn't it? Only I still
don't get it."

"Well," Weigand said, "it was fairly simple, really. He just used
frozen lobster, instead of natural lobster. The kind of lobster they sell
now in little compressed, quick-frozen blocks, each block equal to a
two-pound lobster. You know?"

"Oh," said Mrs. North. "Of course! Of all the *stupid* things. My not
guessing, I mean."

Weigand admitted he hadn't guessed, either, until it was almost over; until, in fact, he had looked in a restaurant window on his way to the North party and seen lobsters lying on beds of ice.

"They looked cold," he said. "Cold lobsters. Then I thought of frozen lobsters and then realized how it could be done. Edwards was always a likely one, it seemed to me, if we could break the alibi."

"But how—?" Mr. North said, still at a loss. Weigand finished his coffee and ordered another cup. He had better, he said, tell them the whole business from the start. There was, first, the motive.

"We didn't get that, really, until after the arrest," he admitted. "Then we knew Edwards had done it, and it was a question of filling in. So I went to Berex." He took a sip of the new coffee. Berex, he explained, because Berex was the only established link between Edwards and his victim.

"Even without the trust fund, which we had had to abandon," he went on, "Berex was somehow the link between Edwards and Brent. Berex himself didn't know how, and we had to dig. Then I remembered something which hadn't seemed to mean anything at the time— that Edwards had sold an invention for Berex. It didn't connect up, at first, even when I found out that it had been sold to Recording Industries, Inc. But the company's name was familiar, and I finally remembered that it was on the list of clients of Brent's firm. So we worked on that line. Then it came out.

"Berex remembered having told Brent of the invention sale, when they were discussing Edwards and the trust fund. Berex had said something about his satisfaction with Edwards' handling of that matter, and told Brent he was getting three thousand a year out of it. Thinking back, he remembered that Brent had looked a little surprised, and said something to the effect that he would have expected it to be more, considering the size of the firm. There Berex stopped. Then we got hold of Recording Industries—this was all day before yesterday, after we had arrested Edwards. It took only a few minutes, there, and we had it. They weren't paying Berex three thousand a year; they were paying him around fifty thousand. Or they thought they were. We subpoenaed Edwards' records and got the whole story. It was straight theft."

Weigand swallowed more coffee and lighted another cigarette. The Norths nodded, encouragingly.

"Edwards," Weigand went on, "was simply rooking Berex. He'd sold the invention, all right, and signed the royalty contract in Berex's name. He had Berex's power of attorney, you see, because Berex was out of the country. The contract provided for royalties running around fifty thousand a year. Then Edwards forged another contract, calling for royalties around three thousand, and that was the one he showed Berex. He kept the difference." Weigand paused. "It was a neat difference," he added. "Now we go back to Brent.

"Brent was surprised that Berex wasn't getting more, but he didn't say anything to Berex about it. Instead, he checked with the corporation, which was easy since his firm were its lawyers. It probably didn't take him as long as it took us to uncover the scheme. His first thought was to go direct to the District Attorney with it, and he called up that Monday and made an appointment. Then—we have to guess a bit here—he decided to give Edwards a chance to explain. Or—" He broke off, and looked at the Norths.

"That is the official version," he said. "The one we're using. It's also possible Brent thought not better, but worse, of it after he had made the appointment with the D.A. Maybe he thought he might get in on it."

"Blackmail?" Mr. North asked.

Weigand nodded, and said it could be.

"But we're not trying to prove it," he said. "All we're going to prove, and we've already proved it at Edwards' office, is that Brent called Edwards on the telephone early Monday afternoon. There's no doubt that, then, he told Edwards enough to show that he had the goods on him. Then Edwards began to think fast. The first result of his thinking was to make an appointment with Brent. He may merely have wanted to have the meeting where nobody would be apt to stumble on it; more likely he decided, almost at once, that Brent would have to be killed. At any rate, he fixed your house—the Buano house—as the place of the meeting, remembering the vacant apartment and the ease of getting in. Then he must have kept on thinking fast; anyway, we can figure out what he did.

"First, he must have prepared the slip to go into the slot by the bell, getting it to size by guesswork, and being sure he made it, if anything, too large. He could always snip it down, after he got there. He cut it out of the top of a letter Berex had written him about the trust fund and was careful to leave part of the X on it. By then, anyway, he knew he was going to kill. He couldn't know that Berex's fingerprints were on it, but there was a good chance. He was careful to see that his own weren't. He printed his own name on it—"

"Why," Mrs. North interrupted. "And why did he leave it?"

"Obviously he had to use his own name, since he was the one Brent was coming to meet," Weigand said. "I'll get to the rest later.

"Then he went home, arranging to get there and receive the lobsters, which he knew pretty well wouldn't get there before the latest hour he'd fixed, three o'clock. He had arranged to have them come by that time merely so he would have time to prepare them, but now it fitted in. He was there when they came, took them into the kitchen, sent Kumi upstairs to clean, and threw the lobsters down the incinerator."

"Oh," said Mrs. North. "Of course!"

"Precisely," Weigand said. "Then he took an old suitcase with him and went down the service stairs and over to the Buano house, which is only a couple of blocks. He had to chance being seen, but he was lucky. We still haven't found anybody who saw him, but we're still looking. The appointment was, probably, for three-thirty, and again he had to chance Brent's being on time. But if Brent wasn't on time, there was no real harm done. Edwards would only have to think up another plan. But Brent kept his appointment.

"Edwards got there a few minutes ahead of time, put the slip in the slot by the bell, and then got in by pretending to be a messenger boy. He disguised his voice, probably by using his handkerchief. When you went back into the apartment after talking to him, Mrs. North, he went on up, quietly—the carpet is heavy, remember—and got into the apartment on the top floor. He probably had to wait a few minutes, and noticed how hot and close it was. He opened one of the windows, sure he wouldn't be seen—the windows on that floor aren't overlooked by any other buildings. Also, since he was going to leave the body there, he wanted an air circulation. Then Brent came.

"I don't imagine Edwards gave Brent any time. He opened the door and stepped to one side, and Brent went in. Then Brent must have stopped, astonished that the apartment wasn't furnished, because Edwards had undoubtedly explained that he had just moved from his old apartment to this one. And that was probably the last thought Brent had, because then Edwards hit him. He'd put the ice-mallet in the suit-case and brought it too, you see. Then Edwards dragged Brent into the bathroom, hit him a couple more times to make sure, banged the face a bit and stripped the body. He put the clothes in the suitcase, wrapped the mallet and wallet and a few other articles up in something—a piece of newspaper he had brought along, perhaps—went over to the subway and checked the case. Then he went by a market in Eighth Street and bought frozen lobster."

"Can you prove that?" Mrs. North wanted to know.

Weigand nodded. They had, he explained, made a store-to-store check when they knew what to look for, and found the clerk who had sold the lobster. He wasn't sure about the time, but he could come close enough, and it was around four. He had, subsequently, identified Edwards as the man who had bought the lobster, remembering him because it was unusual to sell so much lobster to one customer.

"Then Edwards went back to his apartment, up the service stairs, and threw the mallet and other things that would burn down the incin-erator. He'd replaced the mallet with a mechanical ice-crusher by the time I got around, incidentally. Then he thawed the lobster and threw in some other ingredients—probably the ones you named, Mrs. North—and there he was. It wasn't, as you afterward discovered, Mrs. North, very good Spanish lobster, but it looked all right and the chances were a good many to one that nobody would notice—or, if they did, would think anything except that he was a bad cook. He could take that, proud as he was of his cooking, under the circumstances—which were that he had a perfectly good alibi, all the better because it seemed to be such a casual, faulty one—at first glance, that is. When you examined it, it seemed perfect, because he couldn't be doing two things at the same time in different places, and it seemed obvious he had done one of them. He'd eliminated a man who might have sent him to jail, he'd kept his forty-odd thousand dollars and he was probably feeling pretty good—felt pretty good until he remembered something.

"When he went out of the Buano house, with his suitcase, he had, undoubtedly, walked past the mail-carrier, Barnes. Probably he didn't pay any attention at the time, because mail-carriers rather blend into the background, but afterwards he thought of it and realized that Barnes might be able to identify him. So, when he was supposed to be at another cocktail party Wednesday afternoon, he followed Barnes and killed him. That, however, we'll probably never prove; as things stand now, we won't even try to."

"But the slip," Mrs. North said. "I still don't see why he left it. He must have left it when he went out, mustn't he?"

Weigand said, "Yes.

"That was a slip," he said. Mr. North winced visibly, and Weigand grinned at him and said he hadn't meant it. "But probably it seemed like a fine idea at the time," he went on. "He figured it this way:

"His first hope was obviously that we wouldn't find the body until it was too late to identify. That was why he took the clothes, of course. But if nobody found the body, the slip wouldn't be found, either or, as we agreed earlier, wouldn't have any meaning if it were. That was the hope you spoiled, the two of you.

"His second hope was that, if the body was found and identified, the slip *would* be found and *would* mean something; would, as a matter of fact, lead us to him at once. He figured that, if the body was identified, the investigation would come around to him sooner or later, because of Brent's part in the trust fund investigation. He wanted it sooner, if it was coming, for a couple of reasons. For one thing he figured, rightly I think, that if we investigated him with the trust fund in mind, we would be bound to clear him and that, having once given him a clean bill, we would have a tendency to leave him out of it later. He knew we'd have to clear him on that ground, because the trust fund *was* perfectly all right. And, up to a point, it worked out as he had planned.

"His other reason for wanting to be questioned early was even more important. He wanted us to hear and check his alibi as soon as possible, because it was an alibi which depended entirely on the memories of two disinterested people—Kumi, who doesn't seem to have any dog-like devotion to his master, and the boy who delivered the lobsters. He knew—and went so far as to tell me—that Kumi's memory isn't to be depended on, and of course the boy couldn't remember one delivery, out of many, for very long. Edwards wanted us to come after him, if we were coming at all, while those memories were fresh, because while the memories lasted he had an alibi. And that worked out as he planned, too, up to a point."

The Norths thought it over, and nodded. Then Mrs. North thought of another question.

"Would you have caught him if he hadn't tried to—to *get* me?" she said. "Wasn't that foolish of him?"

Weigand said it was very foolish, as it turned out.

"But you have to remember," he said, "that he had no way of knowing I had stumbled on the frozen lobster trick. You were the only danger he saw, and he thought he could get away with it—and with you. As he might have. Nobody knew with certainty where anybody else was at the party, as I gather it. And all the suspects were there. If he wasn't actually caught in the act, it might have been any of them."

Mrs. North thought a moment.

"But how did he know I was going to be up there, alone, where he could get at me?" she said. "Was it just luck?"

Partly, Weigand assumed, it was luck; partly it must have been quick thinking. Naturally, Weigand pointed out, Edwards wasn't saying. Edwards wasn't saying anything.

"But I imagine I can come close to it," Weigand said. "He saw the cat."

The Norths looked at him.

"He may really have intended to go," Weigand explained. "When he guessed that Mrs. North knew, his first thought—almost anybody's first thought—would be to get away. But then he saw that Pete had got out of the apartment and was following upstairs. He followed along to see if what did happen would happen, guessing that any cat would want to explore any place that was dark. He saw Pete slip past you, Mrs. North, and probably heard you speak to him. Then he saw you go back into the apartment after the cat. The rest was easy—he had only to lag behind the others, which was easy in semi-darkness and confusion, and go back upstairs when the rest went into your apartment." Weigand paused. "We can bet it was that way, or close to it," he said. "Edwards liked to plan things out, but he could be an opportunist, too. If he could get you out of the way, he figured, he wouldn't have to run."

"And you think you can convict him?" Mrs. North inquired. Weigand nodded emphatically.

"Verndorf may make it a self-defense plea," he said, "and that may give us trouble, because it will be hard to prove that Brent didn't jump him first. But with the motive and the planned alibi and the attack on you—well, I'm glad I'm not in Mr. Edwards' spot. Very glad."

"And all the others?" Mrs. North said. "They weren't in it at all? They all told the truth?"

"Within reason," Weigand said. "Berex and Claire Brent clipped the truth a bit here and there, undoubtedly, for their own purposes. They certainly tried to hide that they were out together the night Barnes was killed. Mrs. Brent is more conventional than you'd think. The rest undoubtedly told the truth; or thereabouts. For example, North, I really believe you were walking in Central Park when Brent was killed."

Mr. North looked up sharply and then grinned.

"Well," said Mrs. North. "Well—"

They all stood up and Mr. North went over to pay the checks. Mrs. North and Weigand stood waiting for him, and Mrs. North said she had a fine idea.

"Let's go up to the house and have cocktails," Mrs. North said.

They all thought it was a fine idea, and went up to the Norths' apartment and had cocktails. It had turned much cooler, and they could have a fire with only one window open, and it was very comfortable. After the second round, Mrs. North said she didn't know what *they* thought, but she thought this was very nice.

"We must do it again," she said, nodding seriously at Weigand. "Even without murders."

Mr. North, also looking at Weigand, made sounds of approval, faintly tinged with inquiry, and Weigand was a little embarrassed and a good deal pleased and said it certainly seemed like a fine idea to him. So they had another round.

After the third round they remembered to call Mullins up and invite him, too. Mrs. North said it was high time she thanked Mullins for saving her life.

THE END